DIANA WALLIS TAYLOR

Hadassah

QUEEN ESTHER OF PERSIA

WHITAKER
HOUSE

Publisher's Note: This novel is a work of historical fiction and is based on the biblical record. References to real people, events, organizations, and places are used in a fictional context. Any resemblance to actual living persons is entirely coincidental.

All Scripture quotations are taken from *The Complete Jewish Bible*, © 1998 by David H. Stern. Published by Jewish New Testament Publications, Inc. Used by permission. All rights reserved.

HADASSAH, QUEEN ESTHER OF PERSIA

Diana Wallis Taylor
www.dianawallistaylor.com

ISBN: 978-1-64123-213-5
eBook ISBN: 978-1-64123-214-2

Printed in the United States of America
© 2019 by Diana Wallis Taylor

Whitaker House
1030 Hunt Valley Circle
New Kensington, PA 15068
www.whitakerhouse.com

Library of Congress Cataloging-in-Publication Data
Names: Taylor, Diana Wallis, 1938- author.
Title: Hadassah, Queen Esther of Persia / Diana Wallis Taylor.
Description: New Kensington, PA : Whitaker House, 2019. |
Identifiers: LCCN 2019013245 (print) | LCCN 2019015562 (ebook) | ISBN
  9781641232142 (e-book) | ISBN 9781641232135 (paperback)
Subjects: LCSH: Esther, Queen of Persia—Fiction. | Xerxes I, King of Persia,
  519 B.C.-465 B.C. or 464 B.C.—Fiction. | Bible. Old Testament—History of
  Biblical events—Fiction. | Iran—History—To 640—Fiction. | BISAC:
  FICTION / Christian / Historical. | FICTION / Contemporary Women. | GSAFD:
  Bible fiction. | Biographical fiction.
Classification: LCC PS3620.A942 (ebook) | LCC PS3620.A942 H33 2019 (print) |
  DDC 813/.6—dc23
LC record available at https://lccn.loc.gov/2019013245

1 2 3 4 5 6 7 8 9 10 11 **LU** 26 25 24 23 22 21 20 19

DEDICATION

To women everywhere, who though faced with
overwhelming odds, draw on their strength and their God
to accomplish great and mighty things.

PROLOGUE

*H*adassah woke with a start and slowly looked around. She was in her own bed, but the dream puzzled her. In it, she had been alone, walking down a long hall with pillars on every side. She had called out for Mordecai, her guardian, but he did not answer her. She kept walking until the shadows enveloped her.

What could it mean?

Her people believed in dreams and visions. *Was it a portent of something to come?* Perhaps Adonai would reveal its meaning, in time. She shook off the lingering effects of the dream and concentrated on saying her morning prayers.

1

*H*adassah watched the medicine woman, Bardia, put a hand on her mother's brow for a moment and listen to her labored breathing. Shaking her head, Bardia looked down at Hadassah and crouched by her mother's side. The look on her face was grave. Hadassah's mother slowly opened her eyes and motioned for Bardia to come closer.

"She has a cousin... only relative... Mordecai... in Susa." Her mother closed her eyes, her breathing becoming hoarser, then opened her eyes again. "Send for him... he... will come... for her."

She turned glazed eyes to Hadassah. "Mordecai will come. He... is family... will...take care... of you." She slowly reached up and put a hand on Hadassah's tear-streaked face.

"Imah! Don't leave me!" Hadassah frantically clutched her mother's hand, but it became limp and her arm dropped lifelessly on the bed.

First, her papa got sick and died. And now her mama! She threw herself on her mama's body, her grief-stricken cries echoing in the house and outside. The healer quickly lifted her away from her mother's bedside and placed her further away, on the dirt floor.

"You must come away from her. Do you want to catch the fever also? She must be buried immediately."

Bardia stepped to the doorway and nodded to some of the men waiting there. Hadassah could only watch helplessly as her mama was quickly wrapped in a blanket and taken away. Her heart pounded as the healer took her by the hand. "You cannot stay here alone. You will have to stay with a neighbor until this cousin of yours comes."

Their neighbors were Tarig and his wife, Yara. He was not a kind man. He was always angry and Hadassah had heard them fighting many times. When he was drunk, he beat Yara and Hadassah could hear her cries. Fear coursed through her body. *Did this woman mean to take her there?* She cowered back from Bardia, but the healer grasped her hand tightly and pulled her out of the house and through the small courtyard to the home of Tarig and Yara.

"Come—you do not have a choice. If I were you, I'd pray to your God that your cousin comes soon."

Yara came to her doorway. Upon seeing Bardia and Hadassah, she sighed. "So the child's mother is dead?"

"Yes. Before she died, she said there is a relative in Susa. A cousin named Mordecai who works in the King's Treasury. He must be sent for."

Yara's brow creased and she sighed. "It will take days for a message to reach him." She looked down at Hadassah. "You expect me to care for her? She's a Jewish child."

The woman released Hadassah's hand. "I have work to do and others to care for. I cannot take her."

"Are there none of her people here?"

Bardia snorted. "They fled the city when the fever began."

Yara shook her head. "Then they were wiser than us." She studied Hadassah a moment. "You will do as I tell you and stay out of Tarig's way until your cousin comes for you."

Yara looked furtively toward the street. "My husband doesn't like children. I don't know.... What if she has the fever?"

Bardia waved a hand impatiently. "She is well. That is why I took her from the house. Her cousin is well off. You would be compensated for your trouble."

"What if this cousin does not come? Then what?"

"The Jews are fond of their children. I have seen this. He will come for her."

Yara sighed again and stepped back as Bardia almost pushed Hadassah into the house.

Yara waved a hand at Hadassah. "Go, sit over there in the corner until I can think what to do with you."

Bardia hurried away, calling over her shoulder. "I have others to tend to. Send for the cousin."

Yara watched her go and then reluctantly shut the door. She put her hands on her hips. "I do not know what Tarig will say. You better pray that your cousin comes." As she turned away, Hadassah heard her mutter, "If he comes ..."

2

Mordecai stood in the small courtyard of his home reading the papyrus scroll he'd just been handed. Sorrow filled his heart. His father's youngest brother, Abihail, and his wife had died of the fever. His arm dropped to his side.

He knew many of the Jews had chosen to remain in the city of Kish after the dispersal, even when King Darius put out an edict that they could return to Jerusalem. He'd just had news that fever was sweeping in Kish and he'd prayed the danger would pass his uncle's family. Now it was too late.

"I pray there are enough Jews to sit Kiddush for him," he murmured. It was too great a distance for him to go and it would be difficult to leave his work in the treasury for any length of time. As he read the rest of the scroll, the final words sent a jolt through him. His niece, Hadassah, had survived and was being kept by a neighbor until he could come for her. He stroked his beard, frowning as he considered the request. How old was Hadassah now? As well as he could remember, she should be around eight years old.

His wife, Jerusha was nearby, preparing their supper. He called to her and the urgency in his voice caused her to hurry to his side.

"What is wrong, Mordecai? Is it bad news?"

"My uncle Abihail and his wife are dead. The fever. That is grievous news, but there is more." He related the last part of the scroll.

"Oh, husband. A young girl? Are there no relatives to take her in?"

"My uncle was the last of our family. I am Hadassah's only living relative. I must go at once and bring her here." He paused. "I only saw her once, three years ago. A beautiful child."

Jerusha touched his arm. "Oh, my husband. We are to have a child in our home! What a blessing Adonai has bestowed on us."

"Perhaps, but we are still well past the age of child-rearing."

She smiled up at him. "Was not our Father Abraham almost one hundred and Sarai ninety? If Adonai has given us this blessing, surely He has a purpose in it."

Mordecai laughed. "That is true. Adonai has a purpose in everything He does. Leave it to you to see what I did not see."

He pulled on his beard thoughtfully. "I must go to my overseer and tell him what we have to do. He is a good man. I believe he will understand the urgency of the matter. And I must secure passage on a ship. It is the only way, since Kish is on an island."

As he hurried to the treasury, a word entered his mind. *Hurry.*

3

Hadassah sat motionless on a rough pallet, tightly clutching a small, carved toy lamb and listening to Tarig argue with his wife.

"You should have refused. Why are we forced to feed and care for her?"

"I went to the scribe and sent the message as soon as Bardia left. The king's messengers are swift. Hadassah's cousin will come for her."

Hadassah heard the fear in Yara's voice. *Would her cousin really come?*

Tarig pulled on his beard, which was as unkempt as his clothing. "What if he doesn't come for her? Then what?"

"She has no other family here. We can wait a little longer. Surely he will pay us for taking care of her."

He turned his attention to Hadassah, his eyes narrowing. "She is tall for her age and a pretty one at that. She could pass for older." His eyes narrowed. "I could get good money for her."

The tone in Yara's voice suddenly changed. "Her father, Abihail, has always spoken well of his nephew, a man named Mordecai. He works in the King's Treasury. Surely, he has money. Besides, Bardia said the Jews are strong on family. He will pay well for our care of his young cousin. I understand this Mordecai is the child's only living relative."

Tarig stood up suddenly. "It may be as you say, but if her cousin does not show up in a week's time…" He gave his wife a hard look and strode toward the door, then turned back to Hadassah and snarled at her. "If you know what's good for you, you'd better hope your relative comes."

When he had gone, Hadassah turned her eyes back to Yara. "My cousin will come for me." Her voice quavered. She sensed that Yara was not a mean person, but lived in fear of her husband. Her young mind raced. *Would Tarig hit her, too, if he was angry?*

The woman sighed. "I pray to our gods that he will come. If he does not, I do not know what my husband will do. What he has in mind will not be a good thing for you."

Terror gripped Hadassah. He had said he could get money for her. *What did that mean? Selling her? Would she be a slave? Where would she be taken?* She prayed silently, desperately. *Oh, Adonai, save me. Bring my cousin soon.*

Hadassah dreaded Tarig's return. She hugged her toy to her chest as Yara began to put their simple meal together.

As she continued to pray, the peace that came to her from time to time settled on her. Adonai was near, watching over her. The fear abated and she began to entertain herself by thinking about the stories her Abba told her from the *Torah*, the books of the law-giver, Moses. Her Abba taught her to be proud of being a Jew, "for we are a chosen people."

Tarig returned that evening and said little, but kept glancing at Hadassah from time to time and the look in his eyes once again struck fear in her heart. After their meal, she returned to the pallet and curled up for sleep, whispering the evening prayer her Abba had carefully taught her.

Praised are you, Adonai, our God, Ruler of the universe, who closes my eyes in sleep, my eyelids in slumber. May it be your will, Adonai, my God and the God of my ancestors, to lay me down in peace and then raise me up in peace. Let no disturbing thoughts upset me, no evil dream, nor troubling fantasies. May my bed be complete and whole in your sight. Grant me light so that I do not sleep the sleep of death, for it is you who illumines and enlightens. Praised are you, Adonai, whose majesty gives light to the universe.

Suddenly, Tarig stood over her. "What are you whispering? You'll say no prayers to the Jewish God in this house!" For a moment, she thought he would strike her. When she only nodded and shrunk back from him, he glared at her and, to her relief, stalked away.

This time, she prayed silently, in her heart. *Oh, God Who Sees, hear my prayer. Let the cousin come for me soon. Let him be a kind man, not like Tarig.*

Three more days went by and Hadassah sensed that Tarig was getting tired of waiting. After another argument with Yara, he left for his place of work, where he made bricks, his last words ringing in Hadassah's ears. "If the cousin is not here in two more days, I will wait no longer."

It was nearly mid-day when there was a knock firm on the door. Yara hesitated a moment before opening it. A man and woman stood before her.

"I am Mordecai, Hadassah's cousin." He indicated the woman. "This is my wife, Jerusha. We received your message and left right away, but travel was difficult."

Hadassah eyed the pair. The man was tall with a full beard and wore the Jewish *kippah* on his head. He spoke with courtesy, but also with authority.

Yara nodded quickly and looked past them at the street. "I hoped you would come soon. We've lost many people to the fever, including the child's father and now her mother." She glanced back at Hadassah. "My husband is... not disposed towards children... or Jews." She spread a hand inviting them to enter.

"There are not many Jews in the city, but it is difficult for... your people." She pointed at Hadassah. "That is the child."

The man approached Hadassah and crouched down so they were at eye level. "Do you know who I am?"

"You are my cousin, Mordecai." Hadassah's voice was clear and happy. This man had a kind face so she knew Adonai had heard her prayers. Everything would be all right now.

Mordecai gestured to the women who still stood by the door. "This is my wife, Jerusha. We have come to take you home with us."

As the woman approached, Hadassah studied her face. There were crinkle lines by her eyes and smile lines around her lips. Hadassah lost all sense of fear—and now, she was anxious to be out of this house. She looked at Mordecai's wife.

"Do you have children?"

Jerusha shook her head. "No, child, we have not been fortunate in that way. You will be our daughter."

Hadassah rose and put her hand in Jerusha's, smiling up at her.

Yara cleared her throat. "She had no place to go. We took her in." She spread her hands and gave Mordecai a meaningful look.

He nodded and reached inside his tunic. "Of course, you must be compensated for the time and trouble you have gone to. We thank you for caring for Hadassah until we could reach you."

He counted out some coins into her outstretched hand. Yara's eyes widened at the sum. She quickly pocketed the coins and picked up a small bundle.

"Her clothes," she murmured, handing the bundle to Jerusha. Yara then hurried to open the door. "You had best go quickly before my husband returns."

Mordecai raised his eyebrows, but said nothing. He led Jerusha and Hadassah down the narrow street in the direction of the docks.

As they passed through the city, Hadassah looked around. She had not been into the town much except to go to the marketplace with Imah before she got sick. It was not a large city and much of it underground. For the Sabbath, they would walk to a small building that was used as a synagogue. She would hold her mother's hand as they sat in the section for women and listened to the rabbi. She didn't understand much of what he said, but knew he read from the *Torah*. She liked the stories her papa told her from the books.

When papa got sick, Hadassah and Imah couldn't go to the synagogue anymore. Some neighbors left food outside their door, but did not come in. Mama said they were fearful of the fever. So many were dying.

Hadassah didn't feel sad about leaving the city. There was no one here she knew anymore. For a moment, she wondered why no one from the synagogue came for her. Were they all sick, too?

Jerusha gave her hand a gentle squeeze, interrupting her thoughts. Her eyes searched Hadassah's face. "Was her husband unkind to you? Did he hurt you in any way?"

Hadassah shook her head. "No. But he said if you didn't come, he was going to take me away somewhere. I'm glad you came. They argued a lot about me."

Mordecai pulled on his beard. "I wonder if her husband will see the coins at all."

Hadassah looked up at him. "I don't think she will get to keep them."

Jerusha shook her head. "I am glad we came for Hadassah as soon as we did. Oh, Mordecai, how blessed we are to have a child given to us in our old age."

Mordecai glanced at Hadassah and then at his wife. "I believe our lives are in for great changes."

Jerusha brought the bundle that Yara had given her up to her nose and sniffed. Her nose wrinkled and she gave Hadassah a quizzical look. "These are your only extra clothes?"

Hadassah hung her head. "Yes."

"It's all right, child. You will not need these anymore."

At Jerusha's urging, Mordecai stopped at the marketplace to purchase a new shift, a small quilted waistcoat, and a sash for Hadassah as well as some slippers.

Hadassah eyes opened in wonder at the beautiful clothing. "These are for me?"

Jerusha nodded. "You are our daughter now. You must dress as the daughter of Mordecai."

Hadassah's heart was full to bursting. Life in Kish had been difficult; the house was damp and many times, there was little food on the table. But now, she was to have new clothes and likely plenty to eat as well. She sent a silent prayer of thanks to the God Who Sees, who had provided for her.

At the edge of the marketplace was a *hammam*, a bathing house. Jerusha took Hadassah inside and arranged for a bath for her. She disposed of the odious bag of clothing Yara had given her.

Hadassah was embarrassed. Cleanliness was important to her people for it was in the law. Her mother had bathed her before she became ill, but when she took to her bed, no one cared for Hadassah. They were all afraid of the fever.

After her bath, Hadassah put on her new garments. She felt she could hardly speak for the happiness inside. *Oh, Adonai, thank you.* When her new Imah began to brush the dark locks that tumbled in waves down her back, she vowed to be very brave for there were many tangles.

Refreshed, they joined Mordecai and continued on.

As they neared the dock, a sailing ship sat rocking gently from side to side with the sea's current.

"Have you ever been on a ship, Hadassah?"

She shook her head and fearfully approached the large vessel. Jerusha held her hand and murmured encouraging words.

The captain eyed them curiously and questioned Mordecai before agreeing to give them passage.

"Where are you going?"

"We travel to Susa. It is our home."

"What do you do there?"

"I work for the King's Treasury."

The captain raised his eyebrows at the mention of the king. He nodded and took Mordecai's payment for the voyage.

Mordecai unrolled the pallets he'd carried and made a place for them in a corner of the deck. Other passengers did the same. There were no cabins and they would have to ride out the two-day voyage in the open air. At last, the captain began giving orders for the crew to set sail. As the ship moved out from the dock and rocked with the waves, Hadassah felt her stomach doing strange things. Jerusha helped her to the rail just in time.

They had bread, cheese, and some date cakes Mordecai had purchased in the marketplace. It would sustain them until they reached Susa.

Mordecai smiled at Hadassah. "Have some bread with a little salt. You will be all right."

The three of them slept close together in the gathering cold, with Hadassah in the middle. As she dropped off to sleep, for the first time since her parents died, Hadassah felt she was safe.

4

When at last they approached the city of Susa, Hadassah looked with amazement at the great brick buildings and crowds of people moving about the docks. In the distance stood the palace, a sprawling complex of huge buildings perched on a hill like some benevolent giant. The stone and brickwork gleamed in the sun.

Hadassah could not stop staring. Never had she seen something so magnificent. "Is that the home of the king?" She turned to Mordecai. "Have you seen him?"

"Yes, I have seen him. Darius is a good king and has shown kindness to our people, allowing many of them to return to Jerusalem, the holy city."

She frowned. "Did you live in Jerusalem?"

He seemed startled by her question. "My grandfather lived in Jerusalem once, but he and my people were taken as prisoners to Babylon. Years later, he was allowed to return to the holy city, but was captured again by the Persians and brought here to Susa. I was born here in Susa and our people were given our freedom. My father was a learned man and made sure I had a thorough education. I was fortunate to be gifted in learning many languages. Eventually, I was hired to work in the King's Treasury."

Her curiosity grew. "Are you the only one who works there?"

"No, child, I'm one of almost twelve hundred men who work in the treasury."

"What do you do?"

He smiled down at her. "I speak many languages, so it is my job to see that the merchants from the many provinces ruled by King Darius are addressed in their own language. We can transact business with greater ease."

Hadassah nodded. She was glad her cousin Mordecai was not a poor man like Tarig. While she was anxious to see the house where she would now live, her attention was suddenly caught by the sounds coming from the many stalls in the marketplace. Vendors cried out to those passing by, extolling their merchandise. Goats bleated and chickens squawked in wooden cages. One merchant's pen held several pigs. Nearby, hunks of meat hung on hooks. The smells from the pigpen made her pinch her nose shut. She gazed at the stalls displaying beautiful rugs and colorful fabrics that made her catch her breath.

They left the heart of the city and turned down a side street. Soon, Mordecai led them to a wooden door set into a wall. Mordecai produced a large iron key and opened the door. Hadassah was delighted to see a small inner courtyard with plants and flowers. Beyond was the entrance to the house.

Mordecai turned to Jerusha. "I will let my overseer know I have returned." He bent down to Hadassah. "I will be back later, child. Jerusha will show you around your new home."

As they entered the house, Hadassah could not stop turning around and around in excitement. There were colorful woven hangings on the walls, beautiful tile floors with pictures of birds and flowers, and soft Persian rugs. Silk cushions surrounded a low table and a small fireplace set in one wall held kindling ready to burn. A variety of potted plants added greenery to the room.

Hadassah was so taken by it all that she didn't hear Jerusha speak her name. Then the woman tapped her on the shoulder. "Would you like to see your room, child?"

What? She was to have a room of her own? She followed Jerusha down a short hallway to a small room with a table, a clay lamp, and a low bed with a wood framework. It had been covered with a silk fabric and a thin woven rug as a blanket.

Hadassah stared. "This is for me?"

"Yes, child. It is for you. I hope you will be happy here."

"You are my mama now?"

"Yes, Hadassah. If you wish to think of me that way, it would make me very happy."

"I may call you Imah?"

"Mama? Oh, Hadassah…" Tears in her eyes, Jerusha gathered the girl in a warm embrace.

5

When Mordecai was not at work, he enjoyed taking Hadassah on excursions around the city, pointing out places of interest and telling her about King Darius.

"Because of the king, there are good roads throughout the kingdom. Messengers are stationed along the roads only one day apart so no man has to ride more than that distance to carry messages from the king to his officials. They also carry messages from citizen to citizen, just as your message was brought to me."

"Does King Darius have many officials, Abba?"

"Each of the provinces of his kingdom has a governor, called a satrap."

Hadassah's mind was filled with questions, but Mordecai never tired of answering them for her. He was pleased that she had an inquiring mind. She listened attentively as he told her about the benefits of the kingdom.

Mordecai pulled a coin from a pocket in his tunic.

"King Darius designed this coin. We had different coins for the many ethnic peoples, but now, the coins are the same throughout the kingdom."

Mordecai was glad that Abihail and his wife had taught Hadassah both Hebrew and Aramaic, the official language of the kingdom. She was amazingly proficiency in both. Early on, he had cautioned her when to speak each language. "When we are about in the city, it is best to speak in Aramaic, but at home, we will speak Hebrew, as you are used to."

On this day, he pointed out many new buildings that were under construction. "As the city of Susa grows, so does the population."

Mordecai looked out across the city. "Soon, the king and many Persians will move to Persepolis for the summer. Sometimes, there are benefits to less population, at least for our people." He did not elaborate.

Today, Jerusha had asked him to keep Hadassah out of the house for a while so that she could prepare for a special occasion. When they returned, they found Jerusha had prepared Hadassah's favorite meal: fava bean stew with lamb, fresh bread, and bowls of olives, grapes, and cut melons. There was also a platter of sweet date cakes.

Jerusha smiled. "A very happy birthday, Hadassah."

They were celebrating Hadassah's tenth birthday. She had been with Mordecai, now her Abba, and Jerusha, her Imah, for two years. Memories of her life in Kish were hazy and distant. She was saddened to realize that at times, even her mother's face was hard to picture.

Hadassah had blossomed under Mordecai and Jerusha's care, growing taller with each passing year. Dark brows framed her clear hazel eyes; her hair, falling in auburn waves down her back, was like a beautiful cloud around her face.

Mordecai thought she was the most beautiful girl in their synagogue. He was pleased she'd made friends with two girls who lived nearby, Aziel and Talia. They were two years older than Hadassah, but the three enjoyed one another's company.

"It's a shame your friends could not join us on this special occasion."

"It is fine, Abba." Hadassah shook her head. "They talk incessantly about marriage and which boy in the synagogue would make a good choice for a husband."

Mordecai sighed. Her friends were only twelve and it was too soon for a betrothal...but one day, Hadassah would be eligible for marriage herself. He wondered if he would be ready to relinquish her. In the meantime, he avoided the subject of marriage. All Jewish maidens expected to be married. Perhaps things would be different when she was thirteen, but that was three years away.

Mordecai said the blessing and they were just about to enjoy Hadassah's special dinner, when the sound of wailing began to fill the air.

Jerusha put hand on his arm. "Husband, what has happened?"

Someone knocked at the gate. Mordecai frowned and hurried to open it. He spoke with a man who was standing there and then as he shut the gate, he stood for a moment with his head bowed. Then he turned toward them, greatly troubled.

He gathered Jerusha and Hadassah to himself.

"Abba, what is wrong?"

"One of the men in our synagogue, Ezra, has told me sad news. Our king, Darius, is dead. I must go to the palace. There is trouble brewing."

"Trouble, husband?"

"I will find out what is happening."

Mordecai closed the gate and hurried toward the palace. As he crossed the bridge and went through the gatehouse, men were milling about as a sense of gloom pervaded the air. He saw Nadab, one of the men who also worked in the treasury and had a brother working in the palace.

"Nadab, I just learned the king is dead. What is happening?"

"Xerxes, the king's eldest son by queen Atossa, is named the king's heir."

"He is the king's oldest son?"

"The oldest son by Queen Atossa born after Darius became king."

Nadab pulled his beard, frowning. "His right to the throne is being contested by his elder half-brother, Artobarzanes, born of Darius and his commoner first wife before the king rose to power."

Mordecai's brows creased. "How will it be settled?"

Nadab shook his head. "Who knows? Who knows what the coming days will hold for our city…for any of us?"

Mordecai knew he was speaking of their people. Left unspoken was that only Adonai knew what was to come.

When he returned home, Jerusha and Hadassah turned to him with questioning eyes and he told them what he had learned.

"Abba, what will happen now?"

"The matter will have to be settled, hopefully peacefully. We cannot afford a civil war over the throne."

The cloak of mourning was heavy over the city of Susa. Hadassah had overheard Abba and Imah talking quietly about a tower, but they stopped when she approached and began to talk of other things. Almost a week later, the king's body was taken to Persepolis, where the Persian kings held court for the summer months. Mordecai, Jerusha, and Hadassah listened in the marketplace as couriers described the funeral procession in detail for the people in Susa. The king was buried in the tomb he had prepared in Naqsh-e-Rustam, five kilometers from his palace in Persepolis prior to going to war.

The people huddled in groups all over Susa, exchanging any information they could glean. In truth, the entire kingdom was waiting to see what would happen.

Jerusha spoke with the other women at the well, hoping to hear more news. *Would Artobarzanes slay Xerxes to claim the throne? Would troops favorable to him attack the troops of the king?* Fear ran rampant through the city for weeks.

Finally, the Spartan king Demaratus, who was in exile from his own kingdom and living in the palace, argued successfully that under Spartan law, the first son of the reigning king was heir to the throne, no matter if sons had been born before his reign began. Xerxes was also favored because his mother, Atossa, was the daughter of Cyrus the Great, revered by the people. Her influence was great in the kingdom.

The people breathed a sigh of relief when news came that Xerxes planned to follow the ways of his father—benevolent to the different religions of the many provinces of his vast kingdom. His words were carried throughout the kingdom by his special couriers: "God did not create the world, God created happiness for mankind." The new king's words were both strange and promising.

"Does he believe in Adonai, Abba?" Hadassah was curious. How could the new king not believe God created the world?

Mordecai shook his head. "No, child, he is referring to the Zoastrian god, Ahura Mazda."

"That god did not make the world."

Mordecai chuckled. "You are right, my Hadassah. It is Adonai who made the world."

Xerxes was traveling back to the region from Babylonia, where he had served his father as acting governor. The coronation ceremony was to be held in the city of Persepolis, but the entourage would be coming to the palace in Susa later.

Those who had not retreated to Persepolis to escape the summer heat of Susa gathered at the now much smaller marketplace as messengers brought news of the splendid coronation ceremony. Hadassah was fascinated.

"What would it be like to see the king crowned, Abba? What does he look like?"

He smiled indulgently at her. "The king is said to have a pleasing countenance and a warrior's body. I believe he is only in his very early thirties."

The people of Susa looked forward to the grand procession when the king returned to Susa for the winter. It would take place in the fall, at the time of Rosh Hashanah, in the month of Tishri. The king would be carried on a royal throne and paraded through the streets to the palace. His wife, Queen Vashti, and his concubines would follow in their curtained litters.

6

*S*usa was in a state of jubilation. The king and his retinue were approaching the city and sentinels relayed the news of his progress.

When the king's procession entered the city at last, people ran to line the streets and cheer for him. As he passed, the people bowed to pay homage to their new king. Hadassah and Jerusha stood with Mordecai on a porch to watch the grand parade.

Hadassah clapped her hands as she listened to the jubilation of the people. First, came the men called the king's "immortals" nearly ten thousand strong, their wicker shields oiled and shining in the sun. They carried short spears, large daggers, and bows and arrows. They wore special cloth hats of deep purple that could be pulled down to protect their faces from dirt and dust. Today, they wore ceremonial dress garments of orange, red, and purple. Each man wore a gold earring in one or both ears. It was such a fearsome sight that Hadassah scrambled behind Abba and peeked out at them from under the safety of his strong arm.

Next came the queen's bejeweled litter and the crown prince's ornate wagon, which was pulled by four magnificent horses. These were followed by wagons holding the king's concubines and more of the king's household. The people who escaped the summer heat of Susa to travel with the king to Persepolis also returned, with their carts, camels, and horses bearing their household goods.

Hadassah had once asked Mordecai why the Persians left the city in the summer while the Jews and some of the poorer people stayed.

"I believe they are nomads at heart, child. They do not bear the heat well and prefer the cooler climate of Persepolis."

Hadassah remembered languishing in the courtyard one sweltering day in Av and wishing that she and her adoptive parents were Persians, too, and could get away from the heat.

The sound of drumbeats heralded the approach of the royal retinue. When he came into view at last, Hadassah saw the king sitting on a great golden throne atop an ornate platform pulled by six prancing white horses. He wore fabulous purple, red, and gold garments; on his head was a gold crown with glittering rubies and pearls. His right hand held a golden scepter. Hadassah jumped up and down with delight. The king had long curly hair and short beard. She thought him very handsome. He looked straight ahead, but occasionally nodded to people lining the street. As Hadassah watched him pass by, her young heart beating with excitement, she saw him smile. He would be a good king, she decided.

From then on, when Hadassah and her Imah went to the marketplace, she paid close attention whenever anyone mentioned the king. Each evening, she listened as Mordecai shared news from the palace. Hadassah decided that while Xerxes might be a kind king, he seemed to be ruling with an iron hand. On more than one occasion, Mordecai repeated a familiar refrain that was whispered about the treasury and outside the palace walls: "No one challenges the authority of the king and none dare oppose him."

After saying the blessing before their meal one evening, Mordecai broke off a piece of bread, handed it to Hadassah, and then turned to his wife, sighing. "King Xerxes just suppressed a revolt in Egypt in a very short campaign. And then he appointed his brother, Achaemenes, as satrap to govern there."

Rumors flew through the city that Xerxes planned an invasion of Greece, but was delayed by a revolt in Babylonia.

Mordecai faithfully kept his little family updated on news from the palace. He wanted them to know everything that was going on. Although he worked for the treasury, they were Jews, after all. How long would Xerxes continue the tolerance shown by his father if he was so ready to counter the least bit of opposition?

"The people of Babylonia have ignored the new satrap who was assigned to them, so the king has abolished the kingdom of Babel. He also removed and destroyed the golden statue of Bel, their god."

Hadassah frowned. "Bel is the god they worship, Abba?"

"Yes. It is said the Babylonian priest had to seize the hands of the statue at the beginning of each year to beseech their god for its blessings. Now the king has killed their priest. The title 'king of Babel' will be deleted from the king's documents and his title will now be King of Countries."

The rebellion was ended after a short battle and heavy losses among the Babylonians. Hadassah shivered as she thought back to the fierce ten thousand "immortals" who had paraded into Susa. And now, Xerxes might be planning to wage war against Greece. His father, Darius, had been soundly defeated there. The rumors were that Xerxes planned to conquer Greece to restore his father's honor.

7

*H*adassah stopped feeding the chickens for a moment. With one hand, she lifted her long, thick auburn hair off her neck, trying to feel a momentary relief from the heat. The month of Av had begun and she keenly felt the sun's rays beating down on her. At thirteen, her body was already curving into womanhood. Soon, she would be old enough to marry. She was aware of the glances of the young men in the synagogue. Abba told her she was the most beautiful girl in Susa, but she shook her head, attributing that to her guardian's fatherly pride.

She tossed another handful of crumbs and thought of the troubling dream that came again last night, creeping in to disturb her sleep like a thief and startle her awake. In the five years since her first mother died, the memory of her face had slowly faded away, but Hadassah saw her clearly, briefly, in the dream—the same old, unsettling dream in which she was walking alone down a long hallway with pillars on every side. *What could it mean? Was her mother trying to warn her of something? Did the dream foretell a strange future for her?* She shook her head. She was no prophet, no

David. She had a good life and was grateful to her Abba and Imah, who had gathered her in their arms and hearts after her parents died. She could not remember her father at all—he had worked so hard and usually did not get home until she was fast asleep. And she barely remembered her mother...except when she had this dream, which came sporadically, without warning.

She shrugged off the negative thoughts. After gathering the few eggs, she turned her attention to their goat. The doe's sides were swollen with the new life she carried. The goat had been a little bleating thing, only two weeks old, when she had been given to Hadassah shortly after she came to her new home. Abba had thought, and guessed rightly, that it would help Hadassah in her new surroundings and comfort her in her grief. The kid had required care day and night until it gained strength.

Hadassah smiled. Now, unless she penned it up, the goat followed her everywhere. Hadassah was the only mother it had known.

Their house was larger than many of those occupied by her countrymen in the city, but because it was near the palace, they could not keep a large number of animals without inviting complaints about the noises and smells. But six chickens and one goat was fine. They had fresh milk and eggs every day. Hadassah stroked the goat's head.

"Your time will be soon, little mother. You will have another baby to care for." *But not for long*, Hadassah thought sadly. It would be killed for food when it was old enough or, if it was completely unblemished, it would be used as a Passover sacrifice.

With a sigh, she patted the doe on the head again and turned back toward the house, where Imah was setting out the morning meal. Abba would be going to the treasury soon.

Earlier, Hadassah had placed two loaves of bread dough in the stone oven. The smell of freshly baked bread made her realize how hungry she was.

Jerusha paused and looked up. "And how is your little goat this morning?"

Hadassah smiled. "The birth will be soon."

"That is the way with motherhood, child. One day, you will have children of your own and it will be your lot."

Hadassah sighed. Marriage occupied her thoughts lately. Her friends Aziel and Talia married the year before and Talia was already with child. Hadassah daydreamed about who her husband would be one day and secretly looked forward to seeing a certain young man at the synagogue. She sighed again. Abba, to her consternation, did not even want to talk about the subject. "Time enough," he would grouse. Surely, he didn't want her to remain unmarried forever.

Mordecai, having said the morning prayers, reached for some fresh grapes and cheese. Then he tore off a chunk of the warm bread and washed it down with a cup of wine, anxious to hurry to his appointed post. Hadassah was glad of his expertise in several languages. It made him indispensable in dealing with the large crowd of merchants who brought goods to the palace. While Aramaic was still the official language of the kingdom, some people from the far provinces were more comfortable speaking their native tongue. With so many provinces, the great Persian kingdom encompassed many different peoples and languages. As one of the King's accountants, Mordecai helped to keep track of the wealth that poured into the kingdom and made sure that merchants who brought in goods were paid. The position was a good one. Many Jews worked in the Persian city; Abba said the king recognized them as trustworthy.

When he had gone, Hadassah cleared the table and wiped the silver platters. Then she and Jerusha put on their head coverings and Hadassah picked up the water jar as they headed for the well and marketplace. Perhaps they would hear more news of the king's plans for Greece.

Hadassah loved the rich sights and sounds of the market. Vibrant silk and embroidered fabrics were displayed for the women of Susa and stalls carried jewelry of gold and silver inset with precious stones. Hadassah saw a beautiful bracelet inset with rubies and, for a moment, pictured it on her wrist. At a glance from Jerusha, she felt immediately chastened. Some of the Jewish women had adopted Persian clothing and wore jewelry, but her Abba discouraged an outward display of wealth.

Fragrances wafting from the stalls of the perfumers mingled with the smell of fresh leather. Then they made their way down the bakers' street. While most of the Jewish women baked their own bread, many Persian women purchased fragrant loaves and cakes from the bakers.

They came to the stalls of wine merchants and Jerusha purchased two bottles of wine for their table. Hadassah wondered what it would be like to live in a small village and press their own grapes as Imah had done as a girl, mashing the sweet fruit with her feet in a winepress.

As they paused in a silk merchant's stall so Jerusha could examine a bolt of cloth, the sound of a child crying nearby caught Hadassah's attention. She turned to see a small Hebrew boy no more than three, sitting on the stones nearby, his sobs muffled by the noise around him. He looked up at her, his face the picture of woe. Hadassah hurried to him.

"Are you lost?"

"My Imah is lost," he whimpered.

"Ah, I see." She lifted him up into her arms and comforted him. "We will find her. Adonai knows right where she is."

He looked at her with wide eyes. "He knows my Imah?"

She smiled kindly. "Of course. Adonai knows all of us."

Just then, Hadassah spotted a woman moving frantically through the marketplace, her face evidencing her panic as she called out. "Isaac! Isaac!"

Hadassah looked at her small charge. "Is your name Isaac?"

He nodded and sniffed again.

In a moment, the woman spotted Hadassah holding the little boy and, with obvious relief, hurried to them. Hadassah smiled at her. "Isaac tells me his Imah is lost."

The woman gratefully received her small son. "Thank you for caring for him. I only looked away for a moment at one of the merchant's stalls and he was gone. May Adonai bless you for your kindness."

Hadassah nodded. "And may Adonai bless you and your family as well. Shalom." She watched the woman walk away, holding her son tightly. When she had children, Hadassah vowed, she would never let go of their hands.

She spotted Jerusha in animated conversation with her friend, Golda. There must be exciting news in the city. She hurried to join them.

"...and all his officers, satraps, and officials. Such a banquet the city has never seen..."

Hadassah interrupted. "A banquet?"

Bursting with the importance of her news, Golda flung a hand up. "The king is giving a banquet for all the important officers in his kingdom to show his wealth. It may go on for weeks! A huge tented pavilion is being set up outside the palace. It is said it can hold up to ten thousand."

Jerusah shook her head. "So many people! What will happen to our city?"

Hadassah thought back over the past three years. So far, the kingdom had prospered under Xerxes and her people had been relieved to find the new king was as benevolent as his father had been. He was known, however, to be impulsive and vengeful, especially when he had too much wine.

Jerusha, ever practical, shook her head. "And where are all these officials and their servants going to sleep? What will it take to feed them?"

Golda waved one hand in the air. "Who knows? Thousands will be camping outside the city." She gave Jerusha and Hadassah a knowing look. "And you had better secure your animals lest they be taken to help feed all those *goyim!*"

Golda hurried off to share her news with anyone who perchance had not heard. Jerusha shook her head again as they turned toward their home, stopping at the well to fill the water jug.

"Mordecai will be able to tell us more when he returns home this evening, but I do not have a good feeling about this. With all those men and their entourages and animals, the city will never be the same."

As they walked home, Hadassah thought of the king and his queen. It was a world so foreign to her. Though they lived in a Persian city, her people kept mostly to themselves, honoring the Torah and celebrating their own way of life. The king did not interfere with the Hebrew religion; so far, Jews had freedom in the city.

Hadassah listened to the sparrows calling to one another from the rooftops and smiled to herself. Imah shared stories that her own grandmother told her about listening to the birds singing in the mulberry trees near Jerusalem. Hadassah wondered if she would be able to see the holy city someday.

Jerusha began to walk faster. "Sundown is only a few hours away. We have much to do before the Sabbath begins."

Hadassah nodded and also quickened her pace. Tonight, they would take part in the traditional rituals and then they would go to the synagogue for prayers. Her heart beat a little faster. She would be able to see Shamir again. This past year, they had only exchanged a few words, but he seemed to go out of his way to speak to her.

Shamir had celebrated his bar mitzvah three years before and his voice when he recited the Shema was strong and becoming deeper. He was a studious young man and tall like his father. As the rabbi's son, it was likely he would follow in his father's footsteps.

Sometimes, on a Sabbath afternoon, Hadassah daydreamed of Shamir coming with his father and having a betrothal ceremony. Then in a year, the two of them would stand beneath the *chuppah*, the wedding canopy. Would he come one day with his father and seek her as his wife? It was only a daydream, for every other young Jewish girl in Susa had the same dream of marrying Shamir! Hadassah lifted her chin. Abba could not put off her marriage forever. She would be a proper Jewish wife and there would be children.

When Mordecai returned from the King's Gate, his mood was somber. "You have heard the news, wife?"

"Yes, in the marketplace. Everyone is talking about the king's banquet."

Hadassah watched Abba clasp and unclasp his hands. He looked anxious. "The city will be ruined. Too many people and their animals will trample the streets and I can hardly imagine the supplies it will take to feed them all. When I asked how long the banquet might last, no one could give me an answer. It could last a week, or a month—or more. It's at the king's whim. He wishes to impress his officers, officials, and satraps from the various provinces by displaying his wealth."

"But Abba, what is the purpose?"

He turned to Hadassah, his eyes full of concern. "It is about his campaign to conquer Greece. He wishes to avenge the defeat of his father, King Darius. He plans to display his wealth to his satraps to present himself as invincible. His army is larger than that of the Greeks and his armada of ships is the greatest in the world. The king expects total victory."

He paused and put his arm around her. "You must be extra diligent, Hadassah. The men of Susa do not harm our women, but some of the men from other provinces may not hesitate to accost a beautiful young woman, Jew or Persian. When a man is drunk and far from his family, he may do things he may not do when he is sober. If you must go to the marketplace, cover your face and go only with Jerusha. Do nothing to call attention to yourself in any way. Do you understand?"

He started to turn away and as an afterthought, faced her again. "Pass the word to your friends, Hadassah. It is important."

Hadassah nodded her head, and for the first time since coming to live with Abba and Imah, she felt a stab of fear.

8

All day and long into the night, the caravans and entourages came. Servants were assigned to constantly clean the streets from the defecation of the many animals. Every available extra space was commandeered and, as Golda foretold, the plains outside the city were covered with tents, people, and many animals.

They heard about one young Jewish girl who foolishly ventured out to the marketplace alone and was nearly accosted by one of the soldiers. She was saved only by the appearance of two of her brothers, who had noticed her absence and realized the danger. The drunken official backed down and they hurried her back home. The story was repeated to all the families in the synagogue as a warning.

The effects of the influx of people from the various territories seemed incomprehensible to Hadassah. Susa was a large city and the marketplace was usually full of people more than half the year, when the king reigned from his citadel. Now, it was so loud, noisy, and crowded that there scarcely seemed room to breathe. And besides the usual vendors, there were strange, sweaty men with beady eyes who were looking to get rich from the additional population. From morning until night, the streets rang with the sound of their wheedling pleas to passersby.

Servants buying for their visiting households tried to outbid the local populace and many a housewife went home with less than they wanted to purchase. Jewish housewives were the most slighted and it was the talk of every gathering of women Jerusha knew.

Mordecai was working long hours, as were the other men at the King's Treasury. He gazed bleary eyed at Jerusha and Hadassah early one morning after only a few hours of sleep. "The number of animals and supplies is nearly overwhelming." He was expected back at the treasury shortly after dawn.

Hadassah sought to imagine the food that must be collected for such a banquet. "How much food does it take, Abba?"

"Thousands of animals, Hadassah, and vegetables, fruit, beer, eggs... crates and barrels and cages, along with baskets of produce. It is staggering. The merchants come by the hundreds and all must be paid."

He ate his simple breakfast and hurried out the gate.

Jerusha and Hadassah watched him go. Hadassah shook her head. "He cannot keep up this pace, Imah. He looks so tired."

"Yes, but what can we do? We can only pray that this banquet will end soon and all those officials will go home."

⌒

Covering her face carefully to avoid drawing unwanted attention, Hadassah went to the well with Imah and two neighbor women.

Golda raised a waving hand in the air and seemed to be pleading with Adonai. "They use the well to water their horses! How long before they drink it dry?"

Jerusha put a gentle hand on her friend's arm. "We are all concerned about the water, Golda. We must be sure to store as much as possible. Mordecai was able to get two large stone jars similar to those used for purification. We are filling them with water. You must do the same."

Hadassah listened to their conversation with growing alarm. *What if the well ran dry? What would they do for water? Would the king bring water in from other sources?* All of Susa was whispering their fears about the water supply. She and Jerusha hurried into the house and emptied their water pitchers into the large stone vessels that were almost full. The water would last for a while… if they were careful. But how long would the king's banquet last?

～

A weary Mordecai came home late that evening, shaking his head. "There seems to be no end in sight. The word among the cooks and some of the merchants is that the king wants them to prepare for several months."

Jerusha gasped. "Several months? What will it take to feed that many men and their people?"

Mordecai wasn't sure how to respond. He was thinking of the cargo lists of incoming merchandise he had processed this last week.

One thousand stable sheep, 1,000 fattened head of cattle, 1,000 sheep, 15,000 lambs, 500 stags, 500 gazelles, 1,000 ducks, 500 geese, 10,000 doves, 10,000 assorted small birds, 10,000 assorted fish, 10,000 assorted eggs, 10,000 loaves of bread, 10 ,000 jars of beer, 10,000 skins with wine, 1,000 wooden crates with vegetables, 300 containers of olive oil, 300 containers of salted seeds, 100 containers of parched barley, 100 pomegranates, 100 bunches of grapes, 100 pistachio cones, 100 containers of thyme, 10 homers of perfumed oil, ten homers of sweet smelling onions…

The enormity of the process, with merchants to pay and delivery schedules to contend with, was overwhelming. The 1,200 men of the treasury worked long hours with barely time to rest. The king was feeding nearly 47,000 officials, officers, and important persons from the king's provinces.

Just that morning, Moradecai had to deal with merchants from Cappadocia, Pamphylia, Urarto, Armania, Sapagydia, Elam, and Gandara. The noise of the animals and shouting merchants had become a daily, irritating routine that forced Mordecai to use every last drop of patience. Each merchant insisted that his goods were the most important to be processed so he could be paid and on his way home.

Suddenly realizing that Jerusha and Hadassah were still looking at him expectantly, he shrugged. "Hundreds of lambs, fowl, vegetables, rice, fruit, cheeses… We are processing many merchants each day from different provinces."

Mordecai sat down and shook his head. "By the time, the king is satisfied that he has shown them his wealth and power, Susa will be a dead city."

Jerusha sat down next to him. "Husband, we must pray that the king will see this and bring these banquets to an end. Surely he does not wish our city to be destroyed."

"He may not wish it, but he is occupied with his merrymaking and has ignored the advice of his trusted advisors." Mordecai sighed. "Tomorrow night begins the Sabbath. Let us look forward to honoring Adonai. And a day of rest."

After Mordecai left for his post the next morning, Jerusha and Hadassah began to prepare for the Sabbath meal. Hadassah kneaded the dough for the challah bread and divided it into two parts, which she braided before placing it in the clay oven. Then she got the embroidered challah cover out of a small chest.

Jerusha placed the Sabbath candles on the table and set the wooden cup for the wine next to them before going to the storeroom for the wine.

Just as they were despairing that Mordecai might not make it in time, he rushed into the courtyard. When he had washed his hands, they gathered around the table while Jerusha lifted her mantle over her head and lit the Sabbath candles. She covered her eyes with her hands and recited the blessing:

Blessed are you Lord, our God, sovereign of the universe,

Who has sanctified us with His commandments and commanded us

To light the lights of Shabbat.

Hadassah listened to the familiar prayer, thinking of the women of her race, not only in Susa, but in other parts of the empire, who were reciting the Sabbath prayer at the same time. She smiled to herself. One day, she, too, would have a household of her own and light the Sabbath candles.

When they had partaken of the challah bread and the Kiddush had been recited over the wine with the appropriate blessings, they joined their neighbors in walking to the synagogue for the evening service. As she looked through the lattice at the men on the other side, Hadassah frowned. Shamir was not there. The rabbi slowly stepped on the *bimah*, the podium, and addressed the congregation.

"Adonai has been gracious. A miracle. My son, Shamir, while walking to the synagogue, was accosted by some *goyim* from another province. They knocked him down, called him terrible names, and kicked him." The rabbi paused to get his emotions under control. "Who knows what would have happened if an innkeeper and a soldier had not stopped them? My son, may God be praised, has only two broken ribs and a broken arm. I have sent him away from the city to stay with relatives while he heals."

He shook his finger at the congregation. "Men of Israel, protect your wives and children. This is a sad time in our city. Men who are drunk from the king's banquet roam the city looking for amusement. What happened to my son could happen to any one of you. Your wives or daughters could be violated. We must be wise in all our comings and goings until this banquet of the king's comes to an end and may Adonai grant that these people soon leave our city!"

Hadassah's heart beat furiously and she put a hand to her chest. *Danger? Shamir had been hurt? How long would it take his injuries to heal? When would he return to Susa?* She could not tell Abba about her feelings for Shamir, at least not yet. Now, she could only wait and pray that soon, the overwhelming number of visitors would leave.

As the murmurs rose from those listening, the rabbi leaned toward the men and shook his finger again, repeating each word with emphasis. "Watch your wives and daughters. Do not let your sons travel alone in the city until these *goyim* have gone."

One of the men spoke up. "Rabbi, this has been several months. When will they leave? Our city is nearly in shambles!"

The men's voices rose in anger as Hadassah and the other women watched anxiously.

The rabbi shook his head slowly. "No one knows the outcome of this. My advice to all of you as your rabbi is to be as inconspicuous as possible. It is not a time for noisy celebrations that attract attention."

Hadassah suddenly realized the rabbi could be talking about betrothal and wedding ceremonies. *If there were singing and dancing, would the goyim interfere?* The women around her began to fiercely whisper among themselves. This was unwelcome news. After the service, Hadassah hurried home with Mordecai and Jerusha. No one stopped to visit. It seemed everyone had the same idea, to reach the relative safety of their homes.

9

*O*ne evening, when Mordecai returned home from the palace quite late, Hadassah noted his brow furrowed in thought.

"What news do you bring this evening, Abba?"

"The king is moving forward with his battle against Greece. Along with providing food for the king's banquet, we have been sending supplies to his forces. They are digging a channel through the Isthmus of the peninsula of Mount Athos." He unrolled a soft leather scroll that contained a map and pointed out the area to the two women. "We are sending provisions also to stations on the road through Thrace. The king has made an alliance with Carthage..."

Hadassah looked up from the map. "Will they help the king fight?"

"The alliance will deprive Greece of the support of the powerful kings of Syracuse and Argentum. It is said that many of the smaller Greek states have taken our side—Thessaly, I believe, and also Thebes and Argos."

Hadassah loved that her Abba shared this information, not only with Imah, but with her as well. She'd overheard him tell Jerusha that he was pleased she was interested in the city's affairs. He thought she had an excellent mind and grasped the concepts of governing well. As they partook of the evening meal, Jerusha turned to him. "When will the king leave for the battle with Greece?"

He broke a piece of cheese and paused. "Perhaps when he has prepared all his officers for war. It may take almost a year to gather the army he needs from all the provinces."

Hadassah went to her bed that night, wondering about the king preparing for war. *What does a war look like? How would it affect her family? How many soldiers did the king seek to gather?*

She shook her head. Abba had taught her much about running a city, but a waging war? That was beyond her.

The next morning, after Mordecai had gone, Jerusha turned to her. "Our stores are running low, Hadassah. We need to go to the marketplace. I would like to get some more flour, vegetables, and dates." She reached for her mantle and started toward the gate.

"Hurry, Hadassah, we must go quickly. Golda and Rachab will go with us. It is better to go with four than two." Just before she stepped out into the street, she turned back to Hadassah. "Oh, dear. I left the basket in the kitchen. Please get it."

Hadassah retrieved the basket and as she neared the gate, she heard the sound of hoofbeats on the cobblestones. Two riders were racing down the narrow street. Jerusah was startled and as Hadassah tried to grab her arm, her Imah lost her balance and fell backward toward the street. One of the horses reared and his hoof struck her in the head. Blood gushed from the wound as she fell unconscious to the pavement. The man cursed at them and Hadassah screamed. Neighbors rushed to her side and one of the men shook his fist at the two riders, who continued on their way without even a backward glance.

Rachab wrapped her shawl around Jerusha's head to stop the bleeding as her husband, Zeri, carried Jerusha into her home. Another neighbor ran to fetch Mordecai.

Jerusha was laid on her pallet and fear filled Hadassah seeing Imah's pale face and the bloody wound on her head.

Someone sent for Bardia, the local midwife who was also a healer. She arrived just as Mordecai rushed into the house and knelt by his wife's side.

"What happened?" He looked around at those gathered in the house.

"Oh, Abba!" Hadassah bit her lip as she told Mordecai about the accident. "They didn't even stop!" They watched Bardia gently wipe the blood from Jerusha's forehead. Then she used a paste to close up the wound, followed by a poultice from some herbs she carried.

Hadassah looked pleadingly at Bardia. "Can you help her?"

"It would depend on the force of the kick and how hard she struck her head when she fell. I can treat the outside wound, but what has been damaged inside her head, only Adonai knows. You must pray that He will have mercy on her and grant healing."

Murmurs rose from the group of neighbors and friends as they began to beseech God on Jerusha's behalf. Hadassah wept, fear for Jerusha filling her chest so much, it hurt. Mordecai sat nearby, almost in a daze. Jerusha's eyes remained closed and her breathing was shallow.

After the neighbors left to tend to their own families, Hadassah continued to care for the woman who had been like a mother to her all these years. Her tears fell freely as she lovingly wiped her Imah's face. Thoughts of another woman lying on a pallet came to her mind—her first mother, dying of a fever. She brushed the terrible scene from her mind. *Imah must get well.*

In the wee hours of the morning, while Mordecai sat with his head in his hands, quietly praying, Jerusha stopped breathing, slipping away so quietly that Hadassah thought she was still sleeping. She reached out tentatively, putting her hand on Jerusha's chest, and gasped. Her Imah was dead.

A whimper escaped as she turned slowly, tears running down her cheeks. Her eyes met Mordecai's. "Abba, she is gone," she whispered. He rose quickly and knelt by Jerusha's bedside.

Looking at her still form, his face crumpled with grief. He began to cry out, tearing his outer garment. Hadassah did the same. Their cries were heard and there was a knock at the door. Hadassah opened it.

Rachab clasped her hands and bowed her head. "Jerusha?"

Hadassah nodded, too overcome to speak.

"I will gather the women and call for Bardia. You must be strong, Hadassah, and do what is needed for her."

Mordecai, still wailing, stumbled outside to be comforted by the rabbi and the other men who gathered to share his grief.

Bardia arrived and began to cut away Jerusha's bloody clothes with a small knife. She used a strip of cloth to tie Jerusha's jaw and knotted it on her head, closing her mouth. After the body was washed, Hadassah, struggling to contain her tears, carefully anointed Jerusha in olive oil and spices as Bardia directed. When that was completed, Jerusha's hair was trimmed and she was wrapped in a large piece of linen with spices tucked in the folds. As was the custom, she would be buried on the same day she died, so some of the men had already gone ahead to prepare the gravesite. Jerusha's body was carefully moved on to a plank, which Mordecai and three other men carried to the small burial ground the king set aside for the Jews.

When the two pipers arrived, the procession of weeping mourners made their way to the cemetery. Neighbor after neighbor joined them, the men taking turns carrying Jerusha's litter to the grave to show their respect for her and Mordecai. Many could recall the times when Jerusha sat with them in sickness or brought food. Her acts of kindness made her well-loved among the Jews of Susa.

Passersby in the crowded city stopped to stare at the funeral procession of praying men and keening women crying out to Adonai. They shook their heads and turned away.

A weeping Hadassah clung to Rachab for support, while Mordecai's friends surrounded and comforted him as he prayed and grieved. Hadassah bowed her head. She had lost her mother twice.

The mourner's kaddish and psalms of comfort were recited as Jerusha's body was laid to rest. When the sun began its descent, the mourners reluctantly returned to their homes. That evening, *seudat havra'ah,* the meal of condolence consisting of bread and hard-boiled eggs, was brought and left by neighbor women. Mordecai and Hadassah sat bare-footed on low stools and reluctantly ate the food in silence. It was not a time for eating, in spite of tradition.

Mordecai, torn between mourning for the wife he loved and returning to his job at the king's gate, went to share the news about the loss of his wife with Behnam, his Persian overseer. *Would Behnam allow him to be absent from his daily tasks for the seven days of mourning?* Mordecai walked away from the house, his shoulders slumped. Hadassah prayed fervently that the overseer would be kind and agree to respect their customs.

Since there were only two in the family, Hadassah sat with two neighbor women. When Mordecai was present, two of the men joined him. It was a silent circle for neither she nor Mordecai were expected to speak. One of the men read the twenty-third Psalm written by King David, the beloved former king of Israel. The man's low, modulated voice and the familiar words brought some comfort to Hadassah.

Adonai is my shepherd; I lack nothing. He has me lie down in grassy pastures, he leads me by quiet water, he restores my inner person. He guides me in right paths for the sake of his own name. Even if I pass through death-dark ravines, I will fear no disaster; for you are with me; your rod and staff reassure me. You prepare a table for me, even as my enemies watch; you anoint my head with oil from an overflowing cup. Goodness and grace will pursue me every day of my life; and I will live in the house of Adonai for years and years to come.

At the end of the day, as the mourners returned to their own homes, they murmured the familiar words, "May Adonai comfort you with all the mourners of Zion and Jerusalem."

Hadassah was grateful that Abba's overseer, Behnam, lived up to his name, *man of honor.* He was familiar with the Jewish time of mourning and, at his own risk, he allowed Mordecai the seven days that he needed to sit *shiva.*

∽

As the weeks went by, Mordecai grew thinner. Hadassah understood his sorrow, but was surprised one day when he reluctantly put aside his mourning clothes and slowly gathered the garments he had worn to work before Jerusha's passing. When she questioned him, he shook his head sadly.

"Behnam has said that my appearance has jeopardized my position at the treasury. It seems the other men have watched and commented. If it gets back to the king, Behnam would have to let me go. I cannot support us if I lose my position."

With a heavy sigh, he went to bathe and dress.

∽

Susa was a changed city. What Abba had predicted weeks ago had come true. It was as if an enemy had ravaged the once-beautiful city. The fountains sputtered sluggishly and the parks had been trampled to dirt. While the people dared not murmur against the king, there was an undercurrent of distrust and anger.

Then one day, to the people's relief, the news was spread that the unwelcome banquet guests had been ordered back to their provinces—to prepare for war.

Mordecai kept Hadassah appraised of the gossip from the palace.

"Mardonius, the king's cousin, speaks constantly of war with Greece. He feeds the king's ear with talk of punishing the Greeks for what they did to his father. Last year, the king began to mobilize the Persian army. With so many provinces, who knows how long it will take? The officers and officials have been sent back to their provinces to gather their forces."

"What will a war with Greece mean for us, Abba?"

He stroked his beard and sighed. "I believe we need to pray that our king wins the battle."

‿

In the midst of everyone's speculation over the war with Greece, another announcement by the palace shocked the king's subjects. Xerxes appeared to be concerned about the negative effects on his city by his officials from the various provinces. The people were informed that the king was planning another banquet, this time for the other nations and their ambassadors at Susa.

Mordecai put his hand to his brow as he gave Hadassah the news. "Those who work for the king are also invited, along with their families. You will have to set aside your own mourning garments, Hadassah. We must attend or our absence will be noted."

Hadassah sighed. Their king was so capricious!

Mordecai gazed at her solemnly as he recounted the words of his overseer. The man had clapped him on his back in good spirits. "You, my friend, will partake of what is left of the king's bounty. It is to be held in the palace gardens. There will be much wine served in gold goblets. You will eat and drink all you wish. And the queen has been instructed to entertain all the women of the city at the same time."

"Truly, Abba? How did you respond?"

He shrugged. "Oh, *ahuva*, loved one, what could I say but pretend to be enthusiastic about the great honor the king was bestowing on his subjects?"

The following morning, Golda came to pay Hadassah a visit. She mentioned to the older woman that she had often wondered what the inside of the palace looked like. "I truly am looking forward to seeing it for the first time."

Golda's eyes widened. "Ach, we must be ever cautious, Hadassah. There might be a hidden reason for the banquet. We are a people despised by many in the palace. They could be planning something."

The woman was forever negative. Hadassah stifled her retort, smiled at her guest, and offered her another date cake. "I think we will be safe having a banquet with the queen."

"Not if they poison the food!"

After Golda left, still muttering about the banquet, Hadassah picked up the broom and swept the courtyard. She began to daydream as she worked, pondering the queen's banquet, the palace, and the king. *I wonder what the queen's quarters are like...*

10

*M*uch to Hadassah's surprise, Mordecai came home one evening with some new garments for her: an embroidered gown in a soft, light blue fabric, a mantle of fine white lace, and an embroidered vest and a pair of leather slippers dyed a dark blue.

Hadassah felt overwhelmed by the gifts. "Oh, Abba, you got these for me? For the queen's banquet?"

"Though we are in mourning, you must dress befitting your family status. There must be no occasion for comment. Mourning clothes would not be considered acceptable and they would also mark you as one of the Jewish people. That would not do."

"Yes, of course, Abba." Hadassah sensed there was a hidden reason for Mordecai's forceful words and his decision to buy her these beautiful clothes. It occurred to her that the more she fit in with the other women, the less likely she would be noticed. Thankfully, she would be going to the banquet with their neighbors, Rachab, Leah, and Golda. Her friends, Aziel and Talia, would also be there.

When the evening came, Hadassah dressed carefully, braiding her hair and winding it around her head. She kissed the gold earrings and necklace that her dear Imah had once worn before putting them on herself. Then she wound a sash of soft leather around her waist and put the slippers on her feet.

The families hurried toward the palace, where the king's eunuchs met them at the gate.

A tall man, heavily built, with a bald head, stepped forward. "I am Hegai, in charge of the women's quarters. I will escort the women to the queen's banquet." He stood for a moment gazing out at the assembled crowd. "Woman of Susa, follow me." Hegai waved one arm in a sweeping gesture, directing them toward the palace.

Mordecai nodded meaningfully at Hadassah, reminding her of his earlier admonition to remain as inconspicuous as possible. She tilted her head down slightly in return. *I will be cautious, Abba!* Another of the king's servants gestured for the men to follow him toward the court of the king's gardens, where preparations had been made to seat thousands.

Hadassah and the other women followed through great hallways decorated with beautiful inlaid tile floors, with murals of birds and flowers on the walls. They passed massive columns of marble and hangings of the finest, brightly colored silk depicting great battle scenes and fabulous beasts. Hadassah wished she could stop and study them, but of course, that was impossible. On one wall was a massive stone rendition of a majestic, rearing horse. Everywhere they looked was evidence of the king's great wealth. Hadassah and the women around her were all overwhelmed by what they observed, awed by the opulence around them. Hadassah did not even dare to whisper to her friends, so taken aback was she at the splendor.

Surrounded by the other women, Hadassah and her neighbors were led into a banquet hall that was beautifully draped in sheer, floating curtains of gold and white. All around them were vast arrays of flower pots, filling the air with a heady fragrance. The queen sat on a stunning gilded chair on a raised platform. Hadassah had never seen such a beautiful woman. She was dressed in a flowing white gown with flecks of gold, her crown fitted with inset jewels that glittered from the light of the many oil lamps in the hall. Her dark eyes surveyed the group of women thoughtfully. Then she smiled and extended her hand in greeting.

Hadassah wanted to sit closer to observe the queen, but Rachab gave her a knowing look and guided her to one of the low tables in the back of the room. The women sank down on the embroidered cushions and eyed the large bowls of pears, apricots, grapes, and dates placed in the center of each table. In front of them were gold plates and spoons.

Queen Vashti's voice suddenly boomed and echoed in the room. "Welcome, women of Susa! His majesty, King Xerxes, and I wish you to partake of the king's bounty and thank you for your kind hospitality while our...our military guests visited our fair city. Please, enjoy what we have prepared for you."

During the queen's hesitant remarks as she sought to find suitable words to describe the unwelcome "guests" who had nearly devastated the city, Hadassah, Rachab, and Leah glanced apprehensively at Golda, who sat nearby. They breathed a collective sigh of relief when Golda only pursed her lips. Evidently, as outspoken as she was, Golda had the grace and presence of mind to remain silent and enjoy this once-in-a-lifetime occasion.

At the sound of a gong, over two dozen servants entered the banquet hall, bearing platters and bowls of food. A bowl of *khoresh bademjan*, a familiar eggplant and tomato stew flavored with turmeric, lemon juice, and unripe grapes, was placed on their table. Hadassah's mouth watered at the savory smell. The eggplant, fried to a golden brown, was cooked with lamb and seasonings before it was added to the stew. Next to it was an accompanying bowl of fragrant rice. Then came the tantalizing aroma of skewered lamb. *Sabzi khordan*, a dish of edible herbs—mint, tarragon, basil, and cilantro—was mixed with scallions, radishes, walnuts, and feta cheese, and served with *nan*, a flatbread.

Hadassah smiled. *Sabzi Khordan* was one of her favorite dishes. She and Imah had prepared it many times. She loved to fold the herbs, cheese, and other garnishes inside a piece of flatbread and eat it in between bites of stew and rice. Knowing the dishes and what they contained, Hadassah breathed a sigh of relief that they would not be served something strange and foreign.

Hadassah whispered to Leah. "I've never seen a feast like this."

"Nor I, not even at a wedding."

The women dipped their spoons into the thick stew, then into the rice, lifting the delectable bites to their mouths. *Oh, how wonderful! How generous the king is to give us such a bountiful banquet!*

They ate, sipped from goblets of wine, and chattered quietly among themselves, pausing only to bow their heads in respect whenever the queen drew near. She walked slowly among them, speaking to a few of the women she apparently knew, for she asked after their families. Hadassah marveled at Queen Vashti's grace and elegance. She had borne two sons, including the crown prince, and yet her figure was as slim and graceful as a girl's.

Once, while Hadassah was reaching for a small bunch of grapes, she felt someone's eyes on her and suddenly looked up to see Hegai watching her. *When had the head eunuch returned to the queen's quarters? And why is he looking at me?* His gaze was thoughtful and Hadassah's heart began to beat erratically. She quickly looked down at her plate.

After some time had passed and Hadassah was feeling comfortably sated, a final dish was placed before them: steaming rice mixed with pistachios, almonds, orange peel, barberries, carrot slivers, saffron, and honey. Although she felt she couldn't eat another bite, she just had to have a bit of the sweet concoction.

As they were eating the dessert, the gong sounded again and a dozen young women danced into the banquet hall. They were dressed in colorful, flowing silk scarves and dresses that swirled around them as they moved. Tiny bells hanging from their ankles jingled as they whirled around and their small hand cymbals rang in unison. Two other young women played a flute and lyre.

The dancers were sheer poetry in motion and Hadassah was delighted as she watched them sway, leap, and twirl about. But although their movements looked like they were expressing joy, their faces were blank or solemn. Sadness came over Hadassah as she realized that these young women were most likely slaves or concubines. They would spend their lives in the women's quarters and have no freedom to marry or have children. They could only do whatever they were told to do.

When the dancing was over, the gong sounded again and the queen rose.

"Thank you all for coming. I pray you have enjoyed your evening and will think kindly of his majesty the king as you prepare to depart."

The women of Susa rose quickly, understanding that this was the signal to leave the banquet hall. The lovely evening was over. Again, they followed Hegai, bowing low to the queen as they passed her.

Outside the palace, Hadassah quickly reunited with Mordecai and they joined the other families from the synagogue as they made their way back to their homes. There were excited whispers as the men and women shared their thoughts about the different banquets they had experienced and what they had seen. Mordecai seemed deep in thought, for he spoke little as they walked.

"Please, Abba, tell me about the king's banquet for the men."

He sighed. "Extensive gardens with various fruit trees and flowers. There were hangings of white, green, and blue linen with purple material tied to silver rings on marble pillars. We ate well—I believe we were served the same foods you were, Hadassah, as I saw the servants carrying food in all directions—and we drank from goblets of pure gold and silver. The wine was good and plentiful."

She wondered why his description was so brief. She sensed that he only answered her question out of habit, for he always answered her questions. *And he sounds so...* Hadassah glanced up. The look on Mordecai's face seemed almost angry. She touched his arm with concern.

"Did the evening not go well for you, Abba?"

He sighed. "Yes, the evening went well enough, but there is a new face in the palace. His name is Haman." Mordecai paused, then almost spat out his next words. "He is an Amalekite!"

As the door to their house closed behind them, Hadassah turned to him. "An Amalekite in the palace? Why is he there?"

Mordecai waved a hand. "What do you remember about the story of the Amalekites in our people's history?"

She thought for a moment. "When our people left Egypt with our great lawgiver, Moses, it was a long journey and some of our people lagged behind. When we halted at Rephidim, the warriors of Amalek attacked the weak and those that were stragglers."

Mordecai nodded. "Our army rebuffed the Amalekites and fought long and hard in battle, eventually defeating them. After the victory, the Lord instructed Moses to write on a scroll as a permanent reminder and read it to Joshua. The Almighty would erase the memory of Amalek from under heaven. For the Amalekites had raised their fists against His throne, so now the Lord would be at war with Amalek generation after generation."

"But, Abba, were the Amalekites not destroyed?"

"Yes—and no. When our first king, Saul, ruled Israel, the prophet Samuel came to him and told him the Almighty had decided to settle accounts with the nation of Amalek for opposing Israel when they fled Egypt. Saul was ordered to destroy the entire nation of Amalek—all of the people and all the animals. Not a single one was to be left alive."

Hadassah sighed. "I remember now. Saul did not obey the Lord."

"No, he did not. We know that he slaughtered the Amalekites, but kept the best of the sheep and goats, the cattle, the fat calves, and the lambs. Worst of all, he spared the life of Agag, the king of the Amalekites. The Lord told Samuel that he was sorry he had ever made Saul king. When Samuel finally found Saul, the king told him he had followed the Lord's command, but had saved the best of the animals to sacrifice to the Lord."

"And Samuel was angry."

"Yes, he was, because our Lord was angry." Mordecai recited for her the words from the prophet to Saul in the first book of Samuel, chapter fifteen:

> *Does ADONAI take as much pleasure in burnt offerings and sacrifices as in obeying what ADONAI says? Surely obeying is better than sacrifice, and heeding orders than the fat of rams. For rebellion is like the sin of sorcery, stubbornness like the crime of idolatry. Because you have rejected the word of ADONAI, he too has rejected you as king.*

"Then Samuel ordered King Agag to be brought out and Samuel slayed him in front of Saul."

Hadassah frowned, "So then, how does this Haman, an Amalekite, still live?"

"The king was slain, it is true, but there were rumors that the queen, along with a few of her attendants, escaped to a kingdom that sympathized with the Amalekites." Mordecai paused for effect. "And she was with child."

Hadassah gasped. "Then this Haman is a descendent of King Agag?"

"It would seem so, for he calls himself Prince Haman." Mordecai put a hand on her shoulder. "He also is very wealthy. He brought a wife and ten sons with him and purchased an estate here in the city. His presence cannot bode well for our people or for the kingdom. I can only pray that he will not ingratiate himself with the king and his court."

Later, as she lay down upon her bed, Hadassah pondered Abba's words. She looked out the window at the night sky and wondered what it all meant. As the shadows enfolded the room, she felt herself shudder.

11

*M*ordecai hurried through the gate, his mind turning over and over as he considered what he'd heard. Hadassah's lips curved down in apprehension as she observed his countenance. It was hard to hide his distress. *It might be best to ask a tiny, innocent question first...*

"Has the great banquet tent been taken down, Abba?"

"Yes, the king has had it taken down."

"All is well then?"

He shook his head. "I have grievous news. Queen Vashti has been deposed and banished to a separate palace. It is called the *haremsara* and it is for those women who are no longer in favor with the king, but not deserving of death. The king has signed the documents of divorce."

Hadassah looked at him in horror. "The queen deposed? What happened?"

He unrolled a parchment notice, one of hundreds that had been posted throughout the city. He read it for her. "*All wives will*

honor their husbands, whether great or small...every man should be
master in his own house."

Hadassah frowned. "I don't understand. What does it mean?"

"It seems the king sent the seven eunuchs who serve him to
summon the queen, wearing her royal crown, to appear before him
and his guests. He wanted to show her off her beauty."

"Show off her beauty? And so did she go to the king and his
guests?"

He shook his head. "It is against Persian custom for the wife
of the king to appear before strangers in that manner. She refused.
All seven of the king's eunuchs who attend him beseeched her, but
still, she refused. The king was drunk and flew into a rage. His
chief advisor, Memucan, insisted that now the women of Persia
would start treating their husbands with disrespect. There would
be no end to their contempt and anger."

"Oh, Abba, so that's the reason behind this decree."

He pulled on his beard and frowned again. "Haman is increasing in his influence with the king. There is something brewing, but
I have not been able to discover what it is yet."

Hadassah placed the bread and stew on the table. "Let us have
our meal, Abba. You always know what is happening in the palace.
You will learn more, in time. All will be well."

While puzzled at the meaning of the king's edict, the city was
relieved that the thousands of unwelcome visitors were gone. The
banquets that had been held for Susa's citizens were still the talk of
every household. The women gathered in the marketplace to share
what they had seen and heard in the palace. Now, with the loss of
the queen, speculation ran rampant. Would their impulsive king
seek the hand of a princess among one of his allies?

⌒

Once again, there was great fanfare in Susa as the king and
his warriors left the city for Sardis, where he would amass his

enormous army. Mordecai learned that Xerxes had left Artabanus, who commanded the king's guard, in charge of the city. Artabanus had opposed the war with Greece, but the king's most trusted general, Mardonius, his cousin and brother-in-law, urged Xerxes to attack Greece with his superior army. The idea of retaliation for his father's defeat by the Grecian army many years before greatly appealed to Xerxes and Mardonius won the argument. Xerxes would go to war.

Mordecai stood with Hadassah by the side of the road to watch the procession. The people waved banners and cheered their king as he rode his white stallion at the head of the contingent of troops. His immortals, ten thousand strong, marched behind him in battle gear—a formidable sight with all of their weapons and massive shields. They looked invincible and proud. The king nodded to his subjects as he passed them. Mordecai glanced down at Hadassah; her eyes were shining with excitement. With her glorious waves of hair framing her face, she was incredibly lovely. Then his eyes widened in despair as he realized what she was looking at—and who was looking back at her.

Instead of bowing, Hadassah smiled unabashedly and gazed directly at the king, who at that moment had turned his head. His eyes fell on Hadassah and held hers for a moment before he passed by. Mordecai had wanted to hurry Hadassah away before the king reached them. He didn't want Xerxes to even know his adopted daughter existed. Now, it was too late. A sense of unease enveloped him, a portent of something to come. But then the feeling faded and he decided not to let it concern him, or even mention it to Hadassah. After all, the king rode past thousands of people. As beautiful as she was to Mordecai, perhaps she was just another pretty face to the king.

Mothers waved to their sons and wives called out to their husbands as they marched by, but the men's eyes remained fixed straight ahead. Here they were, young men in the prime of their lives, marching off…perhaps to their deaths.

"Oh, Abba, think of all the families of the soldiers passing us. How many of them will come home again?"

How many indeed? As Mordecai spotted familiar, youthful faces from the synagogue mixed among the crowds lining the street, he wondered if the Persians resented them. Xerxes did not require Jews to join his army.

There was an ominous silence when the last of the troops exited the gate. The people watched until the figures were only dots on the horizon, then returned to their homes. They had dutifully cheered their king, but the prospect of war brought no sense of elation.

The palace buzzed with every bit of news brought to the king's advisors by courier. The conscription of men for Xerxes' huge army of thousands had taken place over three years, but it would take over a year to amass them. A vast amount of supplies were gathered as the generals devised their plan of attack.

Mordecai listened as the latest courier shared his news and relayed it to Hadassah that night.

"The king sent representatives throughout Greece to demand the symbolic 'earth and water' from various kingdoms and city-states. If the rulers returned the symbols, they would be agreeing to pledge to honor and serve the Persian king. Xerxes will then agree to spare their people and leave a subordinate ruler to oversee them. Athens and Sparta were not approached, however, for they killed the messengers of his father years earlier." Mordecai shook his head sadly. "Xerxes wants to enslave the people of Athens and Sparta and destroy their cities in retaliation."

Hadassah knew Abba only spoke to her about whatever the couriers reported, no one else. He never talked about the news from the palace or the king's doings to their neighbors or even his friends from the synagogue. The whispered word around the treasury was that Haman, who had joined the king's advisors, had spies throughout the kingdom, ready to report any dissention or complaints against Xerxes.

Mordecai took a sip from his cup of wine. His features looked puzzled, which was so unlike him. "There was a strange bit of news today. Perhaps it was not intended to be shared by the courier. It seems the king tried to cross the mighty Hellespont River and a storm destroyed the bridge his engineers built. In a fit of rage, the king ordered his men to whip the river with three hundred lashes and throw fetters into the water."

Hadassah put down the pear she had been eating and frowned. "How strange! Why would he try to whip the river? Surely, a river can feel no pain. And you said a storm destroyed the bridge."

Mordecai waved a hand. "He was angry and he is temperamental." He shook his head sorrowfully. "Even worse, dear one, the engineers who built the bridge were executed."

Hadassah gasped. "Why? It wasn't their fault a storm came up! Oh, Abba, how cruel."

Mordecai did not respond. He was lost in thought, his mind turning over the rumors he heard that day. It seemed the king's advisors, led by Memucan, had devised a plan to replace the exiled Queen Vashti. Mordecai felt uneasy, although he wasn't sure why, but he knew the answer was prayer, so he spent much time reaching out to Adonai.

O Lord, grant that this night we may sleep in peace. And that in the morning our awakening may also be in peace. May our daytime be cloaked in your peace. Protect us and inspire us to think and act only out of love. Keep far from us all evil; may our paths be free from all obstacles from when we go out until we return home.

The very lives of Mordecai's people in the city of Susa depended on the king's benevolence. Xerxes' erratic and willful behavior did not bode well for their future. *What if the king changed his mind about the Jews in the city?* Some had gone with Nehemiah years earlier to return to Jerusalem. *What about the Jews who remained here in Susa?*

These thoughts occupied Mordecai's mind more and more as the months went by and Haman's influence seemed to be increasing. Right now, he was acquiescing to Artabanus, who served as regent in place of the king, but Mordecai felt Haman was only biding his time.

⟜

Word finally came that a second bridge had been constructed and the Persian army had crossed into northern Greece. The people of Susa felt this was a sign of future victory and listened anxiously for every bit of news the messengers brought.

The king's army was now a multinational hoard of 300,000 to 500,000 men from each of the 127 provinces, headed for the pass at Thermopylae. The whispered words from the palace were that the troops had devastated every crop and resource on their way to Greece. Advancing through Thessaly and Macedonia, Xerxes' army stripped all the edible crops from the fields and the fruits of every tree, whether ripe or not. All sources of water had been appropriated, leaving wells dry and turning small streams into beds of mud.

Mordecai opened a crude map of Greece he'd purchased in the marketplace and pointed out the king's progress for Hadassah. While he was keenly interested in the war and how the king would fare, he was alarmed to learn that Haman was rising in importance in the kingdom. Slyly and with great expertise, the Amalekite was using his fortune to ingratiate himself with the king's advisors. To Mordecai's dismay, it was rumored that when Xerxes returned from Greece, Haman would be named grand vizer—the king's second in command.

Yet there were other rumors among the palace servants that were passed on to Mordecai by his contacts. Memucan, the king's cousin, felt Haman was a threat to his own role as prime minister. Both men wanted power. Did the rumors foreshadow an eventual clash between the two?

One of them would not survive—and Mordecai feared it was Memucan who would lose his life. Haman would find a way to get rid of the one man who stood in his way. Mordecai brooded over these thoughts, but did not share them with Hadassah. He could see in her facial expressions that she was worried enough about him.

12

As she entered the synagogue with Mordecai on the Sabbath, Hadassah noticed that Shamir was back. Her heart began to beat faster. She watched through the lattice from the women's section and could not take her eyes off him. Her mind began to race. *Was he ready to choose a wife? Would he come with his father to her? Did the few words and the looks they exchanged in the past mean he was considering her for his bride?* She anxiously awaited the close of the service and was puzzled that the men gathered together in what appeared to be an urgent conversation. She waited, wondering what they were talking about.

Shamir lingered also and finally approached her. His dark eyes looked deep into hers.

"You are well now, Shamir?"

"I am well, Hadassah." The way he said her name made her feel light-headed. They stared at each other for a moment. Finally, he spoke. "I have missed seeing you."

Dare she speak out loud? Dare she say it? "I have missed seeing you also, Shamir. I am glad you are back." *Could he hear her heart pounding? The tremble in her voice as she spoke those mundane words?*

Shamir smiled then and nodded. "We will see each other soon."

And then Hadassah knew and her heart danced within her. He would be coming with his father to seek her hand. Of course, the rabbi and Abba would negotiate the dowry first. She smiled and nodded. "Of course, Shamir. I look forward to that day."

~

"Hadassah, are you coming?" It was not like Abba to sound so impatient. He almost rushed Hadassah to their home and when they had entered, he closed and barred the door.

She grew alarmed. "Abba, what's wrong?"

He took her hand and she was startled to see tears forming in his eyes.

"Hadassah, one of the men in the synagogue has a brother who is a servant in the palace." He dropped her hand and began to pace the floor, glancing at the door from time to time. "There is terrible news."

Hadassah covered her mouth with her hand. "Oh, no, Abba, has something else happened to the queen? She was so kind and gracious at the banquet she gave us..."

He shook his head. "This will punish Vashti even more, yes, but its effect is more far-reaching."

Mordecai studied her face and then drew her close. "You are more precious to me than all the gold in the kingdom, Hadassah. This news will greatly affect us and I fear for your safety—and your future."

Hadassah's eyes widened in alarm. *What had happened to cause Abba so much concern?*

He took her by the shoulders. "You must stay home. I know you must go to the marketplace now and then, but you can only do so when you are disguised so that your features and your figure cannot be seen. And you must only go out with the neighbor women, never alone."

She frowned. "Abba, what are you saying? Why must I disguise myself?"

"It is the king's new edict, his advisors' solution to finding him a new queen."

Hadassah could only stare at him, a lump rising in her throat.

"Along with the decree that all wives must respect their husbands and that every man must rule over his own household, to punish Vashti for disobeying the king, there is a new decree in the works." Tears formed in Mordecai's eyes as he spoke. "The word in the palace, if I understand it correctly, is that while the king is off to battle Greece, his advisors suggested they comb the kingdom for the most beautiful virgins to be gathered into the palace for his return. The maidens are to beautify themselves for a year and then when the king comes back, one by one, they will go to his chambers. The one who pleases the king will become the new queen."

The impact of his words took Hadassah's breath away. But still, she misunderstood his meaning.

"Those poor young women, taken from their families, to become perhaps just another concubine for the king! No hope of marriage, unless they are the one the king chooses. And what kind of marriage would it be to such a temperamental man as King Xerxes? Why, he may wed a maiden one day and banish her the next!"

He sighed. "My Hadassah, daughter of my heart, you must know that you are beautiful. I have told you so many times. And you are beautiful inside as well. But this is one time I would have you be the ugliest maiden in the kingdom. I do not know how long I can hide you. This new decree apparently will not stipulate that the maidens must be Persian. It will merely say that all the young, good-looking maidens are to be gathered from all the provinces of the kingdom. Sooner or later, you, my dearest Hadassah, may be taken to the palace, rounded up with the other maidens like so much chattel!"

"Abba!" She clung to him. Now she understood. "I will not even go outside to the marketplace. Surely Rachab or Golda would be willing to shop for us, for a little while. I will stay here in the house. They will not know I am here." She sobbed and buried her head against his chest. "I could not bear to leave you!"

He patted her on the back. "His soldiers are going to comb all of the provinces, including our own city, Hadassah," he whispered. He let go of her and sank down on a low stool, his head in his hands.

The realization what might come was almost suffocating in its import. "What you are telling me is that I could be taken from our home to the palace?"

"Yes, *ahuva*. And in time, one of the couriers could summon you to spend the night with the king."

She gasped. "And if I don't please the king, I become a concubine in the palace, never to marry or have children?" She began to weep softly. "Oh, Abba, what can I do?"

"We can only pray to Adonai that this virgin hunt will end in time and you will be spared. From now on, you must remain in the house. You are right; I'm sure the good women of our neighborhood will do us the *mitzvah* of shopping for us. If need be, I will go to the marketplace myself."

⌣

The months went by and with the king's representatives searching the far reaches of the kingdom, it was easy to forget about the maiden-gathering decree. Life seemed to go on as usual in Susa. Hadassah, approaching her fifteenth birthday, was restless, having obeyed Mordecai and stayed in the house out of sight for months. All of the Jewish fathers had attempted to hide their unwed daughters who might be taken by Xerxes' men.

Each evening, Mordecai shared news about the king's progress on the battlefront and the virgin roundup in the far-off provinces. Sooner or later, the men would begin searching the city of Susa. The king's spies were everywhere, watching and gleaning information about any eligible girls in the city.

That evening, Mordecai rushed in the gate. He looked around as if searching for something and sat down at their low table, deep in thought.

He stood suddenly, startling her. "That is the answer! You must marry, Hadassah, at once. It will not be the celebration you would choose, for it must be done quietly."

"But, Abba, I am still not even betrothed. I am fifteen, so of course, I am ready, but should there not be a betrothal ceremony before a wedding?"

He sighed and bowed his head. "I was not anxious to lose you. You are the only family I have now. This has not been fair to you. I will go to the rabbi and arrange it. It is the only way to save you." He crouched down beside her and hugged her. "You are so precious to me, Hadassah, a blessing to me and your late Imah, the daughter we never had. I do not know what I would do if you were taken from me."

Apprehension filled her. It was a solution to what would be a terrible fate otherwise. *Did he have someone in mind? Could it be Shamir?* Realization dawned. If Abba was going to the rabbi, then surely he was arranging a marriage between her and Shamir.

⌒

Arrangements took time, but meanwhile, each day when Mordecai left for the treasury, Hadassah was careful to remain in the house. He went to the synagogue alone, as did many of the other men who had eligible daughters. He sensed he was being watched. *Would his overseer remember he had a daughter and tell the soldiers?*

Hadassah could only wait to see what Mordecai arranged for her. *Would she have to be betrothed in secret?* A ceremony would attract attention and if they were aware of Jewish customs, the king's men would know that the marriage was only arranged, not consummated. One young girl had already been claimed by the king's guards and dragged away from her weeping family.

Then Mordecai brought the alarming news that Shamir and his father had traveled to another city to mourn the death of a relative. When she knew the reason for the delay, it brought her a small amount of joy. Abba *was* planning her betrothal to Sharmir. Hadassah waited anxiously for word of their return.

One evening, as she was preparing the evening meal for the two of them, there was a pounding on the gate. Hadassah bit her lip and looked at Mordecai.

"Quickly, remove your dishes from the table and stay in your room."

She did as he bid her and rushed to her room, fear coursing through her body.

"You have a daughter," said a gruff voice from the courtyard. "She will come with us."

Mordecai lied. "She is betrothed, a married woman."

"We are aware of your customs. If she is only betrothed, the marriage has not been consummated."

Hadassah waited for Mordecai to speak. *Would he lie again to save her?*

Heavy footsteps sounded in the hall and her door was thrown open. Two of the king's soldiers stood staring at her.

One smirked at Hadassah. "Hegai will be pleased with this prize."

They seized her by the arm and forced her to come with them. Mordecai stood in front of them to stop their progress.

"Stand aside, old man, or we will be forced to do you harm. We are following the king's orders."

Mordecai put up a hand, taking on a respectful stance. "Please, let me at least say goodbye to my daughter, to ease my sorrow. I am a loyal servant of the king, working in his treasury."

The soldiers looked at him and finally nodded. "It is permitted, but we will be waiting outside the gate. You have only a few moments."

When they had gone, Mordecai took Hadassah in his arms, his tears running down his cheeks and into his beard. "My daughter, I could not save you. I am so sorry."

"You were waiting for Shamir to return and I will always be grateful that you wished me to have the one I wanted for my husband."

He nodded. "How could I know they would leave for the death of a relative? I will grieve the rest of my days."

He clasped her to himself again. "Know that I will be nearby and friends who work in the palace will keep me apprised of all that is happening for you."

Hadassah reached up and put a gentle hand on his face. "Are we not in the hands of Adonai, Abba? He knows my way. We must trust Him for the outcome of all this."

He nodded. "That is true. We must trust Adonai. We cannot see the way, but He goes ahead of us. We must pray and trust Him." As he released her, he stepped back and glanced toward the gate. "You must go, Hadassah, but I would request something from you."

"What is it? I will do anything you ask, Abba."

"Do not give your name as Hadassah, but tell them it is Esther, which is a Persian name. I would have you hide your Jewish heritage for now. I don't know why, but I feel this is something you must do. Will you remember?"

She gave him a puzzled look, but answered, "Yes, Abba. I will do as you wish. I will take the name Esther."

He led her to the gate and the soldiers helped her up into a donkey cart, where another young woman sat quietly weeping. Hadassah moved to comfort the girl, but just then, she looked up the street and gasped. Mordecai, still standing at the gate, followed her anguished look. Shamir and the rabbi, dressed in their Sabbath clothes, were coming toward her home.

Seeing the soldiers and Hadassah sitting in the cart, their eyes widened as they grasped what was happening. As one soldier hit the donkey with a branch and the cart moved away, Shamir mouthed her name and took a step forward, his face the picture of anguish. She lifted a hand in farewell and they could only gaze hopelessly at each other until the cart turned the corner. Hadassah put her face in her hands. As tears slipped through her fingers, she felt an arm around her shoulders. Tears slipped down their cheeks and on to their clothing as the two young women comforted each other and wept for the life and families that would never be.

13

*A*s the cart moved along the road toward the palace, Hadassah looked up, remembering the night of the banquet when she and the other women dined in the queen's quarters. *How many women had the soldiers gathered and where would they be housed?* The cart went through a gate in the wall surrounding the palace and stopped at the entrance to the main hall. Once again, Hegai, the eunuch in charge of the king's harem, who had introduced himself the night of the great banquet, came to meet them.

"You are fortunate to be chosen from all the women in the kingdom. Come with me."

The two women followed the eunuch through the hall where Hadassah once walked in anticipation of seeing the queen. Two guards walked behind them, perhaps to keep them from turning around and running away. *Had any of the women tried to do that? What happened to any who did?* Her thoughts tumbled in her head. When the great bronze doors closed behind them, all thoughts of escape seemed futile. Hadassah lifted her head. She must trust

Adonai, who had brought her to this point. She did not understand, but she knew she must place her trust in her God for whatever the future would bring.

Hegai faced them. "What are your names?"

The other girl looked down at the tile floor. "I am Amiram."

Hegai frowned. "A Jewish name." He turned to one of the guards. "Take her to the section of the harem with the other Jewish women."

He peered intently at Hadassah. "What name do you go by?"

She lifted her head and returned his gaze. "I am Esther."

He contemplated her for a long moment. "I will take this woman to the other quarters."

He thought she was Persian! Hadassah didn't know Abba's reasons, but perhaps the Persian name would protect her in some way.

Hegai seemed very interested in Esther. His voice was kind as he spoke with her and led her along a corridor, where they passed other rooms filled with women of all nationalities. They came to another bronze door. She could hear the voices of women murmuring and as he opened it, a small group of women turned to look at her. She felt their eyes silently appraising her; some with open interest, some with sympathy, and others with calculating shrewdness.

Hegai led her across the room and into another section of the harem. The tiles on the floor depicted an array of beautiful flowers. Silk hangings separated the sleeping area from the rest of the room. Several young women lounged about, their eyes following Hegai, some fearfully, as he glanced around the room.

He spread one hand. "This will be your quarters until the time you go before the king." He began to point to some of the women. "Your name?"

"Nadia."

"Yasmin."

"Mamisa."

"Amirah."

"Karani."

"Parisa."

"Razak."

As he pointed to each one in turn and they gave their names, he studied them thoughtfully. "Those who gave me their names, remain. All the rest of you, return to the main harem."

When the others had gone, the seven women who gave their names glanced at each other. Esther wondered what it all meant. She stood quietly, waiting for the eunuch to tell her what to do.

"You seven have been chosen will attend this woman. Her name is Esther. I will go now to arrange for your meal. You will introduce yourselves to Esther and tell her about yourselves."

She was to have seven handmaids? Why had she been chosen for such an honor? She tried not to show surprise, but gathered her wits and smiled warmly at each of them. "Please, have no fear. I am a captive, just as you are, taken from my guardian. Let us get to know one another. Please tell me your names again."

"I am Parisa. I was purchased for the king's household in Babylon, but truthfully, they have treated me well here, mistress. Are you a princess?"

Esther thought about her heritage, from the clan of Benjamin and the clan of their first king, Saul. "I am descended from a king," she told them truthfully.

"I am Nadia, from Media. Do you know how many women were brought to the palace?"

Another young woman spoke up. "I heard Hegai tell someone that there were nearly four hundred."

Four hundred women. Esther suddenly realized it could be years before she was taken to the king. She looked at the young women chosen to attend her. She wondered if they were all servants or if any had been taken from their homes just as she had been. She nodded at one with a smile, encouraging her to speak.

"I am Amirah, mistress. I am only a maidservant. I served one of the king's wives. I was taken from my home when the king's army defeated Babylon."

"I am Razak, also a maid who served one of the king's wives."

Esther lowered her voice. "Were any of you planning to be married before you were taken?"

Amirah began to weep as she slowly nodded her head. Esther moved to put a gentle hand on Amirah's shoulder.

She had to let them know she understood their plight and sympathized with them. She wanted them to realize that they were in this situation together, even if they were to be her handmaids. "I was to be betrothed the evening I was captured. My uncle wanted to have me married to prevent the soldiers from taking me, but it was too late."

In her mind, she still saw the look on Shamir's face as she rode away in the cart. He and the rabbi were coming to speak to Abba for her. Her heart felt heavy at the knowledge, but she pushed those thoughts away. Adonai knew her way and mourning her loss would do no good. She must trust Adonai for strength to face her future. Tears would be of no avail now. As she listened to the young women chosen to attend her, she realized they were only servants, purchased or captured by the king's forces and brought to the palace. They were not part of the group of virgins selected for the chance to become the new queen. Again, she wondered why she had been chosen to have seven maids attend her. *Surely all four hundred virgins did not have a retinue like this!*

It was not too long before Hegai returned, bringing a bowl of fresh fruit. Other eunuchs followed with trays of bread, goat cheese, figs, dates, and wine. They did not look at Esther or her handmaids as they placed the food on the low tables.

After they left the room, the young women fell on the food, devouring every morsel.

Esther asked each maid gentle, innocuous questions about her homeland, favorite foods, culture, and the like, listening attentively to their answers and making sure to speak to them by name both to let them know they were important to her and also to help her remember who was who. All seven had come from various provinces and conquered peoples.

She thought of the young Jewish girl who had come to the palace with her. *Why were the Jewish maidens kept in another part of the harem, separated from the other women?* Perhaps in time, Hegai could be prevailed upon to answer her questions. *Why was she given special treatment, if indeed that was the case?* Esther could only hope that she would somehow learn the answer. All she knew for certain was that the king was attacking Greece and would not return until the war was over.

With the strong wine and so much to eat, combined with the stress of the day's events, Esther felt a great weariness overtake her. She made sure each girl was comfortable on the cushioned pallets that had been placed around the room before climbing into the bed that had been reserved for her. Yet no matter how tired she was, her mind kept racing as she stared up at the floral tiled ceiling. *How long before the king returned? What must Abba be thinking? Would he remember to eat? What would happen when she was taken to the king?* And the biggest question of all—because it could be an indicator of how the king treated his women—*what happened to Queen Vashti?*

Esther prayed silently to Adonai for strength and then recited the prayer Jerusha had taught her so many years before:

Praised are you, Adonai, our God, Ruler of the universe, who closes my eyes in sleep, my eyelids in slumber....

The familiar prayer comforted her. She could be assured Adonai would watch over her. She closed her eyes and gave herself to sleep.

14

*M*ordecai sat at the table, his head in his hands. He had failed Hadassah and now she was in the king's harem. *How could he ever see her again?* No man could go near the harem or that part of the palace. Anyone who was caught doing so would be slain immediately.

After mourning the loss of his beloved wife, he'd been comforted by his beautiful, young, vibrant daughter—so intelligent, thoughtful, and ready with a smile whenever he had a trying day. Now, his Hadassah was lost to him, too.

Mordecai recalled the brief conversation he'd had with young Shamir and the rabbi.

"We should have come sooner," Shamir had repeated over and over.

"The Almighty knows His way, my son." But the rabbi's words brought Shamir no comfort.

"I loved her! I have loved her all my life. I was only waiting for her to be old enough to wed." Still weeping, Shamir had turned and fled down the street.

Watching his son go, the rabbi had placed a hand on Mordecai's shoulder. "We must trust Adonai, my friend. Circumstances kept them apart, but all is in the hands of our God."

Mordecai had only nodded. Then he and the rabbi had bid each other *shalom* and parted.

The house was so silent and empty now, yet memories of Jerusha and Hadassah laughing and chatting as they prepared meals, mended clothes, or swept the floors seemed to echo in the rooms. Mordecai had not eaten in two days. He had no appetite.

There was a knock at the gate and, reluctantly, he rose to answer it. Rachab stood with a cloth-covered tray in her hands. He could smell the lentil stew and fresh bread.

She scolded him. "You must eat! Would Hadassah want you to starve yourself to death? Eat!" She handed him the tray and turned away to return to her house.

Mordecai stood for a moment, staring down at the tray in his hands. Then, he turned, went back into the house, and placed the tray on the table. *How could he eat at a time like this?* Gradually, however, his stomach betrayed him, sending out soft growls of hunger. And the tantalizing smells of Rachab's thoughtful meal made his mouth water.

Rachab was right, Mordecai knew. Hadassah would not want him to starve to death—and he could not possibly help her by doing so. He thanked God for the meal and as he ate, he tried to think of a plan, some way to get Hadassah out of the harem. Yet, even as he sought an answer, he knew it was hopeless. He finished his small meal and bowed his head to pray again.

As Mordecai poured out his heart and sorrow to Adonai, a strange peace enveloped him. Words formed in the back of his mind as though a voice had spoken to him aloud. *Trust Me.*

He had trusted in Adonai all his life. He would continue to do so. He nodded and whispered. "Yes, Lord."

⌒

While Mordecai was at work on the accounts the next day, another courier came. It seemed the king was anxious to let his people know of his successes. He had started out from Sardis with a fleet of ships and an army of 60,000 combatants, along with his 10,000 elite "immortal" warriors. It was an immense army that must surely outnumber the forces of Greece. Victory seemed certain.

The only news Mordecai received in answer to his tactful inquiries regarding Esther was that she was being well cared for in the harem. He tried to alleviate his concerns by reminding himself that it might be years before Esther's time came to go to the king. She might just live out her life in the harem, never seen by the king or any other man save for the eunuchs. Not the life he would choose for her, but he had to trust in Adonai.

Mordecai had hired Anna, one of the local Jewish widows, to keep his house and prepare meals for him. Each evening when he returned, his food was covered with a cloth and waiting on the table for him, sometimes cold if he was delayed at the treasury. Nevertheless, he was grateful for Anna and gave thanks to Adonai for her help.

When the time came for Passover, there was no one to recite the Passover story with him, no one to share the simple meal of unleavened bread, herbs, a small apple, and a hard-boiled egg. Mordecai ate in silence and then walked to the synagogue.

Amos, whose daughter had also been taken, greeted him anxiously. "Have you had word, Mordecai?"

"A week ago. Hadassah is well, under the circumstances. I am sorry, friend, but the only thing I could learn about Amiram is that she is housed with the other women of the harem."

Amos's eyes started to tear up and Mordecai put a comforting hand on his shoulder. "We must trust the Most High, my friend. We can do nothing else."

Amos nodded and turned away. All they could do was wait for the return of the temperamental king.

15

In the morning, Hegai brought additional garments for Esther and her maids. "Change into these." He turned his back on them. They hurriedly washed in the shallow pool and put on the fresh robes and tunics. When their rustling noises had ceased, he called over his shoulder. "You will come with me."

Hegai led them through the hall to another compartment that was more spacious and elegant than the one they left. Esther looked around in amazement. *They were taken to the best part of the harem?*

Breakfast was supplied on large trays—breads, a variety of fresh fruit, dates, meat from a fowl of some kind, and wine. Hegai watched them as they ate and they all glanced at him shyly from time to time. *Why was he watching them? What was he thinking? What were his plans concerning them?*

After their meal, they had their answer.

"Who among you plays a musical instrument, dances, or sings?"

Nadia spoke up. "I play the *ney*." She bowed her head. "Our king is kind. I was allowed to bring it with me when I came to Susa."

Esther was surprised to learn her maids were so musical. Besides Nadia's Persian flute, Karani played the tambourine and Yasmin played the *chang*, a Persian harp. However, neither had their instruments at the palace. Although Esther had occasionally played the *kinnor*, she knew she could not mention that. *For why would a Persian maid play a Jewish harp? But should she say that she enjoyed singing? Was her voice worthy?* Then Hegai looked directly at her, his gaze expectant.

"I like to tell stories and sing."

Hegai seemed pleased with her response. Then his countenance changed.

"All of you must learn the dances that please the king. Instructors will be brought to teach these to you, as well as palace etiquette. Musical instruments will be brought for you and you will practice to perfect your skills. And you will be supplied with ointments, creams, and perfumes with which to prepare Esther for the king." He wrinkled his nose and sniffed. "A year should suffice."

After he left them, the young women around Esther began to speak at once.

"The king won't return until he is victorious over Greece. How long will that take?"

"You could be preparing for two or three years!"

Razak snorted. "Even that may not be enough! Our king can be very critical. Why, the wife I served was sent out of his chambers almost the instant she walked in, even though she was more beautiful than a prized rose."

Esther sighed. "With four hundred women, I may not see the king for years."

The women began to murmur.

"We will have instruments, so we have something to do."

"Must I learn to dance if I play an instrument?"

Shy Mamisa, who rarely spoke, chimed in. "I will be happy to learn court etiquette. I feel so out of place…"

Esther gave her a gentle smile. "We will all do well, I'm sure of it. We cannot change our circumstances, nor lament what is past. But if we make the most of each day, we can rest our heads in peace at night."

Yasmin glanced at the doorway, as if making sure Hegai was not nearby. "At least I will not be called to the king." When Esther raised her eyebrows, Yasmin looked at her sympathetically. "We are only servants. With four hundred women gathered for him to choose a new queen, your chances of being selected are slim. You will go to his bed and if he is not pleased with you, you will be returned to the harem, never to see him again. That is no life to look forward to. It would be no better than ours." All of the other maids had gathered around them, wondering at Yasmin's boldness—and what Esther's reaction would be.

Esther carefully considered Yasmin's words. She would never see Shamir again and would have no hope for a family. The king would use her for one night and she would live out her days among dozens of other women who had suffered the same fate. It was not a happy prospect. She could only trust that Adonai had a purpose for her life. He knew His way. *What could she do but submit herself to Him and trust in His plan for her?* And yet…

"What you say is true, Yasmin, and you are very kind to share your thoughts with me about what's at stake. But for whatever reason, fate has thrown us together. And if you maidens help me to be my very best when I am called to the king's chambers, if he honors me by selecting me as his queen, I will not forget you, who helped to put the crown on my head."

The women's demeanor perceptibly changed at Esther's courteous reply. They realized that they, too, would advance if their mistress became queen.

Eunuchs brought in the bag that held Nadia's *ney* as well as a *chang* for Yasmin and a tambourine for Karani.

Yasmin looked down at the beautifully carved harp for a long moment and then began to tenderly pluck its strings. Her features softened and a small smile came to her lips. Esther could see that it was a comfort to her to be able to once again play her favorite instrument.

Nadia removed her *ney* from the bag, caressed the flute, and lifted it to her lips. She played a few tentative notes. And then she began to play a melody that was both beautiful and mournful. As she played, every young woman in the room could hear the sadness and cry of the girl's heart.

Karani took up her tambourine and gave it a few tentative shakes, but when the eunuchs left, she laid it down. Esther thought about how the tambourine made a joyous sound at weddings and special occasions, but Karani evidently had no interest in playing at this moment, in the king's harem. Esther resolved to quietly speak to her, lest Karani get into trouble with Hegai.

Amirah turned to Esther and reached out to touch her hand. "Will you sing for us, Esther? A song of your people?"

With a start, Esther wondered if Amirah knew she was Jewish...but then she realized the girl probably meant a song that her parents taught her. She could not sing the Hebrew version she learned from Jerusha, but she could sing it in Aramaic. She closed her eyes and sang:

Sleep my child, sleep my darling.
All too soon my song will cease.
When you have left my arms so loving,
May you then find a life of peace.
When you have left my arms so loving,

May you then find a life of peace.
Though life offers pain and sorrow,
To the humble, lowly born,
Yet, there will be for all a bright tomorrow
Work, my child, for that happy morn.
Yet, there will be for all a bright tomorrow.
Work, my child, for that happy morn.
Work and love your toiling brother
While you sing a song of peace.
When workers clasp hands with each other,
Then the whole world will be at peace.
When workers clasp hands with each other,
Then the whole world will be at peace.

Her clear, lovely voice carried throughout the harem, although she wasn't singing nearly as loud as she could. Women appeared from the other quarters to stand and listen. When Esther ended her song, the murmurs of many voices made her open her eyes. They widened in surprise to see so many women had gathered to hear her. Some had tears in their eyes. She nodded her head in thanks for their being there. And with a jolt, she discovered that another had watched her as well.

Hegai.

16

*M*ordecai hurried toward the treasury early one morning. His overseer had told him the night before that if he walked by the courtyard of the harem, someone would meet him there and give him news of his ward. The courtyard walls were thick and there was no way to converse with Esther personally without jeopardizing his life or hers. He approached the courtyard and waited, his heart beating rapidly. *Was she all right?* Presently, one of the eunuchs appeared.

"I am Hathach. You are Mordecai?"

"Yes. Have you news for me?"

"My master, Hegai, is in charge of the harem and has allowed me to speak to you. He asked me to tell you that the maiden Esther is well. She has found favor with my master and has been given seven maidens to tend to her needs."

Bewilderment as well as relief flooded Mordecai. "Thank you. May I come again and inquire of her?"

"I will give your words to my master. If he is willing, you will receive word."

As Mordecai nodded, Hathach turned and left him.

Seven maidens assigned to her? Mordecai puzzled over that. Given the number of women taken, it seemed unusual for Esther to have any attendants, let alone seven. *Why would the head eunuch appoint seven maids just for Esther? She had somehow won the favor of Hegai—but why?*

From then on, each day at the same time, before reporting for work at the treasury, Mordecai went to the courtyard by the harem, hoping for news about Esther. Sometimes, Hathach came and gave him little tidbits of information. Many times, Hathach would either not appear or pass Mordecai to merely whisper: "No news."

The king was still in Greece, so Mordecai reasoned that there was still time. Somehow, he would have to think of a way to get Hadassah out of the harem. Yet even as these thoughts crossed his mind, his shoulders slumped. Her fate was sealed. And if by some chance she managed to avoid the king's bedchambers, she would still spend the rest of her life in the harem. It would appear that she would be well-treated, but what kind of life was that? And how could he ever see her again? He returned home that evening and sat with his head in his hands, his meal untouched.

Finally, he looked up. "Oh God Who Sees Me, I cannot understand Your ways. She could have had a home and husband and I would have had grandchildren to bounce on my knees. I failed her. I didn't move quickly enough. What could I have done? Now Hadassah is lost to me forever. I can only look forward to occasional messages. That is to be my life. I have served You, trusted You…" Mordecai sighed and from deep within came a quiet, subdued voice:

My ways are higher than your ways.

"Yes, Lord. You are Adonai, the beginning and the end. I do not understand, but I will trust You. I must or I cannot go on."

He thanked God for the food on his table and the kind hands that had prepared it for him. At last, he ate, feeling better than he'd felt for days. Then he lay down on his bed and slept in peace.

17

*E*ach time a courier came home from the battlefront, everyone gathered in the marketplace. When it appeared that their king was winning the battle, the people smiled and cheered. When the report was unfavorable, many wrung their hands and shook their heads in disbelief. Fear appeared on many faces.

Mordecai shook his head after the latest courier had moved on, wondering what to believe. The treasury buzzed with rumors and opinions. Was the king going to return triumphant after all... or in defeat?

A few days later, another courier brought news that the king, who feared their bridge over the Hellespont would be destroyed and his army trapped in Europe, had retreated. He moved into Asia, taking the greater part of the army with him.

After services that Sabbath, the men of the synagogue gathered in groups to talk among themselves.

"This does not sound promising, Mordecai."

Ezra harrumphed. "He has more worries. Babylon is rebelling and now, it would seem, requires the intervention of the king."

Mordecai shook his head. "True. The king left his top general, Mardonius, in charge of the contingent left in Greece. It was Mardonius who suggested the retreat in the first place."

Simon spoke up. "Have you not heard? Mardonius has been killed in battle. The king has lost one of his finest generals."

Another man joined the conversation. "The news is good, the news is bad—we can only listen and hope. What do we really know?"

The men began talking all at once.

"The war with Greece was doomed from the start. Our king had to finish his father's war!"

One man scowled and spoke up in a harsh whisper. "Hush! Would you bring trouble on us? Who knows who might be listening?"

"What will this mean for us?" Simon wrung his hands, his eyes fearful.

The rabbi joined their conversation. "All I feel is a sense of unrest. If the king comes back in defeat, what will he do? Will he take his shame out on our people as rulers have done in ages past? Will we once again become a target for a ruler's anger?"

Mordecai spread his hands. "We can only wait and pray until the king's return. Does not the Most High God know our way? We must place our fears in His hands."

The rabbi put a hand on Mordecai's shoulder. "Wise words, my friend. You have borne your loss well. We do not know the mind of Adonai. We can only trust."

As Mordecai left the synagogue he watched the other men take the hands of their children and grandchildren as they joined their families. Once again, he felt the enormity of his loss. With heavy steps, he made his way home.

The next day, Hathach let him know that Hegai had ordered special foods for Esther, foods she had requested "if it was not too much trouble." Mordecai smiled as he made his way to the treasury. He was sure she was doing her best to keep kosher.

A couple days later, however, as he passed by the harem courtyard, Hathach let him know that Esther was being given special creams and ointments. Although he smiled and thanked the eunuch for that bit of information, when he was out of sight, Mordecai beat his breast with his fist. He wanted to cry out in his pain. She was being pampered so she could be deflowered by their pagan king!

After another day at the treasury—thankfully a slow one— Mordecai hurried home and closed the gate behind him. Only then did he let the tears fall. "Hadassah," he murmured over and over. Sinking down on a stone bench in his small courtyard, he bowed his head, once more seeking strength from his God.

Nashon, a palace servant who had become Mordecai's friend, kept him apprised of Haman's words and actions.

"As soon as the king returns, there will be trouble, Mordecai. He plots against Memucan. The king's advisor seeks power, but so does Haman. He will ingratiate himself with the king. Sooner or later, the two will clash. Haman is everywhere in the palace, sneaking around, watching and listening." And although the two men were meeting in a little-used pantry and the noise from the kitchens likely suppressed their whispered conversation, Nashon still looked uneasy. "We must be careful with our words. Some of the servants who spoke against Haman have disappeared. We live in fear of him." He shook his head. "It is not good. We all wish the king to return—and soon. He has been gone too long."

"I will pray that the situation improves for you, my friend. These are dark times indeed for Susa. Haman is not to be trusted."

Mordecai was convinced in his heart that as soon as the king returned, Haman would continue to wheedle Xerxes and ply him with gifts to try to win his favor. It was obvious that the Amalekite had his sights set on becoming prime minister. Mordecai listened to what was enfolding in the palace with growing alarm. He knew Haman hated the Jews and if he was in a position of power, what might he do? At the synagogue, there was much discussion and murmuring. The only thing Mordecai and his people could do was wait and watch, but there was a sense of unrest and, for some, a sense of dread.

18

The summons was unexpected and Esther's heart filled with anxiety. *The queen mother, Atossa, wanted to see her? Why? Had she been watching the women in the harem to determine who would make the best wife for her son?*

Esther followed Hegai through the marbled halls of the harem and as she walked, her long-forgotten dream came to mind. The hall and the pillars! She lifted her chin and took a deep breath. *Now was the time to show calm and rely on the strength of Adonai!* They turned at last to another wing of the palace, more resplendent than any of the other rooms Esther had seen. She knew at once it was the quarters of the queen mother. *Where was the former queen, Vashti? Why did no one speak of her anymore? Where was the hall where she entertained the women of the city?*

Two eunuchs guarded a huge ornate door overlaid with gold filigree. With their curved swords at their sides, the guards looked fierce indeed. At Hegai's approach, they turned and opened the massive doors. Esther meekly followed the head eunuch into an atrium, which she presumed must serve as a waiting room for Atossa.

Esther took another deep breath, hoping to still her rapidly beating heart. *Oh, Adonai, give me grace and favor with the queen mother!*

Hegai indicated she was to wait. He disappeared through a smaller door, which he closed behind him. After a few moments, the door opened again and Hegai gestured for her to follow him. As they entered the room, a tall, stately woman turned from where she was speaking with one of her attendants, and regarded Esther. Atossa.

Esther sank to her knees and bowed her head before the older woman.

"Stand up, so I can see you better."

Esther complied and stood quietly. Somehow, she sensed she had nothing to fear from Atossa...at least not at this moment. She waited.

"Hegai has good judgment. I understand seven maids have been assigned to you?"

"Yes, your majesty, though I do not understand why I am so honored."

A tiny smile seemed to play about Atossa's lips. "Humility becomes you. Come closer."

With her head lowered, Esther walked slowly to the queen mother and stopped a short distance away. Atossa reached out, lifted Esther's chin, and looked her over appraisingly.

"You do not enhance your eyes with the kohl. In fact, you do not seem to enhance your appearance with any pigments, oils, or powders at all. Why is that?"

"I have never done so, your majesty. My guardian felt it was not necessary."

"A guardian? What province are you from?"

"From here in Susa, your majesty."

The queen mother turned and sat down on a bench with a silk-embroidered cushion. She indicated Esther was to take the one across from her.

As Esther sank gracefully on to the bench, she raised her chin and looked directly at Atossa, then lowered her eyes shyly. *It wouldn't do to appear so bold!*

And yet the queen mother gave her a small, fleeting smile. "You have spirit. Perhaps that is a good thing, provided one understands how to use it. Tell me all about yourself and your family."

"I am an orphan, your majesty. My father and mother died of a fever in Kish. My only living relative, my father's nephew, came with his wife and brought me to Susa to live with them. My cousin is a lot older than I am, so they raised me like a daughter. My adopted mother was killed in front of our house. Two soldiers were galloping down our street and she accidentally stepped out, startling one of the horses. She was struck down and died. My cousin is now my only family."

Atossa sat silently as Esther gave her this brief life story. Nothing in her features gave away her feelings or thoughts about what she had heard. Finally, she motioned to an attendant, who hurried over with a cup for her. She did not offer any beverage to Esther. *Nor should she be expected to!* Esther reminded herself. She was only one of four hundred, after all.

"He has done well by you. You are as Hegai has described you. I'm surprised you were not married yet. How is that?"

"I was to be betrothed, your majesty, but I was taken by the king's men and brought here. I can only wait on the king's pleasure."

Atossa raised her eyebrows. "You are outspoken as well. Are you mourning your intended?"

Esther lowered her eyes. *Had she offended the queen?* "At first, I did, it is true, your majesty. But mourning a lost love will not change my circumstances now. I can only pray that the king finds another queen to his liking."

Atossa studied her for a moment and Esther wondered if she had said the wrong thing.

"How do are you faring in the palace?"

Another tack? "I am being treated well, your majesty."

Atossa sighed. "Let me be frank, child. Vashti was vain and foolish. It was her undoing. But this idea of my son's advisors to gather up all these women from his kingdom to choose a new queen is ridiculous. There are noble families to choose from across his kingdom, alliances to be made. Now he is fighting Greece and who knows how long this war will take."

Esther wondered why the queen mother had shared these thoughts with her. Perhaps no one but Atossa could speak so forthrightly about the kingdom. She had learned in the harem that the king looked on his mother with great favor.

Noting the surprised look that Esther had done her best to hide, Atossa chuckled. "Do not be alarmed. As his mother, I can say what I wish."

Then, she again changed the subject abruptly. "Did you attend the banquet?"

"Yes, your majesty. It was most gracious of the king to serve the people of his city such a feast."

"Ah, so you did not mind the effects of our officials on this city?"

Esther thought quickly. *Was this a trap? Was Atossa testing her loyalty?* She sensed that she had to be very careful in her response.

"My guardian told me that the king was preparing his officers and governors for the war with Greece. He said it was important for the king to demonstrate that he could provide for the troops from the different countries, to show that he was not only wealthy, but strong."

Atossa's eyes narrowed. "That's a very tactful answer. Your guardian kept you apprised of the king's preparations?"

Esther quickly thought back to Abba's words of caution when they learned about the roundup of the maidens. Since most of the men who worked in the treasury were Jews, she could not say that he worked there, for fear of giving herself away.

"He deals with many merchants, your majesty. And, of course, we are all interested in the king's progress toward victory. My guardian shared any news that arrived from the couriers."

Atossa half-closed her eyes, feigning boredom. "You find news interesting? Most young women your age have other things on their mind."

"Too true, your majesty, but since I am an only child and my adopted mother is deceased, he talked to me in the evenings when he came home. He has always shared the news of the city."

Atossa was about to speak again when a eunuch entered and bowed, holding out a parchment. As she opened it and read the contents briefly, her eyes flashed.

"Democedes!"

Hegai, who had been respectfully standing against a wall, stepped forward. "Does he send bad news, my queen?"

"He was to survey the Greek coasts for the king, yet he has taken the opportunity to desert us and defect to the Greeks!"

The queen mother rose suddenly and nodded to Hegai. "She may return."

To Esther, she waved a hand absentmindedly. "We will talk again one day."

Esther was dismissed. She bowed and left Atossa's chamber, many thoughts running through her mind. She turned to Hegai and whispered. "Who is Democedes?"

Hegai shook his head. "He was the royal physician for King Xerxes and the queen mother."

Gathering her courage, she dared to ask Hagai another question. "Has the queen mother talked with other girls from the harem?"

He paused, his dark eyes studying her for a moment. "Yes." And he said no more as he showed her back to her quarters.

⌒

Her maidens gathered around her.

"What was the queen mother like?"

"Did she say what happened to Queen Vashti?"

"Why did she want to see you?"

Esther smiled. "She wanted to know more about me and where I came from. I believe she has also talked with some of the other young women in the harem."

Later, when her maidens were occupied, Esther went out to the garden. The sun was setting; it was her favorite time of the day. She watched a small flock of birds gathering seeds and turned over the last hour in her mind. *Atossa said they would talk again, but why? Why did she call Vashti "vain and foolish"? Why didn't she ask Esther to tell her who her guardian was? Was it because she already knew? And if that were the case, what would she do with that information?*

A butterfly lit on a nearby flower for a long moment. Its life was freer and more carefree than hers. Mordecai had sent word that several young couples in their neighborhood had married and there were children on the way. It was his way of letting her know that Shamir had moved on with his life. She wondered about her friends and if they thought of her. They would not envy her, in spite of her special treatment. Life was far better for them, with husbands and children to take care of. No one would want her fate. A tear made its way down her cheek and she quickly brushed it off with her hand.

Unbidden, part of a psalm from King David came to her mind: *Tears may linger for the night, but with dawn come cries of joy.*

Where had that come from? With a sigh, Esther turned her thoughts over to Adonai. There were too many questions...and she had no answers.

19

*S*ome of the women from the harem gathered unobtrusively on a high balcony, where they could not be seen but could still hear the messenger from the battlefront in the hall below. Voices carried upward and Esther listened, remembering how Mordecai had shared the news of the city, the palace, and the king with her when he came home in the evening. He told her the messengers had a long ride as the news was relayed from post to post. *As swift as they were, how old was the news?* For the king's sake, she hoped he would win the war. Yet that also meant he would be returning home and might call for her to spend the night with him.

Esther had learned from the royal tutor that the king's advisors, led by his cousin Memucan, were all nobles of the kingdom and, of course, knew all of the Persian laws and customs. Whenever the king needed to make a decision, he consulted them. These men held the highest positions in the kingdom, save for Xerxes himself.

On this day, after the messenger had left, they were still in the hall below, arguing over the news. Xerxes had defeated the small force of Greek warriors led by their king, Leonidas of Sparta.

Esther had listened to their conversations for weeks now, so she learned to know each man by the sound of his voice.

"It is to the king's advantage," Memucan was saying. "The king was fortunate that Ephialtes betrayed his own people by telling our forces of another pass around the mountains."

"Ahura Mazda has indeed smiled on us," said another adviser. "With the storms destroying the Greek ships at Artemisia…"

"…And Xerxes burning Thermopylae and capturing Athens," Memucan interjected, "so those cowards abandoned their city and fled to the island of Salamis."

"One group did try to defend the Acropolis," Marsena pointed out.

Memucan snorted. "Ridiculous! Since they were defeated and the city was burnt to the ground, we can be confident that the king has control of the Greek mainland to the north of the Isthmus of Corinth."

There was silence at this bold statement, so Esther dared to peek over the balcony to take a look at the men. They were merely nodding their heads in approval. *So the king was indeed winning the battle against Greece?*

Tarshish, another of the king's advisors, entered the courtyard. "I have just received more news. The king's generals advised him to send part of the fleet to the Peloponnesus to await the dissolution of the Greek armies, but instead, the king chose to attack their fleet. The conditions are not favorable." He spread his hands in a gesture of helplessness. "Ahriman is showing his might. He whispered into the Greeks' ears an ingenious plan to lure our ships into a bottleneck, so we could only attack two at a time."

Memucan shook his head gravely. "This is not good. I fear for our king." Since he was the king's cousin and prime minister, Memucan ruled in the king's place. Should anything happen to Xerxes, he would rule as regent until the crown prince came of age.

Esther watched Memucan's face as he spoke. His countenance did not match his words. As she and her maidens withdrew quietly, a movement in the hall across from them caught her eye. They hadn't been the only ones listening to the advisers' conversation. Another stood in the shadows and as he moved away, she recognized the back of his head: Haman, the Amalekite.

A shudder passed through her body. Esther always kept Abba's warnings about Haman in the back of her mind. He moved about the palace like an animal on the prowl, watching and listening. Esther hurried her maidens back to their quarters in the harem, and then walked out to the garden. She sought her favorite secluded corner, so she could be alone and pray.

20

*M*ordecai shook his head after talking with other men at the treasury. The king was winning. The king was retreating. The king was pleased. The king was furious. *Who could guess whether the king would return triumphant after all...or straggle back to Susa in defeat?*

To Mordecai, the news did not sound promising. On top of the trouble with the Greeks, there were rumors that Babylon was rebelling and would require the king's attention. Mordecai considered the news in growing concern. Xerxes was reckless—and it had cost him dearly. He thought again of Mardonius, a well-respected and seasoned soldier, dead because of his cousin's rash decisions. Xerxes should have listened to him.

Two weeks later, the news all of Susa had waited for finally came. A courier stood by the marketplace and read from his scroll. "The king's offensive against Greece has come to an end. The war with Greece is over."

When the people of the city heard the news, there was rejoicing in the streets. But Mordecai and the men of the synagogue felt uneasy.

Throughout the Torah were stories of their people being enslaved and persecuted. The messenger's words did not make it sound as if Persia had won the war. And if Xerxes was returning in defeat, would he take out his anger and shame on the people, in particular the Jews? Would Mordecai's people once again become the target of a vengeful ruler? They could only wait and pray until the king returned.

Over two months went by and at last, word came that the king was nearing Susa with his immortals and what was left of the army. The people lined the streets, but the king's return was nothing like the day he left for battle. He entered the city quietly and although people cheered his return, it was not with the enthusiasm of his departure.

Mordecai observed the king as he rode his white horse, looking straight ahead, his face drawn and somber. Xerxes had aged and yet it was only the seventh year of his reign. He was no longer the cocky young king who had ridden out to battle. His immortals marched with their chins up, their countenances as fierce as ever. Behind them, the army marched stoically, many of them wounded. The ragtag group was considerably smaller than the one that had marched out of the city years before.

Women anxiously searched for the faces of loved ones. Those who recognized their husbands, brothers, and sons cried out their names with relief.

Soldiers were released to go to their homes and barracks. Most of the immortals returned to their quarters, but a small contingent of them followed the king up the ramp to the palace gates. When they had all gone through, the gates closed behind them, leaving a heavy silence, broken only by the weeping of the women whose loved ones had not returned.

Little by little, the streets emptied of the crowds as people returned to their daily affairs.

The following day, the men in the King's Treasury were given the task of salvaging the king's fortune. Much had been spent on the campaign against Greece and the king was raising taxes to begin to refill his coffers.

21

*H*egai had supplied Esther with the best of the creams and ointments, but during the king's two-year absence, she noticed that some of the other women in the harem were less diligent. Now, there was a flurry of activity. Xerxes was beginning to call for the young women who had been captured first.

Hegai took small groups of women to the room where the jewels and ornaments were kept. Each was told she could take whatever she wanted to wear for the king and would be able to keep what she had chosen when he dismissed her.

When Esther's turn came, she was overwhelmed with the plethora of jeweled bracelets, necklaces, and other glittering jewelry. The room was filled with fine gold and silver bangles and baubles. Esther had seen some of the women pass her quarters so laden with jewelry they could hardly walk. She wanted to laugh out loud, but suppressed even a smile. *Who was she to judge their choices? But would a woman laden with jewels impress a king who ruled a vast empire and had more gold than he could count?*

She turned to Hegai. "What should I choose?"

"Whatever you like, Esther." But he watched her carefully.

"Can you please show me what the king would like?"

The eunuch was visibly pleased. "You have spoken wisely. I will show you."

He chose a simple pair of silver earrings inset with stones of lapis lazuli. Then he glanced over the endless array of jewelry and lifted out something the other women had missed: a large matching pendant on a thick silver chain.

Esther held the earrings and the necklace in her right hand and with her left, turned the stones this way and that, admiring their rich, deep blue hues with unique golden sparkles. Then she looked up and smiled at Hegai. "It is enough, Hegai. Thank you."

In a similar manner, the women were then taken in small groups to another room that held silk tunics, jeweled jackets, and gowns so sheer, they were light as air to hold. The other women giggled like schoolgirls and draped garment after garment across themselves for approval. In triumph, they carried away great piles of clothing.

Again, Esther turned to Hegai. "What should I choose?"

"When it is time, I will bring you a gown," he murmured as he led her away and back to her chambers, where her handmaids waited in anticipation. They cooed appreciatively over the jewelry.

Esther watched as, one by one, young women passed by their quarters in the cool of the evening—some anxious, some weeping, and some visibly frightened. They did not return to the virgins' harem. Instead, Hegai said they were sent to another harem, the quarters of the king's concubines, to live out their lives in seclusion…awaiting a summons from the king that might never come.

❧

Queen Atossa wanted to see Esther again. As she followed Hegai to the queen mother's quarters, Esther puzzled over the request.

The queen mother was sitting in an ornate gold chair with a deep red velvet cushion. There were no other servants in the room. This time, she had an expectant look on her face.

Esther sank to her knees and prostrated herself before the queen.

"Stand up, child. Come and sit by me." She indicated a nearby bench upholstered in blue silk.

Esther rose to her feet and sat where Atossa indicated.

"Leave us, Hegai."

He raised his eyebrows slightly, but bowed and left the room.

"You wished to see me, your majesty?"

Atossa studied her a moment. "Hegai tells me you are helping the other girls in the harem and your servants are devoted to you."

"We have become friends."

Atossa huffed. "Servants are not friends, Esther. They will betray you when the opportunity arises."

"Your majesty, I am only a young woman, just like they are. I have no rank over them. They are homesick, as I have been at times, and I only sought to comfort them."

"You say you have no rank, yet you bear yourself with dignity. That is obvious. Your guardian must have taught you well."

"I am descended from a king, majesty, but far back in my family line. At present, I am only a citizen of Susa."

At the mention of the word "king," Atossa's eyes narrowed. "You are descended from a king? What king?"

Esther took a deep breath. "His name was Saul. His descendants ruled Jerusalem many, many years ago, before the Babylonians destroyed the city."

Atossa frowned. She had obviously not heard of Saul, to Esther's relief. *Why had she been so bold as to tie herself to her Jewish heritage against the wishes of Mordecai?*

"Now my son, Xerxes, rules 127 provinces, including Jerusalem!"

"Yes, your majesty. He has ruled well."

This pleased the queen mother. Her face softened and she regarded Esther again thoughtfully. "How much do you know of the Persian Empire?"

"The Persian Empire is strong, your majesty. They defeated the Babylonians by cleverly entering the city through the water channel. The Babylonian king, Balthazar, was captured and killed."

Atossa gave her a slight smile that swiftly vanished. "So you know your history. That is well. But perhaps you don't know that Vashti is the daughter of Balthazar. She was taken captive that night and my son, pleased with her beauty, made her his queen. She had everything—and lost it all. I will say she had courage. Xerxes does not like his plans thwarted."

It was an opening and Esther seized on it. "Your majesty, what happens to a queen who is deposed? Where is Vashti now?"

Atossa sighed. "The Palace of Tears, also called the *haremsara*. She is isolated in a small apartment, kept from the other women there, with only one servant to attend her."

"The Palace of Tears?"

"It is a place for those of rank who are out of favor with the king but not condemned to death. It is on the other side of the palace in a separate building. If her parents lived, Vashti would have been returned to them since she was royal blood. But both her father and mother are dead."

"And the princes, Darius and Artaxerxes? Are they with her?"

Atossa's eyes narrowed. "You ask many bold questions."

Esther bowed her head. "My apologies, your majesty. It's simply that I've felt sad for her."

"She had a hard choice: either defy the king or break the law of the Medes and Persians and appear like a concubine before a mob of drunken men! It was not for a queen to do so."

Esther was surprised at the vehemence in Atossa's words.

Yet Atossa answered her question. "The crown prince and his brother remain here in the main palace with the other children of the king. They are being tutored, especially Darius, for one day, he will succeed his father as king." She sighed. "Darius and Artaxerxes are too old to be with the other children. I must speak to my son about giving them their own quarters."

"I've not seen any children since I've been here. I believe I have heard them playing though."

"They are with their mothers in a different part of the harem."

By now, Esther was getting a sense of the enormity of the palace grounds. So many areas and the section where she was housed could hold over four hundred women.

Atossa sat back and for once, her face showed her nearly seventy years. "Hegai says you sing. Sing for me. A song of your people."

Esther hesitated. *A song of her people?* Once again, she wondered how much Atossa knew of her heritage. She searched her mind quickly for one that might please the queen mother. What came to mind was *Yedid Nefesh*, a song sometimes sung between *Minchah*, afternoon prayer on Friday, and the beginning of *Kabbalat Shabbat*, sung to welcome in the Sabbath. It spoke of her people's intense love of God.

She sent a quick prayer to Adonai to give her strength and help her to sing the song in Aramaic, rather than Hebrew.

Beloved of the Soul, Compassionate Father
Draw your servant to Your Will.
Then Your servant will hurry like a deer
To bow before Your majesty;
To Him Your friendship will be sweeter
Than the dripping of the honeycomb and any taste.
Majestic, beautiful, Radiance of the universe,
My soul is sick for your love.
Please O God, heal her now

By showing her the pleasantness of Your radiance;
Then she will be strengthened and healed,
And eternal gladness will be hers.
Enduring One, may Your mercy be aroused
And please take pity on the son of Your beloved,
Because it is so very long that I have yearned intensely
To see speedily the splendor of your strength;
Only these my heart desired,
So please take pity and do not conceal Yourself.
Please my Beloved, reveal Yourself and spread upon me
The shelter of Your peace;
Illuminate the Earth with Your glory,
That we may rejoice and be glad with You;
Hasten, show love, for the time has come,
And show us grace as in days of old.

Atossa listened with her eyes closed as Esther's voice filled the room. When the song was over, Atossa opened her eyes and regarded Esther for a long moment. Finally, she spoke.

"It is as a queen might sing to her king, a love song. I have never heard it before. It is quite beautiful." She stood suddenly and Esther knew the interview was over.

Atossa rang a small gong nearby and Hegai once again entered the room.

"My queen?"

"She may return to her quarters."

As Esther bowed and turned to leave, Atossa spoke once more. "When you come to the king, sing that for him."

Esther caught her breath and bowed her head in acknowledgement. As she followed Hegai down the corridor again, she thought of the queen mother's last words. A reminder that one day soon, she would be taken to the king.

*M*ordecai kept his ears open to everything he could glean about what was going on in the palace. One of his sources told him that Haman had been made one of the king's advisors against the wishes of Memucan. *Did Memucan feel threatened?* Perhaps with good reason.

"Haman hides his ambition well," the friend told Mordecai. "He makes himself indispensable."

It was as Mordecai had feared. Haman wanted to be second in command to the king—prime minister, grand vizer. But that meant disposing of Memucan. The Amalekite was cunning. When his informant had gone, Mordecai stroked his beard thoughtfully. *How vulnerable was Memucan?*

He had not seen Hathach, the eunuch assigned to carry messages regarding Esther, in several days. There was nothing he could do but go to the courtyard each morning before reporting to the treasury. One day, surely, he would know his cousin's status.

Xerxes had only been in Susa for two months when he left again, this time for the summer palace in Persepolis. *Would the king take some of his concubines…or would he take some of the virgins still waiting to be sent to him?* Mordecai went to the courtyard by the harem at his usual time to learn how Esther was faring and when she would be going to the king. He waited but no one came. Then, as he was about to leave, Hathach came from the palace to meet him. Mordecai felt his stomach tighten.

"Your daughter will not go to the king until he returns from Persepolis. The king takes only some of his concubines."

When the eunuch had gone, Mordecai rejoiced. Esther had been given another reprieve; she would not be ravished by the king in a strange city. At least here in Susa, she knew her Abba was near, if only in prayer for her.

The king usually spent four months in Persepolis, first to celebrate the Persian New Year, *Nowruz*, or "new day," and then to escape the summer heat of Susa.

⁓

The king rode out of the city again, almost quietly. His face was drawn and tired. As Mordecai watched, he almost felt sorry for Xerxes. Perhaps the king would be able to rest and recoup his strength.

The caravan of soldiers and concubines seemed smaller than in years past. The king took only what he felt he needed. Four curtained litters of his concubines passed and Mordecai looked for the young princes, but they did not appear to be going for there was no sign of them. He turned away and walked to the treasury building. As he passed Haman's large estate, a great house almost in the heart of the city, he felt anger rise again. The man had ten sons, five of whom rode with Haman through the city on their way to who knows where. There were rumors but none had been substantiated yet. *Why was this man here?*

With the king gone, the flood of merchants was reduced to a trickle. There were no great banquets to prepare for. Mordecai's overseer kept the men busy, however, for even with 1,200 men in the treasury, there was always tax money to process and monetary portions going to the officials in the various provinces. He settled down to his tasks, but his thoughts were on Esther. The palace as well as the city seemed to settle down to a slower pace. Mordecai thought of his conversation recently with his friend Nashon. The palace may be quiet, but the intrigue had not abated—not as long as Haman skulked the halls.

Today, Mordecai also thought of Jerusalem. The Babylonians had taken captive his grandfather, for whom he'd been named, along with the other people of the city. The Jews had been resettled in other parts of the Babylonian empire and the beautiful city of Jerusalem destroyed. His uncles had settled in Kish, but his grandfather had come here to Susa. Now they were all gone. He and Hadassah were the only ones left of his family. He sighed. There would be no sons from Hadassah to carry on the family now and he himself had no thought of remarrying. Hadassah had been his joy, the only child he and Jerusha had raised.

Reluctantly, he turned his thoughts away from where Hadassah was now. It only brought sorrow.

He considered Jerusalem again. Some of the Jews had returned, but there were not enough men to do much to rebuild the city. They would have to have the permission of King Xerxes to do any of that. He'd thought of returning himself, but he could not leave Hadassah alone in Susa, awaiting a summons from the king.

He concentrated on the tasks at hand. Better to be absorbed in his work than his memories.

⌇

In the palace, Esther was also thinking over her past and her future. Her thoughts of Shamir no longer brought pain and anguish, for she wished him well in his marriage. Dwelling on negative thoughts had never been her way. She was where she was and Adonai knew her future. She could rest in His love and care. Just knowing Mordecai was near and praying for her helped her through the days when she was tempted to be discouraged. With the king gone, the atmosphere in the harem of the virgins was lighter. Many of the girls had made friends and they all knew that even if the king sent them to the second harem after their night with him, there was always the possibility of a child to nurture, even an illegitimate one, since they were not wives. They would also be reunited with the other girls they had met and formed friendships with over the last few years.

The favoritism that Hegai showed to Esther had not gone unnoticed, and each of the captured virgins reacted to Esther's elevated status according to her nature. Some were envious, some surprised, some made catty remarks, and others just welcomed her. Some stood in awe of the fact that Hegai treated Esther so well and it led to much speculation.

Esther was grateful for her maids and loved each one of them; she felt loved by them in return. Her kindness seemed to bring out the best in them. Then a troubling thought occurred to her. *If she was sent to the second harem, would they go with her or be assigned to someone else?* This was just one more aspect of her life that depended solely on the king.

23

*W*ord came that King Xerxes was returning. The city, like a giant sleeping in the sun, began to awaken. Merchants poured in and the anticipation of the king's coming was felt not only in the city but also in the palace. The young women, aware that they would be sent to the king sometime in the next few months, began to apply the creams and ointments in earnest. Clothing was discussed and sorted through in anticipation. Some of the more timid girls began to weep in fear. Others, saucily confident they would be the one to impress the king, sorted through the jewelry they had been allowed to keep.

Esther went to her secret corner of the garden to draw strength from Adonai. She could not escape her night with the king, but her God could see her through it. She bowed her head and entrusted her care to Him.

Mordecai went to the courtyard daily after the king's return, but it was nearly three months later that Hathach approached him slowly, a grave expression on his face. Mordecai's heart sank. He could only guess the news.

"Your daughter goes to the king at sundown tomorrow." Seeing Mordecai's face, the eunuch seemed about to say something more, but merely shook his head and returned to the palace.

Mordecai stood quietly, his shoulders slumped. The day he had dreaded was coming to pass. Like a lamb led to the slaughter, a pagan king would ravage his beautiful Hadassah. His footsteps slow, Mordecai started towards the treasury. Then he lifted up his eyes. *Oh God Who Sees Me, give my Hadassah grace and favor in the eyes of the king. Let the sweetness of her beauty touch his heart. Let her not be cast aside like an old wineskin. You have placed her there, for a reason I cannot imagine. Be with her tonight, Lord God, give her strength to bear what she must.*

Then, like the soft, morning breeze that brushed his face, a single word echoed in his mind. *Peace.*

He hurried to the treasury to begin his work for the day. The other workers were checking scrolls and calling each merchant to process his goods. Merchants were lined up for many blocks at the entrance to the palace, with goats bleating, chickens squawking, and pigeons cooing, protesting being crowded into wooden cages. The king's butchers were examining the animals it would be their task to kill and prepare for the palace cooks. Carts of produce, large stone crocks of olive oil and wine, all waited to be processed. The spice merchant paced beside his fragrant-smelling baskets, eager to get his money and be on his way. Mordecai sighed, knowing it was going to be another long day before all the merchants had been taken care of. He went to his post to listen to the language of the next merchant so he could deal with the merchant's goods. When one had been taken care of and the scroll of purchase prepared, the merchant made his mark and was paid for his goods. Mordecai did not mind this day. It would keep his mind off Hadassah.

24

*E*sther awakened that morning and realized it was Tebeth, the tenth month of the Jewish year. Years and months had gone by and she had almost become resigned to her life in the harem. She sensed that somehow, this day would be different. She silently said her morning prayers and then slipped from her bed to greet her maids, who had waited expectantly for her to rise for the day.

Later in the morning, Esther was in the middle of telling a story as her maids listened eagerly. They didn't know the characters came from the Torah, for Esther disguised them carefully. Today, she was telling the story of Shimshon, who was so strong, he tore a lion to pieces with his bare hands as easily as if it had been a young goat.

Hegai entered their chambers, as he did frequently. Seeing his face, Esther paused and waited expectantly. Over the past two years, she had come to realize that he was a man who liked to hide his thoughts behind a stern countenance. And for whatever reason, he found favor with her. He put her in the best part of the harem and gave her the most expensive creams and oils, the foods she preferred, and seven servant girls to attend her. No more did she wonder, *What is this leading up to? Surely there are many women who are just as deserving?* She was simply grateful for his benevolence.

He nodded unperceptively...and Esther knew. It was her turn to go to the king.

"Tonight when the sun goes down, I will take you to my master." He nodded to Hathach, who came behind him, holding a garment over one arm. It was soft, almost sheer white silk with silver trimmings, simple and yet beautifully made. Small birds were embroidered around the hem of the gown.

Her servant girls gathered to touch the material and exclaim over it.

"So beautiful!"

"I have never seen anything like this gown."

"The king will be pleased with you, mistress."

Esther let their murmuring fade into the background of her thoughts. Tonight, she would go as the maidens had gone before her. *How many had he been with so far?* Righteous anger rose up within her. She would just be another captured virgin to share his bed. *Was there some way she could be spared this humiliation?* Then her mind turned in a different direction. *What would it be like to see the king alone, face-to-face? Would he be kind, gentle? Or would he just take her roughly?* She did not want to think of what the night might hold. She closed her eyes and beseeched Adonai to give her courage to face what she must.

Her maids helped her bathe and massaged her with special perfumed ointments. She felt like a lamb being prepared for the evening meal. Nadia, who was the most skillful, added a small amount of shadow to Esther's eyes. Her flawless skin needed little makeup.

As they prepared her, Esther recollected the words of the visitor Hegai had brought to her quarters the night before, an older woman who moved gracefully across the room toward her. Hegai had dismissed Esther's maids and made sure the two were not disturbed. Sitting on a cushioned bench, Esther had gestured to another bench beside her and waited for the woman to speak.

"I am Samira. I came to the king's father many times and bore him two sons. I am only a concubine and my sons are illegitimate, having no rights to the royal line, but I have been treated well over the years. Hegai tells me you are an orphan, raised by a guardian. You had no mother to teach you certain things. Hegai has asked me to speak with you as your mother would have spoken to you on the secrets of men."

Esther had felt a knot in her throat as she realized why Hegai had brought Samira. There was no thought to the passing of time as Samira had shared knowledge that women taught their daughters for centuries. Esther had found herself blushing as Samira raised certain subjects. She had been kind, but thorough.

As Samira concluded, she had placed a hand on Esther's arm. "I know of Xerxes. He can be willful and cruel, but he can be gentle and compassionate also. He desires what every man desires: to be loved...for himself. Look beyond the man, Esther, and look into his heart."

Now, as her maids prepared her for a night with the king, Esther reflected on Samira's advice and the knowledge she had shared about the mysteries of love between a man and a woman. *Could she live up to all that was expected of her?*

The shadows deepened. Nightfall was approaching. Esther stood and her maidens slipped the beautiful gown over her head. It swirled gracefully as she moved, catching the light. Her hair was brushed until it gleamed and her dark tresses fell like a waterfall about her shoulders and down her back. A sheer veil covered the lower part of her face. When they were finished, her maidens stood back and smiled.

Razak, always outspoken, nodded her head. "Mistress, you will be the most beautiful maiden the king has ever seen. How can he not be pleased with you?"

And what if he was not pleased with her? What difference would it make in her life if he was? He would discard her to spend the rest of her life in the second harem with the rest of his concubines.

Esther remembered Vashti and how lovely she was; yet on a momentary whim, fueled by too much wine, the king cast her aside. Although Vashti was the mother of the crown prince, Darius, and his brother, Artaxerxes, she had been stripped of her title and banished to the Palace of Tears.

Her heart beating rapidly, Esther strove to calm her thoughts as she followed Hegai down another ornate hallway to a part of the palace she had never entered before—the king's quarters. Bigthana and Teresh, the two eunuchs who guarded the king, stood on either side of the ornate door, silently appraising her. In an effort to still her trembling hands, she clasped them in front of her and again prayed silently. *Oh, Lord God, my Adonai, give me courage to face this night.*

Two lamps burned, leaving most of the room in shadows. A voice, tinged with sarcasm, spoke from somewhere in the darkness. "Who have you brought me tonight, Hegai? I don't hear the clanking of a dozen gold ankle bracelets."

"This one needs little adornment, my king."

Hegai indicated that Esther should sit a cushioned bench and wait. And then he left her.

"Who are you, silent one? Are you going to dance for me? Play the flute or a harp? What shall you do to entertain me?"

She looked around in the direction of his voice, but saw no one.

"I do not play the flute or harp, your majesty," she answered softly. "I can tell you a story or sing for you."

"Sing for me then. A song that will sooth me, for it has been a difficult day."

She rose and took a deep breath, remembering the words of the queen mother: "When you come to the king, sing that for him…"

Esther's heart stopped fluttering as she felt strength pour into her. She stood quietly and began to sing, in Aramaic, each note floating clearly on the still evening air.

Beloved of the soul, compassionate Father…..

All was silent for a moment, then she heard footsteps on the marble floor, moving slowly toward the curtain that separated where she stood from the king's inner room. He stopped, still behind the curtain, and listened to her sing.

She reached the last verse,

Illuminate the earth with Your glory
That we may rejoice and be glad with You;
Hasten, show love, for the time has come,
And show us grace as in time of old.

As the final note died, Xerxes pulled the curtain aside and she found herself face to face with him. He wore a garment about his waist, his chest bare in the lamplight. He moved toward her and slowly removed the veil from her face. Then he took a step back and studied her for a moment.

"I have seen you before, but you have not come to me here."

Esther thought quickly. *Where had he seen her?* Then the memory came back. On the day the king rode off to gather his troops for the battle with Greece, he had looked directly at her in the crowd…and she had dared to gaze right back at him.

"I was only a girl, watching you ride off to war. I wanted to see what you looked like and as I raised my head, you looked at me."

Recognition came. "Ah, the maiden in the crowd. I thought about you many times." He moved closer. "I remember your hair, like a cloud around your face." He reached out and touched her long, auburn locks, moving her hair between his fingers.

Esther gasped; she had forgotten the proper etiquette for meeting the king! "Forgive me, your majesty! I should have bowed before you."

He chuckled. "You were singing. It's hard to do that with your face on the floor."

She looked into his face. He was still as handsome as she remembered, but the war had taken its toll on him. There were lines about his mouth and a tired look in his eyes.

Xerxes gently turned her chin and touched the lapis lazuli earring dangling from her right lobe. He smiled then and ran his hand down her throat and neck to the pendant nestled between her breasts. She suppressed a shiver.

"Did you know that this is my favorite stone? Most try to dazzle me by wearing half my treasury."

"I did not know, your majesty, but I do think it's most beautiful. I asked Hegai to help me select the right jewelry."

"Ah, a woman who listens to advice. He chose the gown also?"

"Yes, your majesty." She waited, her heart starting to beat rapidly again. "Forgive me, I have never been alone with a man before."

"You did not dress to impress me." He tilted his head to the side. "You are different from the other maidens. Simpering women, I am weary of them." Xerxes reached out an arm and drew her to him. "Ah, sweet Esther. That is your name, is it not?" He leaned down and kissed her eyes, her ears, her neck...and finally her lips. His kiss was gentle, not demanding.

As she stood in the circle of his arms, he reached for the clasp behind her neck and the shimmering gown dropped to the floor. She stood before him in a simple silk shift. He kissed her again and she responded, surprising herself. *What were these feelings, so new and so different?* Standing there, the king's arms around her, she was submissive yet receptive, willing but not bold, letting her body guide her as Samira had encouraged her to do.

"You are like a beautiful flower, fresh as the morning," he murmured. There was no lust in his eyes, only a question.

"Come, my beautiful Esther, let me teach you of love." He picked her up in his arms as if she weighed nothing at all and carried her behind the curtain. As he pressed her against him, she could feel the steady beat of his heart.

25

*E*sther awoke to someone gently shaking her arm. She looked up sleepily at Hegai. She was in the king's bed and the sun was coming up.

"Come, Esther. You must return."

Suddenly an arm was flung across her chest, preventing her from rising. "Leave us. For once, I would like to wake up with the one who has shared my bed through the night."

Hegai raised his eyebrows, but assumed his usual mask again and quickly left the room.

Xerxes drew her to him. "My beautiful Esther, you have captured me. I do not wish to let you go. You did not just submit to me—you gave yourself to me without reservation. Why?"

"You were kind to me, your majesty. You did not just take me to satisfy your desires. You gently showed me what it was like to be a woman, loved by a man."

"Loved," he savored the word. His eyes searched hers. "Can you love me, Esther?"

And she knew the answer. She did not have to pretend. She put a hand on his cheek and smiled. "I can love you, my king, for now and for all my days."

He studied her face. "I see truth in your eyes. You cannot understand what that does for me." He tilted her chin with one finger. "I would choose you to be my queen. Beautiful Esther, share my kingdom and rule with me."

"Your queen?" She searched his face, wonder filling her mind. "You would make me your queen?"

"You are like a beautiful rose that unfolds its petals when the sun touches it. Even when I was at war, I saw your face in my mind. I could not forget you. Now that you are here, in my arms, I will not let you go." He lovingly caressed her cheek. "Marry me, Esther of Susa."

She nodded, savoring the strange feeling of elation when he touched her. She looked into his eyes and saw what she had never expected and moved closer to him. "Yes, my lord," she whispered.

"I will send for Hegai." He kissed her again. "But just not yet."

～

Hegai did not take her to Shaashgaz, keeper of the second harem. Instead, he led her back to the quarters she shared with her maidens. As they gathered around her, she sensed their deference. Esther was sure the palace was already alive with the news. The king had chosen a queen.

"We knew he would choose you."

"You are the most fortunate of women, mistress."

"You will make a great queen. You will give him sons."

Sensing her new authority, Esther told Hegai that she wished to keep the seven maidens who had served her all this time.

He nodded, "We are even now preparing the queen's quarters for you to occupy after the wedding." Then he bowed his head in respect. As he turned to go, she saw a small wisp of a smile as he strode purposefully from the room.

⌒

Mordecai did not have to go to the courtyard by the wall to inquire after Esther. As he left his home on the way to the treasury, his friend Amos hurried up to him. "Mordecai, have you heard the news?"

"How could I?" he retorted somewhat grumpily. "I'm just leaving for the treasury."

"Prepare yourself, my friend. The king has chosen a queen. Her name is Esther, from right here in Susa."

Esther? Mordecai took a step backward. *His Hadassah had been chosen as the new queen?*

"We hear she is more beautiful than Vashti." Amos thought a moment and then hung his head. "My daughter was returned, as were most of the Jewish girls. I'm sorry about Hadassah. Have you any more word on her?"

Mordecai caught himself almost blurting out that this new queen was Hadassah. Yet it was not for him to reveal the secret. The Almighty had a purpose. He marveled. Of all the maidens taken, a Jewish girl was to become queen of Persia.

As Amos hurried away, Mordecai savored the news. The ways of Adonai were beyond understanding. *Was this why he felt led to tell her to change her name? What would come of this? If the king eventually found out she was Jewish, would it make a difference? Would she be in danger?* He sent a prayer of thankfulness for the goodness of the Most High. Still considering the implications, he hurried to the treasury.

26

*M*ordecai was informed by Hathach that the Zoroastrian priest would determine the most auspicious time for the royal wedding. He was not surprised to learn that, evidently encouraged by the king, the priest picked a day only three weeks hence.

The preparations for the great event reminded Mordecai of the food preparations for the king's prolonged banquet several years before. Merchants came by the hundreds and the men of the King's Treasury were hard pressed to process them as quickly as possible. A steady parade of animals, carts of produce, bags of grain and fruit, spices, and other goods entered the palace in an endless stream. Couriers rode at great speed to spread the announcement to the provinces and Mordecai imagined that those satraps and high military officials who were able would hasten to Susa as fast as they could get there. Those in the farthest provinces could only send gifts to the king to express their congratulations.

Mordecai longed for word from Hadassah. Surely now, she would be allowed to contact him directly. But though he came to the courtyard for three days, he heard nothing. Then on the fourth day, Hathach was waiting for him. He handed Mordecai a scroll, bowed, and returned to the palace.

Mordecai quickly unrolled the missive and read:

"Abba, I am well. It was not my decision to be queen, but I am in the hands of the Most High and He has given me peace. I do not know the purpose for the turn my life has taken, but I trust Adonai. The king has been gentle and kind to me and he is not what I thought he would be like. I have asked Adonai to show me his heart. I will not have the beautiful wedding of our people that I dreamed of, but at least I will be married and not live as a concubine somewhere in the palace harem. The other young women who were taken as I was have been moved to the second harem. I cannot speak to you, but you will be among the officials who line the great hall to witness the wedding. Hathach cannot read, so my words are safe and he is trustworthy. Esther."

Mordecai read the message several times and found tears running down his cheeks and into his beard.

That evening, a messenger arrived at his home and handed him a small scroll—an invitation to enter the king's great hall as a guest for the wedding. *Would he be able to see Hadassah? Or at least let her know somehow that he was nearby?* Mordecai decided that when the day came, with much pomp and the blowing of trumpets, he would find a spot where she could see him when she entered the hall. Neither of them chose a marriage such as this for her, but he would be there for her, just as he had always been.

Rumors ran like an undercurrent throughout the palace. Through his sources, Mordecai became aware of the worsening conflict between Haman and Memucan. Their mutual distaste was almost tangible when they were in the same room. The king, occupied with other matters, including his approaching wedding to Esther, seemed oblivious to the coming storm. They might appear friendly toward each other in light of the king's upcoming marriage, but what would happen afterward?

Memucan was cautious and his spies kept him apprised of Haman's movements in the palace. Apparently, however, Haman had his own spies who kept him informed of any conversations Memucan had with the king. Intrigue was a way of life in the palace, but the servants watched and listened with a growing sense of dread. If Haman and Memucan's sour relations were not resolved, one of them would end up dead—and Mordecai feared it would be not be the Amalekite who fell.

Haman wanted the king's ear and the prestige of being prime minister; it appeared he would stop at nothing to achieve his goal. Mordecai listened to the bits of news without commenting. He had always found it better to listen more than weigh in with his opinion, even if he trusted the speaker. It stood him in good stead and allowed him to remain inconspicuous. It was clear that Haman was a cunning adversary who was biding his time.

What concerned Mordecai more than anything was that his Hadassah, as Queen Esther, was going to be in the thick of the trouble brewing in the palace—and there was nothing he could do about it.

27

The days seemed to pass quickly. For a third time, Atossa sent for Esther. In light of Esther's new status as her son's future bride, the queen mother was more welcoming than she had been before, waving her hand quickly to prevent Esther from bowing. She gestured and Esther gratefully sat on the cushioned bench beside her. A small table held two silver goblets of wine and a plate of date cakes. They enjoyed the refreshments for a few minutes, exchanging only a few pleasantries about the weather, when Atossa put down her goblet and raised the reason for the visit.

"I have spoken with my son and told him I approve of his choice. You have the courage and strength to be queen at his side." She paused. "When you came to the palace, I took the initiative to make sure you were well-versed in protocol. However, while you have been taught some things about palace life and all that entails, as were the other maidens, it is necessary for you to understand your authority and what will be expected of you as queen."

As if to answer Esther's unspoken question, the queen added, "When Xerxes ordered Vashti to come before his drunken guests, she refused on the grounds of Persian law. Which the king well knew but ignored."

Atossa waited for those words to sink in. "You have great power over my son. He is besotted with you—as he never was with Vashti—and you must handle this very carefully. You must know your place, yet use your authority as queen delicately. A man in love, even a king, can be manipulated." She paused again.

Esther could only nod her head. *Was Atossa suggesting that she had more power than Vashti did? And if he ever ordered her to appear before drunken guests, what should her response be? What was she hinting at?*

"There will be times, Esther, when the king will not send for you, but call for one of his concubines instead. He is the king and you must learn to be there when he needs you and not be upset when he does not. Do you understand what I am saying? No judgment. No reproaches or tearful accusations. He would see it as rebelling against his authority."

Esther bit her lip. *So Xerxes could love her and yet choose one of his concubines for the evening? That was a difficult notion, hard to understand...*

Atossa reached out a hand and placed it on Esther's. "Do you love my son, Esther?"

"To be honest, your majesty, I did not expect to because of the manner in which I was brought to the palace. I thought I would be his for one night and returned to the second harem as the other young women were." She looked away a moment, remembering that night with Xerxes. "Yet there was something between us from the moment he looked at me. I did not see him as a king, but a man, a gentle man. I... I found that I could love him."

Atossa smiled. "You are a wise woman for your youth." She sat back. "Now let us discuss your role in the wedding and what it will entail."

When the queen had finished, Esther felt more comfortable about what was expected of her on her wedding day. The king would be sitting on his throne and a throne would be placed to his left. She would enter the hall, dressed as the queen she was to be, and walk forward alone to greet the king. He would indicate the second throne and she would ascend the steps and seat herself. The priest would perform the ceremony and the queen's crown would be placed on her head.

"When the notable guests have acknowledged the marriage, you will receive their good wishes. The king will dismiss them to the courtyard, which will be decorated for the banquet, and he will lead you there to share the wedding feast with him. After an appropriate time, Hegai will come for you and lead you to the king's chamber, where you will await your husband. When the king has performed his duties at the banquet, he will come to you."

He will come to me. Esther considered these words. Before, she had gone to the king, trembling with dread at what was to come. It had been nothing like she expected. She had found love so unexpectedly. It had been with great reluctance that he had let her return to the harem. She understood that she would not see him again until the wedding, which he vowed to hasten and arrange as soon as possible. Now she turned back to the queen mother.

"Thank you for your kindness to me, your majesty. I am greatly honored."

Atossa rose. As Esther also stood, the queen put a gentle hand on her shoulder.

"There is trouble brewing in the palace. Do not think that in this far corner, I am not aware. I have many who keep me informed. The man who seeks to ingratiate himself to my son is like a viper who bides his time and then strikes unexpectedly."

Esther drew in a sharp breath. "Haman."

Atossa's eyes narrowed. "What do you know of Haman?"

"When he came to Susa, my guardian told me that he was an Amalekite. The news of him was not good. It did not trouble us for he was in the palace and we were in the city. There are many rumors of him. He is a prince and has great wealth. My guardian felt he was an ambitious man." Esther guarded her words, for she could say nothing of the Amalekite's hatred for the Jews.

Atossa sighed. "Yes, he is ambitious. It may be his undoing." She thought a moment and then made a decisive pronouncement. "You have much to learn, Esther, but I am your friend. If you ever need to talk with me, I am here."

Esther bowed her head. "Thank you, your majesty. That means a great deal to me."

As Esther once more followed Hegai back to the harem, she thought of Xerxes. He was no longer just her king—he was to be her husband and she was to be his wife, queen of the Persian Empire. The thoughts running rampant through her head kept her silent all the way back to her quarters.

Just before he left her, Hegai murmured, "The king will not send for you again before the wedding, but he impatiently awaits that day."

Esther smiled. "Thank you, Hegai. Thank you for everything you have done for me. I will never forget your kindness."

He reached out and touched her arm. "And a word of caution, Esther," he said softly. "The queen mother still carries great power. As the daughter of King Cyrus and the widow of King Darius, she is much revered. She will help you and you must trust her. Betray her, however, and she would be a formidable enemy."

Esther nodded. "Again, my thanks, Hegai. I will remember."

He left her and she turned to greet her maidens, who crowded around her. "I have asked Hegai to allow you to remain as my attendants once I am married to the king. You shall move with me to the queen's quarters and prepare for me after the wedding."

Several of the girls began to weep with joy, as others beamed.

"You have been so kind to us."

"Will we get to hear more of your stories after you are queen?"

"I'm so happy! We wanted to stay with you."

She embraced each one, laughing with them.

The ever-observant Yasmin piped up. "Can you not see how weary she is? Let us prepare our future queen for the night. She will need her strength for all that is ahead of her."

The days passed quickly. Esther's mind was occupied with the things Atossa had shared with her. As she walked in the garden, she found herself longing for the wedding and searching her heart. She was a Jewish girl—yet no more a girl, no more a virgin, but a woman now. It seemed strange to no longer be a virgin when she was not yet married. Soon, she would be a wife—yet not the wife of a Jewish man, nor the rabbi's son, as she had once hoped, but the wife of a pagan king. Esther knew with certainty now that she had not come here by accident; she felt the hand of Adonai upon her. *Yet was her God pleased with her?* The Jewish holidays had gone by—Passover, the Feast of Tabernacles, Hanukkah—all without her being able to participate. She missed the synagogue and the rabbi's teachings. She missed lighting the Sabbath candles on Shabbat with Mordecai. And she sorely missed him. Now, she had her maids and the love of the king, while he had no one. She could only pray he was well.

She thought of Shamir, knowing that by now, he had married and fathered children. Children. *Would she have any by Xerxes?* That was in the hands of Adonai. Esther knew there was purpose in all that had happened to her. She didn't understand why the God she had trusted from childhood had allowed her to be taken to the palace and now had her betrothed to the Persian king, but somehow, she felt His hand. As the shadows of the afternoon began to spread, she found her quiet place in the corner of the garden, where her maids knew they were not to disturb her, and bowed her head. Always aware someone might be listening, she prayed silently, in Hebrew.

28

*M*ordecai made his way, along with other officials from the city, up the long stone ramp to the gate of the palace, which stood open to admit them. Flags flew from every balcony and pole, for King Xerxes had proclaimed it a royal holiday. Flowers filled pots all over the city and their fragrance wafted through the late morning air.

As they entered the great hall, banners were draped from the upper railings and a long, beautiful carpet had been placed from the entrance to the foot of the steps leading up to the throne, which was used only on state occasions and carefully stored away when not in use. Today, the new queen would walk along the carpet to the dais and Xerxes' throne. Another throne for her had been placed to the left of his. To his right, some ten feet away, was a stately chair carved and decorated with gold, reserved for the queen mother. Attendants led Atossa led to this chair and she sat, watching the festivities. Crown Prince Darius and his brother, Artaxerxes, stood to one side with their men-at-arms.

The king's advisors were stationed near the foot of the dais. Mordecai noted that Haman was among them, seated a short distance from Memucan. Neither man regarded each other, but kept their eyes on the king. On either side of the thrones stood two of the king's immortals, swords at their sides, alertly watching the crowd.

Mordecai and the other guests sat on cushions on either side of the hall.

The great doors were closed and the sound of a gong interrupted his thoughts. Then trumpets announced the arrival of the king. The guests stood and bowed their heads as Xerxes, resplendent in a gold tunic embroidered with precious jewels, took his place on his throne. He held the golden scepter indicating his authority. Despite of the war with Greece, Xerxes, in his late thirties, was still handsome and his muscular body portrayed strength and virility.

He nodded to those assembled and they once more sat down in their places. Then he nodded to Atossa, acknowledging the queen mother.

Mordecai had taken a seat closer to the entrance, so as not to appear more important than he was. At least he was visible. He hoped somehow Esther would see him.

The trumpets sounded and the doors opened once again. As they did, Esther stood in the doorway, alone.

Mordecai almost did not recognize his adopted daughter. Her glorious hair was swept up behind her head and she wore a gown of gold silk. A jeweled girdle emphasized her small waist. Her head was covered with a sheer veil that sparkled with tiny diamonds. A pendant had been draped on her head coming just to the middle of her forehead, which held the veil in place. She wore an ermine-trimmed robe and held her head high as she slowly walked into the hall. As she neared the place where Mordecai sat, she inclined her head so imperceptibly that only Mordecai knew she had seen him.

He watched her walk past, every inch a queen, and his heart nearly burst with fatherly pride. She was the most beautiful woman he'd ever seen—and she was his Hadassah! But mingled with his pride was sorrow. *For now, how could he ever hope to speak to her again? How could he ever be a part of her life?* Although near, she surely was more lost to him than before.

Xerxes intently followed Esther's progress, love and pride radiating from his eyes as she approached. The guests murmured all around Mordecai.

"She is truly beautiful. Where did he find her?"

"Look how regally she walks! She must have royal blood."

"A wise choice by our king."

Mordecai basked silently in their obvious approval. *How would they react if they knew she was only a simple Jewish girl, raised here in Susa?* He smiled to himself. They would never know.

Esther reached the foot of the steps to the king's dais and he himself rose and came to meet her, escorting her up the steps and to her throne. She took her place on it and faced their guests. From the side, a Zoroastrian priest appeared and bowed to the king. Servants held a green canopy over the heads of Xerxes and Esther. Mordecai was reminded of the similarity to the canopy used at Jewish weddings, which pleased him greatly.

Trying to remember what he knew of the Zoroastrian religion, Mordecai found his attention wandering from the words of the ceremony. He knew the king was a Zoroastrian. It was a monotheistic faith, founded by the prophet Zoroaster, which believed in a single creator god. Those who followed this teaching believed in good and evil, judgment after death, and free will. They also believed in the ultimate destruction of evil. In his studies, Mordecai found there were some elements similar to the Jewish religion. At least they both believed in a single creator God. Mordecai knew that though the Zoroastrians worshiped one god, their practices were far different from the Jewish faith. He had studied the teachings of

Zoroaster to help him understand what Hadassah must contend with. He still had many questions…

Xerxes was placing a crown on Esther's head. Her veil had been folded back revealing her face—the face of a young, beautiful woman. The king and his new queen turned to acknowledge their subjects and shouts of approval went up from those gathered in the great hall.

Xerxes spoke with obvious pride: "I present to you, Esther, queen of Persia."

Again the crowd roared with enthusiasm. Esther smiled, nodding toward each side of the room and acknowledging them.

Xerxes raised his scepter for silence. "I have chosen the most beautiful woman in my kingdom to become my queen. You will honor her as you honor me as your king."

As the officials and his advisors applauded, Mordecai glanced at Haman, who was standing off to one side, facing the crowd. The man's head turned slightly, his eyes traveling all over Esther's body, his face alight with obvious admiration. A jolt went through Mordecai's heart. *Would he be a threat to Esther?* He prayed she would not get caught up in any of Haman's plans. Mordecai clenched his fists, hidden at his side. Haman would dispose of anyone who thwarted him…even a queen.

Xerxes waved his scepter. "Come, help us celebrate this great occasion. A banquet is prepared for you in the courtyard."

Esther placed her hand on the king's arm and together they walked through the great hall and led their guests to the banquet.

Mordecai entered the courtyard and mingled with the crowd, marveling at the flowers, more silk banners, and other decorations that surrounded him. Once again, the king had spared no expense to entertain his guests. Each received a golden goblet, a gift from the king in honor of his marriage. *The goldsmiths must have been working night and day to produce these.*

Mordecai settled himself on a cushion at one of the low tables, felt a prickle along his neck, and looked up to find Esther's eyes upon him. She gave a slight smile and then nodded and smiled at others at his table so it would not be obvious that she had singled him out. He longed to speak with her but knew he could not do so without breaking protocol. He would have to be satisfied just being near her, even for this one moment.

While the king tended to his guests and received congratulations from his various high officials, his eyes turned to Esther time and again. It was clear the king was in love with his bride. Mordecai listened to murmured comments around him.

"I would be beside myself with joy if I had such a wife."

"Never have I seen a woman of such beauty."

"She bears herself well. She must be from a royal line."

Then a voice behind Mordecai chuckled. "I would gladly take the king's place this night."

It was all Mordecai could do to keep silent. He wanted to shout at them, "She is my daughter! Show some respect!" But he had to bear it all in silence. He could not even tell one of his own people that Esther and Hadassah were one in the same, lest he put her in danger—especially with the hated Amalekite sulking in the palace halls.

On each of the tables was a platter of *noone' sangak*, a specially baked flatbread in the shape of flowers, and a basket of *tokhme'morgh*, the decorated eggs that represent fertility. Seeing the eggs, Mordecai was reminded of his desperate prayer to Adonai.

Along with the eggs were bowls of crystallized sugar, representing sweetness in the lives of the bride and groom. Bowls of gold coins were everywhere, representing prosperity, but Mordecai felt it was more to show the opulence of the king. Baskets of apples and pomegranates had been placed to represent a joyous and fruitful future for the couple. Finally, there were small trays of spices in seven different colors to represent the spiciness of life. Each spice carried a meaning and significance.

Servants began to enter the expansive garden area bearing tray after tray. There were succulent meats: *akkadian*, beef cooked in liquid with leeks and garlic; and *fesenjan*, a stew made with walnuts, chicken, pomegranate paste, and onions, slowly simmered to a thick sauce as saffron and cinnamon were added. Platters of *tandig*, Persian crispy rice, were placed on the table for each guest to serve himself. There were plates of *sabzi khordan*—a mixture of mint, tarragon, basil, and cilantro with walnuts, scallions, radishes, and feta cheese—served with *nan*, a warm flat bread.

Mordecai had enjoyed the *bademjan* that was served at the king's banquet for the men of Susa and Anna gamely tried to prepare it for him once. But the tart stew she made—consisting of tomatoes, fried eggplant, onions, and lamb, seasoned with turmeric, lemon juice, and some young grapes—was nothing like the king's cooks had prepared.

Mordecai broke off a piece of *nan*, scooped a bit of the herb mixture, then folded it into the bread and began to eat. Servants deftly slid kabobs of lamb off skewers and on to each guest's plate. Some of the guests, including Mordecai, brought out small, sharp, stiletto knives to cut the meat into smaller pieces to spear and eat. Empty bowls and platters were whisked away and yet another dish was served: *ghormeh sabzi*, a mixture of stewed greens, spinach, leeks, coriander, kidney beans, and dried lemon, seasoned with turmeric and spicy lamb.

Finally, gold platters of *bamieh*—Persian doughnuts—were placed before them. Mordecai had a fondness for the fried dough soaked in a rosewater and saffron syrup. He sighed, remembering Hadassah fixing them for him.

Just when the guests felt they could eat no more, the servants brought out *ranginak*, a date and walnut pie. Dates stuffed with toasted walnuts were bathed in burnt butter and a flour mixture, then topped with cinnamon, cardamom, and pistachios.

Throughout the banquet, Mordecai made polite conversation with some of the other men, asking casual, attentive questions to glean what he could from them without giving any clues about himself. Indeed, he asked so many friendly questions that perhaps it didn't occur to them that the flow of information was only going one way. His ability to speak many languages caused them to defer to him, perhaps assuming he was one of the king's counselors.

Mordecai surreptitiously eyed Memucan and Haman across the patio and noted again they were studiously avoiding each other. Watching them, Mordecai wondered what the next few months would hold. *When would Haman make his move?*

Casually, he turned to look in the direction of the king and queen to see how Esther was faring. To his surprise, she was gone. He looked around to see if she was anywhere nearby, but to no avail. Then he realized that she would have been taken to the king's chambers. Once again, anger rose in his heart. She was now the wife of a pagan king. If she had any children, they would be raised in the harem with the other children. He knew the former queen, Vashti, had given Xerxes two sons, Darius, the crown prince, and Artaxerxes. If Esther had any children, they would be in danger from those who supported Darius. Once again, Mordecai prayed silently.

Let there be no issue of this marriage, Lord God. May the blood of our people not be tainted with pagan blood. A child could cost Hadassah her life. Spare her, Holy One of Israel. I never thought I would pray for a Jewish girl to be barren, but that is my prayer. Hear my prayer, Oh Holy One of Israel.

He had a sudden desire to return home. Nodding to several guests, he made his way toward the entrance to the gardens. He smiled widely, holding up his golden goblet as if pleased with the gift and the luxurious banquet he had attended. Noting that some others were leaving, he followed them through the huge iron gates and walked silently toward home. When he finally was inside and closed the door behind him, he sank to his knees and prayed with all of his being for his Hadassah.

29

For Esther, the days passed with great happiness. Xerxes called for her frequently and was pleased that she listened intently when he shared matters of the kingdom with her. He continued to be an ardent lover as well. Some evenings, she sang songs of love and hope to him, songs she'd learned as a young girl. Again, she sang in Aramaic and the king seemed to be pleased. Some evenings, she read to him from the epic of Gilgamesh, or told him stories she'd adapted from the Hebrew.

Xerxes had seen to it that she learned archery. He stood behind her, helping her to hold the bow and line the arrow up with her nose. He showed her how to pull back with just the right tension before releasing the arrow. They then went hunting for wild boar and Esther was amazed to see Xerxes drop one with a single arrow. He was a skilled hunter and while he did not take her often, she went willingly, grateful to be out of the queen's quarters. She had to express her admiration for his hunting skills, though on the inside, she hated to see the death of a beautiful deer or ram.

Esther spent weeks learning the art of riding a horse. She never lost her love for animals and Farah, the beautiful, gentle mare that Xerxes had given her, was calm, steady, and well-behaved. One day, Xerxes took her riding on the plains outside the city. They were accompanied by several of the king's immortals, who were always at his side or nearby. Later that evening, they stood on the balcony outside his quarters and looked over the sleepy city of Susa.

"Your kingdom is so vast, my lord. It is hard to imagine all the lands and peoples it covers."

He was silent a moment, his arm around her waist. Then he spoke. "It is a blessing and a burden, my love. I wish for peace, yet there is no sooner one matter settled or an issue dealt with than there is something else." He turned her to him, looking down at her upturned face. "You are a sea of peace amidst the turmoil. The gods have blessed me beyond my dreams."

"I wish always to be here when you need me, my lord." She sighed and he searched her face.

"What is it that troubles you, Esther?"

"The months go by and I do not carry your child."

He chuckled. "My love, I have other wives and concubines and many children. I did not marry you for a child. I have a crown prince, Darius, and also his brother, Artexerxes. Darius will take the throne when I die."

A shudder went through her body. "May you live long, my lord! I am not anxious to lose you or to be a widow."

He chuckled again. "I am glad to hear that." Then his voice became husky. "Come, my beautiful Esther, the night is still young and it is ours."

And he led her inside.

⌒

Standing on the rooftop of his home, Mordecai looked at the night sky and thought of Hadassah. Word from Hathach was that she was happy and loved by the king. He called for her often and even shared matters of the kingdom with her, Hathach reported.

This night, Mordecai also thought of Shamir. He saw the young man at the synagogue every Sabbath and while the rabbi's son seemed happy with his wife and child, there were times when Mordecai caught Shamir glancing his way with a sad expression on his face. He would look away quickly, but his pain was evident. Mordecai's heart hurt for the young man who had loved his Hadassah and had finally come to ask for her hand, only to watch her being taken away by the king's men. To be forever confined to the king's harem.

Many times, Mordecai puzzled over why the Most High had prompted him to tell her to go by the Persian name of Esther. The other Jewish girls had been released even before the king returned from the conflict in Greece…but not Hadassah. He did not understand the ways of the Most High, but knew His prompting. Adonai wanted Hadassah to be known as Esther. That was as clear as His renaming of father Abraham. While Mordecai had obeyed, he still found himself asking over and over: *Why?*

Slowly, he descended the narrow steps and entered his house. He passed Hadassah's room, still as she had left it on that auspicious day, and wearily made his way to his bed. Despite the many questions fighting for a place in his mind, he said his evening prayers, then closed his eyes and fell into a deep sleep.

The next morning, when Esther returned to the beautiful quarters she occupied as queen, her maids were waiting anxiously to attend her. She was bathed in a pool in the center of the room and then Parisa massaged her with special oils. Nadia and Yasmin played a tune for her while Amirah gently brushed her abundant hair and braided it before winding it around her head and affixing a small jewel crown. Although she had spent the night with Xerxes, he could call for her at any moment of the day at his whim and she must be ready. Esther complimented Amirah on the beautiful way she fixed her hair, but she smiled to herself. The king always took her hair down when she came to him. He loved to run his fingers through her thick tresses.

As Esther settled on a cushioned bench, Hegai, followed by Hethach, escorted her tutor, Marcellus, into the room. They had waited patiently outside her door until one of her maids indicated the queen was ready and they could enter.

Esther was learning about the countries and languages of the 127 provinces of the Persian Empire. She wanted to know about the peoples and city-states her husband ruled. When he learned of her quest, Xerxes seemed pleased and made sure the best tutor was acquired for her enlightenment. She remembered the facts about Susa that Mordecai had shared with her, along with different aspects of the battle with Greece and news of the kingdom. She had a good memory and as her tutor questioned her on past lessons, times and places came quickly to her mind. She was also aware of reports sent to the king of her progress and she wanted him to be proud of her.

Knowing that remaining in Xerxes' good graces was important to all aspects of her life now, Esther applied herself to her studies. It also filled up the long days when he didn't call for her. When Queen Atossa sent for her from time to time, they ate the noon meal together. Atossa was also pleased with the studies Esther had undertaken.

"You learn what is important to your king, Esther. He is pleased that you have such a good mind and apply yourself."

"I knew some history from my guardian, but there is so much more, your majesty. The kingdom is so large and encompasses so many people and languages. I can see why his father instigated Aramaic as the language of the kingdom. It unites the people in many ways."

"True, Esther. Keeping the peace in so far-reaching a kingdom is a never-ending task. Xerxes must constantly be alert to problems in a province and listen carefully to the messages brought to him by his couriers."

"We followed the war with Greece as each messenger brought the news."

Atossa looked up at the window. "He was so sure of victory, the means to avenge his father. It was a hard blow to return home and face his people with so many losses."

Esther nodded. "I remember hearing the cheers when he rode back into the city. The people were not as loud as they had been when he rode out to battle."

Atossa studied her and tilted her head to one side. "It has been over a year and there is no sign of a child. Surely you do not prevent it?"

Esther hung her head. "No, ma'am. I do not know why I have not yet conceived. The king tells me he does not need a child from me, that he has other children already, including the crown prince."

"Ah, but a king often feels he must prove his virility." Atossa put a hand on Esther's arm. "Perhaps you need to pray to the gods to grant you a child."

"Yes, your majesty."

And, as always, Atossa abruptly changed the subject. "How much do you know of Memucan?"

As used to the queen mother's ways as she was, the question startled Esther. "He is the king's prime minister and his cousin. I've heard he gives wise counsel."

Atossa pursed her lips and peered into Esther's eyes. Finally, she sighed. "Haman also wishes to be prime minister. Beware of him, Esther. Do not trust him at any time. Do you understand?"

"Yes, your majesty." Esther cleared her throat. "I must confess I do not like him at all. He always seems to be lurking about the palace, watching and listening."

Atossa raised her eyebrows, but did not comment further. She rose, signaling their time together was over. Just as Esther bowed her head and turned to leave, Atossa stopped her.

"We will be leaving for Persepolis soon. It is the summer palace."

Esther thought a moment. "It is to celebrate the Persian New Year? I remember the king always leaving the city at the beginning of spring."

"It is nearly six hundred kilometers to Persepolis from Susa. It will be an arduous trip. The king must move most of his household with him."

"I will be ready, your majesty."

Esther returned to her quarters with Hegai and Hathach. The latter had been assigned to her from the very beginning and she knew he watched over her with a keen eye. *Was she in danger from Haman? If he was hoping to influence the king, would he try to do so through her?*

30

The months went by and to Esther's sorrow, there was still no evidence of a child. While she had sought Adonai many times, she remained barren. Fortunately, it did not seem to bother the king.

Xerxes gave her permission to meet the royal children: Vashti's sons, Crown Prince Darius and his brother, Prince Artaxerxes, as well as the children of the king's lesser wives.

Esther sat on a bench in the garden and waited until she heard the muffled voices of children approaching. They were led by a eunuch Esther hadn't seen before.

He silenced the children with a look and addressed her. "I am Shamach, keeper of the harem of the wives of the king and their children. As you have requested, I have brought them to meet you."

Two tall young men stepped forward. She smiled at them in acknowledgement. They were unmistakably the royal princes, eighteen-year-old Darius and sixteen-year-old Artaxerxes.

Darius gave her a perfunctory bow, his eyes blazing with suppressed anger. "My mother should be queen," he said, gauging the effect of his words.

"I understand, Darius. And I'm sorry that you cannot be with her."

At the kindness in her voice, he frowned and stared at her a moment. "Did you want to be queen?"

Startled by the audacity of his question, she looked at Shamach. He was frowning and ready to pull the prince aside. She gave an imperceptible shake of her head. "I did not choose to be queen, Darius. Your father chose me to be his queen. I, too, lost my mother and my father. I was raised by a guardian, just as you are."

Suddenly, the young man's eyes filled with tears and he bowed quickly before walking to the side of the garden. Her heart went out to him.

Artaxerxes' demeanor was more open and friendly. Perhaps because he had no hope of being king, his future was not set in stone. He bowed and regarded Esther with open curiosity. "You *are* very beautiful."

She smiled at him. "How very kind of you to say that, my prince."

He stepped aside. One by one, each of the other sons and daughters of Xerxes came forward to be introduced. She acknowledged each one with a smile and a kind remark.

One of the younger children spoke up. "We have heard that you tell stories, majesty. Would you tell us a story?"

Esther looked up at Shamach, who bowed his head. "You may if it pleases you to do so, your majesty."

The children crowded around her but Darius and Artaxerxes hung back. She sensed that they felt they were too old to be listening to children's stories.

Esther decided to tell the story of Jonah and the whale. As she began, the princes' interest increased and they moved closer to the perimeter of the children to listen.

"Once upon a time, there was a man named Jonah. He was a good man and obedient to his God, but…he did not always like to do things he was told. One day, the voice of his God spoke and said to him, 'I want you to go to a very great city that is very wicked. I will direct you. You are to tell them how wicked they have been and that I am going to destroy them unless they are sorry for the bad things they had done.' Jonah did not like the people of that city and he did not want it to be saved from destruction. So he did not obey his God. He got on a ship that was sailing away in the opposite direction."

She paused and smiled to herself. She could see Darius and Artaxerxes were interested in the story. "Well, Jonah's ship was caught in a big storm. To save the ship from going down into the deeps, the sailors began to throw the cargo over the side. They hoped that by making the ship lighter, it would be able to ride out the storm. But the storm only became worse. Every man prayed to his god. Then they drew lots to see who had caused this bad luck. The lot fell on Jonah and he had to stand there on the storm-lashed deck and tell the sailors he had offended his God, who had sent the storm. 'What shall we do to appease him?' they cried. Jonah replied, 'Throw me into the sea and the storm will stop.'"

She looked around at the children. "The sailors did not want to throw Jonah into the sea, but they had no choice. As soon as he entered the water, the storm stopped and the sea was calm."

"Was he drowned?" one of the children asked.

"No. He sank down in the water but his God sent a great fish to swallow him. He was in the belly of the fish for three days and nights and finally repented. He cried out to his God to save him. He promised to go to the great wicked city to tell them of their bad ways."

Darius interrupted. "This is a funny tale. How could a fish swallow a man?"

"It was a very great fish. I have heard fishermen say there are such creatures in the sea."

Another child spoke up. "Have you ever seen a fish like that?'

"No, I have never been to the sea. I would like to see one though."

Artaxerxes moved closer. "What happened to Jonah then?"

"Well, Jonah's God caused the great fish to spit Jonah out on a sandy shore. He was so happy to be free of the fish that he hurried to the great city as fast as he could to tell them what his God had told him to say. It took him four days to walk throughout the city as he cried out to them, 'Stop your wicked ways and repent or my God will destroy your city.'"

"What did the people do?"

She leaned toward them. "The king of that city heard the message that Jonah had brought and proclaimed that everyone was to put on sackcloth and ashes and repent of the terrible things they had done. He told them that perhaps Jonah's God would have mercy on them and spare the city. Everyone obeyed the king and Jonah's God did spare the city."

The children clapped spontaneously.

Darius frowned. "Why did they listen to this man? They did not know him."

"True, but understand, he had been in the belly of the fish for three days. Can you imagine what Jonah looked like? What his clothes looked like? He must have looked like a dead man, all covered in slime with his clothes messy and torn. I think that is why the people listened."

Artaxerxes spoke up. "What happened when the people listened to Jonah and were sorry for what they had done? He didn't like them."

She shook her head. "He went off and sulked. He camped by a stream and felt sorry for himself. He knew his God could spare the city and he wasn't happy."

Artaxerxes was going to ask another question when a gong sounded in the distance. Shamach stepped up. "It is time for the evening meal. Please excuse us, my queen."

The children smiled at her and thanked her for the story. "I will tell you another story again sometime," she assured them. She glanced at Darius and Artaxerxes. They only inclined their heads briefly in respect before turning away and leaving.

Returning to her own quarters, she thought of the littlest children. Her heart felt hollow. *Would she ever hold a child of her own in her arms? Why had Adonai closed her womb?*

⌒

Mordecai made his way through the marketplace toward his home. It had been another long day and he looked forward to a quiet evening to eat his meal and study the Torah for a while before retiring.

As he paused to look at some new Persian rugs that were displayed, he heard voices in the shadows nearby. He would not have paid much attention, but was startled to realize they were speaking in Akkadian, the language of Babylon. He leaned against the wall out of sight and listened, his curiosity peaked.

"Bigthana, have you purchased what we need?"

"Only just now in the shop of the apothecary."

"What did you tell him?"

"Only that we had rats in an area and wanted to be rid of them."

"Did he believe you?"

"You are too anxious, Teresh. Our plan will not fail. When the king is distracted tomorrow evening, I will add it to his wine. It does not work right away. His guards will think he died of natural causes."

Mordecai's heart began to pound. *The king's guards were planning to poison him tomorrow night?* He must find a way to get a message to Esther as soon as possible. Her own life could also be in danger. *What if she was accused of poisoning the king?* He slipped away quietly and stopped by one of the scribes to purchase a small blank scroll. The scribe offered to write his message for him, but he shook his head. "I want to consider what to write."

This was not a message to dictate to an ordinary scribe!

He went home and quickly penned the message:

Your Majesty, I overheard two of the king's guards, Bigthana and Teresh, in the marketplace speaking in Akkadian, the language of Babylon, so they could not be understood. They couldn't know I am versed in that language. They are plotting to poison the king tonight. You must warn him immediately. Your Servant, Mordecai

Mordecai arose before the dawn so that he would arrive at the palace as the sun's rays hit the gates. He approached the guards at the entrance. "I am Mordecai, who serves in the King's Treasury. I have an urgent message for the queen, a matter of grave importance. I must speak with her servant Hathach as soon as possible. I will be waiting at our usual meeting place."

The chief guard frowned but was evidently moved by the urgency in Mordecai's words. He nodded and opened one of the doors to speak to a guard inside. Mordecai thanked him and hurried to the courtyard where Hathach usually met him. It was only a short time before Hathach appeared.

"When the queen heard your name, she urged me to go to you immediately. What is your message?"

"The king is in danger. Take this scroll to the queen. She will know what to do." He handed the missive to Hathach, who hurried back to the palace.

Esther could not imagine what Mordecai had to tell her and quickly opened the scroll. Reading the words, she gasped and looked up at Hathach.

"I must go to the king immediately. Please find Hegai for me."

"Yes, majesty." The eunuch hurried away and soon reappeared with Hegai.

Esther held out the scroll to him. "Read this. It is from someone I know well, who can be trusted. I must see the king."

Hegai read the words and his eyes widened. "Come with me, majesty. We will go at once. Wait for him in his chambers. The king is currently in the inner court with his advisors. I can only hope he will be able to speak to me...privately."

He escorted Esther to the king's chambers and bowed before hurrying away to the court.

She did not have to wait long. The king strode into the room and approached her. "Esther? Are you ill? Hegai said it was a matter of life and death."

Esther handed him the scroll, her eyes wet with unshed tears. After Xerxes read the message, he exploded with anger and paced the room, his fists clenched.

"My trusted servants? The men who guard the door to my chambers would assassinate me?" Then he turned to Esther. "You trust the word of the man who sent this message?"

"Yes, my lord, I know him well and he is a good man, loyal to you. He speaks many languages, including Akkadian, the language of Babylon. That was what they were whispering in."

"Those two men are from Babylon..." Xerxes murmured and resumed his pacing, then stopped short and shouted. "Guards!"

Two of his immortals, who were ever nearby, immediately stepped into the room.

"Arrest Bigthana and Teresh immediately and question them carefully, individually, about a plot to poison me. Find out if anyone else is involved."

The two soldiers bowed and strode quickly away.

The king turned to Esther. "How is it you know this man, this Mordecai?"

"He is well-known in the community where I lived, my lord, and a friend of my family. We have known him for many years. He would not send such a message without cause." She looked up at him, her heart still thumping in her chest. "I was so afraid for you."

Xerxes wrapped her in his arms. "So he is not a young man, then? That is good. I am jealous for my queen." He kissed her on the forehead. "And grateful for her concern for my safety."

She leaned against him. "I don't want anything to happen to you."

"Then wait with me until I have word on the outcome of their questioning."

He walked with her out to the balcony and they stood together for a while, looking out over the city. Finally, he sighed. "A king is always in danger from those who either disagree with him on political matters or want his throne."

Esther thought of Haman and Memucan. The king's death would not benefit Haman. He could only aspire to be a trusted advisor to the king...for his own purposes. She considered Memucan, the king's cousin. In order to take the throne, he would have to get rid of Xerxes and his royal heirs, Darius and Artaxerxes. Then another more ominous thought occurred to her. If Xerxes was the sole target of those plotting to murder him, Crown Prince Darius would become king and his mother, Vashti, would become queen mother, regaining a position of power.

Esther strove to remain outwardly calm and kept her thoughts to herself. She knew it was best for the king to get to the bottom of this plot by Bigthana and Teresh on his own, without her involvement. She could not speak her concerns to her husband, for if she were wrong, it would mean more trouble. Her heart still beat with fear for Xerxes, who paced the floor, glancing from time to time at the door to his chambers.

Sometimes, Esther thought back to her simple life as a Jewish girl, far from the plots and intrigues of the palace. Life as a queen was certainly complicated. *How many times had the king's life been in danger through the years?* She was grateful for the hand of Adonai, who had placed Mordecai in the marketplace in the right spot, at the right time, to hear the plot of the two men. These were men who guarded the entrance to the king's chambers. She had passed them many times. This morning, others had taken their place and she was told they had gone on an errand for the king. A shadow had crossed her mind, but she dismissed it. *Were the men guilty?* She shuddered to think of their fate if they were. There would be no mercy.

A servant brought fruit and sweetbreads, along with a flagon of wine, but she and the king ate little, the waiting becoming almost unbearable. The moments seemed to drag on as they waited for news. Esther did not wish to be sent to her quarters and was glad Xerxes seemed to want her to remain.

She sought to distract him from the matter at hand, talking to him about hunting and her studies with her tutor.

"There is so much to learn, my lord. Your kingdom seems boundless. Your father made Aramaic the official language, but there are merchants from far away who have not mastered it. Mordecai, the one who sent the message, sits at the king's gate and I understand works in your treasury. He is not the only one who must deal with many languages in the course of working with traveling merchants every day."

He nodded absentmindedly, his thoughts on the dangerous situation he was facing.

Esther placed her hand on his arm. "How frightening, my husband, to feel the ones who watched over you while you slept were planning to kill you. It is a time one must trust their god."

He turned to her, considering her words, and took her hand, lifting it to his lips. Her heart melted for him. He loved her, not just for her body, but for the love that she gave him unconditionally. She reached up and touched his cheek. He gave her a half smile as he turned again to look out over the city and the distant countryside, his face haggard.

It was nearly two hours before the two immortals returned to the king. Xerxes rose quickly to meet them, Esther close behind.

"Majesty, the two men have confessed their guilt. One of them had a small bag of poison hidden in his garment."

"Did they implicate anyone else?"

"Yes, majesty. It took a little more persuasion, but one confessed."

"And…?"

"Memucan."

Esther gasped and Xerxes took a step backward as though he had been struck in the chest. His face crumpled in anguish. "Memucan?" He stood dumbstruck for just a moment before he transformed into an explosion of rage.

"My own cousin? Who is around me that I can trust? Execute the two men immediately and bring me Memucan."

"Yes, majesty."

Esther shuddered. She knew what kind of execution the two men faced. They would be impaled on sharp poles to die like a worm on a fishing hook. It was a horrible death, but it was the means of execution for criminals in Persia.

Xerxes turned to Esther, his eyes full of pain. "Leave me for now, beloved. There are things I must do."

She bowed her head, "Yes, my lord."

Hathach was waiting in the corridor to escort her. She could only look at him with tears in her eyes and silently follow him back to her apartment.

31

Whispers spread through the palace like a small storm. Upon receiving her summons, Hegai faced Esther. Her maids retired to a respectful distance, but still kept their ears open to hear the fate of the king's foremost advisor.

"Memucan is dead, majesty."

Esther's hand went to her chest. "By the king's hand?"

"No, majesty. When we finally found him, he had swallowed poison. He was taken to his chambers and could only speak a few words to the king before he died."

"Did he say anyone else was involved?"

Hegai shook his head sadly. "He could only tell the king he was sorry."

What would the king do now? Would Xerxes have Memucan's body impaled, even though he was already dead? Esther was almost afraid to ask. "What did the king do?"

"He was with Memucan for a long while, ordering all of us to leave the room. He grieves for his cousin, majesty."

She sighed. "I am sad for him. To be betrayed like that…"

Hegai hesitated a moment, and then murmured, "The king has ordered his men to bury Memucan."

Esther frowned. "Bury him? Wouldn't they do that anyway?"

Hegai's eyebrows raised almost imperceptibly, but his face was otherwise expressionless. "You have lived in Susa, majesty, and thus should know, the king is Zoroastrian, as are all the Persians. They believe that the soil, water, and fire are sacred. Burial in the ground is regarded as a punishment for the wicked, for it denies the body exposure to the rays of the morning sun on the fourth day after death. With his body placed in the ground, Memucan's soul cannot ascend to god and will be doomed to an eternity in the underworld of shadows, remaining forever in the darkness of the earth. It is a fitting punishment for Memucan's betrayal of the king."

Esther remembered what Abba had told her about Persian burial customs. He'd merely said that the dead were taken to a tower. Perhaps he wanted to spare her the details of their burial practices.

"I see. I did not have occasion to understand those rites, but I thank you for clarifying them to me."

Hegai bowed and left her to her thoughts.

It was a sad ending for a man who had been like a father to Xerxes. *How different those beliefs are from those of our people,* Esther thought. *Adonai is more forgiving.* She prayed for a time when she could talk to Xerxes about Adonai...yet that would reveal her identity as a Jew. Each time she prayed for such an occasion, she felt a check in her spirit. *There would come a time—but when?*

Without a word, Esther nodded to Yasmin and Nadia. They understood and reached for their instruments. The music of the flute and harp provided a soothing balm to her heavy heart. As her maidens played, Esther went to the window. She walked a fine line as queen. She must stay in the king's good graces or she too was doomed to a sad fate: the rest of her life in the secondary quarters of the king's concubines under Shaashgaz, or like Vashti, sent to the *Harensara*, isolated with only one servant to care for her needs and no contact with other women. She walked slowly out to the garden and found her quiet, secluded corner. She could only place her fears and concerns in Adonai's care.

That evening, the king sent for her. He needed the comfort of his queen after all of the sorrows of the day. When she came and quietly stood before him, he rose and gathered her in an embrace, burying his face in her hair.

The next morning, Esther sent a message to Mordecai, telling him that the two men had been found guilty and executed. The only word from the palace regarding Memucan was that he had died. No details were given. The king had forbidden the guards and Hegai to speak about the attempt on his life. No good could come from such a discussion.

The king was not himself for many weeks after Memucan's death. It was hard to believe that men he trusted, most especially his cousin, had betrayed him in such a way.

Xerxes needed a distraction and Esther was finally able to convince him to go hunting. She was glad to go with him. Their quarry this time was deer. To help her pass the long days when she wasn't by his side, she was tutored by an expert archer and spent many hours practicing her skills. The king was so pleased with her prowess that she was given her own bow and quiver of arrows.

On this day, Esther wore a divided skirt that allowed her to sit comfortably on her horse. She wore a beaded jacket and leather boots that had been especially made for her feet. An embroidered leather vest kept her warm in the morning chill. To observe protocol, a veil covered the lower half of her face.

To her surprise, when a young deer was sighted, the king nodded to her to take the first shot. She raised her eyebrows, disconcerted for a moment. *He wished her to shoot first?* She truly hated the idea of killing animals. *But how else could one eat meat?* She drew the arrow back, even with her nose as she had been taught, and let it fly. To her amazement, she hit the mark and the small deer dropped to the ground.

She turned quickly to see Xerxes grinning broadly. "What a woman I have married! Well done, my queen, well done."

As servants hurried to collect Esther's deer, they rode on. From astride his horse, the king spotted and took down a buck. Esther breathed a sigh of relief that his deer was larger than hers. The king was an excellent archer and she knew he needed to prove his own skills before his men.

Making their way back to the palace, the king glanced over at her. "I have decided to replace Memucan. One of my advisors has proved trustworthy and wise in his advice. I intend to promote him to prime minister."

A sense of foreboding came over her. "And who is that to be, my lord?"

"I have chosen Haman."

Esther looked down at her horse, endeavoring to master her turbulent emotions. She couldn't let Xerxes detect how upset she was.

They rode on in silence, which the king appeared to take for agreement. Esther was grateful that she did not to have to speak, for it would be difficult to hide her feelings concerning the Amalekite. When they at last returned to the palace and dismounted, the king took her hand and lifted it to his lips, murmuring, "Refresh yourself, beloved. I will send for you later this evening."

She did not trust herself to speak, but only smiled and nodded.

As she hurried to her quarters behind Hathach, her thoughts tumbled inside her head. *Haman!* He had finally wormed his way into the king's good graces and achieved the power he craved. He would be second in command to the king. She knew Haman, as an Amalekite, hated her people. *How would he wield the power he'd been given?*

32

The streets were crowded with the citizens of Suza dutifully waiting to pay homage to the king's new prime minister. Most people in the city did not like Haman. He was rude with merchants and rode roughshod through the streets without regard to people or goods. Mordecai and the other elders in the synagogue wondered how the king had chosen him...but knew better than to ask anyone.

As Haman rode one of the king's finest horses through the streets, he was resplendent in elegant clothes and wore the king's ring of authority. As he passed by, the citizens bowed in respect. Mordecai, observing the smug face of his enemy, remained standing, albeit in the shadows. Haman, looking the other way, did not see his act of rebellion.

When Haman was further down the street, Mordecai's friend Ezra turned to him. "Don't be foolish! The next time he comes by, you must give him respect. Do you wish to call attention to yourself? It will only bring you trouble."

"I will not bow to a man who is the sworn enemy of our people. He does not deserve my respect." Mordecai brushed Ezra's hand from his arm and strode away.

As the months passed, Mordecai's friends attempted to distract him and keep him away from the street when Haman was coming though. They pretended they needed his advice on a matter, or directed him inside one of the shops on one excuse or another. He appreciated their concern for him, but realized they were also worried about their own safety. *What could the Jewish people expect from this Amalekite as prime minister?*

⌒

Xerxes ordered all of the palace officials to bow to Haman to show him respect as he went about his affairs. Esther, as the queen, did not have to so. Instead, Haman bowed to her when he passed by. Sometimes, he smiled, but it did not reach his eyes and his expression was unreadable.

She strove to be courteous, hiding her revulsion for the man she felt would, in time, present a danger to the king. She knew Haman was too ambitious. Sometimes, he addressed her with a smug look on his face and she resisted the urge to slap him. Everywhere she went about the palace, she continued to watch and listen carefully so she could keep track of his movements and actions.

As the months went by, Esther became aware that Haman and a group of soldiers that had been assigned to him were making many excursions outside the palace. It was said he was handling trouble spots for the king and putting down small rebellions.

At one point, she mentioned the subject to Xerxes. "My lord, it is said that Haman handles many small uprisings in the nearby provinces. It is good you have a trusted official to take care of these matters for you."

"He says they are inconsequential matters in the villages. It is one less thing I have to deal with."

But something nagged at Esther's spirit and she determined to send a message soon to Mordecai to see what he knew about these forays of Haman's.

⌒

The elders in the synagogue murmured among themselves, many anxiously looking over their shoulders. Should anyone learn this news, there could be bloodshed.

The rabbi shook his head. "My sister's son may not survive the night. He was badly wounded. That he got away to come to us is a miracle. Haman will not leave survivors to get word to the king."

Mordecai stroked his beard. "So Haman is ravishing the small villages and taking plunder he is not reporting to the king?"

The rabbi nodded. "My nephew hid out for two days, making sure Haman and his men had returned to Susa before venturing out. He rode his donkey all the way here and waited until darkness before collapsing just inside our gate."

Mordecai exploded angrily. "So the people are afraid to speak up. Haman would threaten their families if anyone told the officials?"

"Yes. That is what my nephew told us."

Simon pounded his fist in his hand. "That son of a camel driver! He gains his wealth on the backs of our people."

Ezra put a hand on his arm. "Shhhh! Should someone hear you, we could all be in danger."

Mordecai looked around at the small group of frightened men. *He could go to the queen with this news, but would he put Hadassah in more danger?* Haman was ruthless. Spring was rapidly approaching and the king and his court would travel to Persepolis for the Persian New Year. They could only hope that Haman would accompany the king and give them some months of respite.

The small group of elders slipped away to their homes. Each vowed to pray into the night for their friends and fellow Jews in surrounding villages.

As Mordecai walked through the gathering shadows, he again considered sending a message to Hadassah. *But she would be getting ready to accompany the king to Persepolis—and if the message got into wrong hands, it could be dangerous for both of them.* He thought of Nashon, who told him the palace servants lived in fear of Haman. They hardly talked among themselves anymore, not knowing who could be a spy.

Mordecai shook his head. *What a terrible way to live—fearful of your own shadow, wondering if any of your words could be construed against you.* He raised his eyes toward the twilight sky above. *You have a plan, Adonai. You see the peril of your people. Send us a deliverer, Oh Most High.* He sighed. *The Messiah was to be a conquering king, but who could possibly challenge an empire the size and strength of Persia?*

The streets were silent and he glanced at the shadows around him. Had the message from the rabbi not seemed urgent, he would not have ventured out. To anyone watching, it was only a prayer meeting at the synagogue. *Yet with Haman's spies all around, who knew what had been reported? Had anyone overheard them?* Mordecai braced his shoulders. He would not live in fear of this Amalekite. He lifted his chin and strode home with purpose.

Earlier, when he returned home from the treasury, to his surprise, there had been a lamb stew in the pot on his small clay stove. The warm meal bolstered his spirits. After eating, he had searched through his scrolls and found the scroll of the Prophet Yesha'Yahu, the one the Gentiles called Isaiah, and had been reading it when the messenger from the rabbi came.

Now as he sat, looking around his quiet house, voices of the past seemed to whisper around him. Hadassah as a laughing child. Jerusha admonishing him to get ready for the Sabbath meal. He half expected them to appear, perhaps from another room in the house, but there was only silence, only his imagination.

He again considered returning to Jerusalem, their holy city. The temple had been rebuilt, not to the grandeur of King Solomon, but he still longed to see it. He sighed. He could not abandon Hadassah. Although they could only speak through an occasional message, she knew he was there. If it were any comfort to her with all she faced, he would remain.

Kneeling beside his bed, Mordecai covered his head and prayed the *Hashkiveinu*, one of the evening prayers of his people.

Lay us down to sleep in peace, Adonai our God, and raise us up again, our Ruler, in life.

Spread over us Your Sukkah of peace, direct us with Your good counsel,

And save us for Your own Name's sake.

Shield us, remove from us every enemy, pestilence, sword, famine or sorrow.

Remove all adversaries from before us or behind us, and shelter us in the shadow of Your wings.

For You are our guarding and saving God, yes, a gracious and compassionate God and King.

Guard our going out and our coming in for life and peace, now and always.

Mordecai remained in prayer for a long time, lifting up Hadassah to their God and giving over his fears to the One who could carry them.

33

*E*sther awakened in the dark, for the morning had not yet brushed away the shadows of the night. Winter was withdrawing and the spring equinox would be arriving in less than a month. Tomorrow, she and her maids would travel with Xerxes and the royal entourage from Susa to Persepolis, where they would celebrate the Persian New Year. She had been out of the palace on the hunting trips with her husband, but never to another city. Esther smiled to herself at the thought of traveling in a veiled cart pulled by mules. Crown Prince Darius, Prince Artaxerxes, and a large number of servants and a few concubines would be going as well. She had taken Atossa's advice concerning the concubines to heart and while a sense of jealousy sometimes prevailed, she never spoke to Xerxes about the nights he did not call for her.

Looking out the window at the city below, she wondered if the king's advisors would join the caravan. If Haman stayed, while she would be relieved that she didn't have to deal with him, it could mean trouble for her people or anyone who got in his way. If he went, life would be easier for those left behind. She could only wait to see what the king had decided.

There was a flurry of activity all over the palace as preparations were made for the annual move. To her surprise, Xerxes sent for her. Her maidens quickly dressed her and Hegai escorted her to the king's quarters.

When Hegai had gone, Xerxes took her in his arms. He smiled down at her and with a twinkle in his eyes, announced, "You will ride with me as we leave the city."

She gave a cry of joy. "My king, you surprise me! I thought I would have to remain in a cart the entire journey."

He shook his head and tilted her chin up with one finger. "You are my queen and I wish you by my side as we journey."

"It will give me the greatest pleasure to do so, my lord." She debated a moment before posing the question that had been uppermost in her mind. "Will the entire court accompany us?"

"A few, but I leave Haman in charge until I return. There needs to be some semblance of authority while I am gone."

She could only nod.

"We will leave at dawn tomorrow." He drew a finger down her cheek. "But I may see you before that."

As she returned to her quarters to oversee preparations, she prayed silently for Mordecai and her people. Xerxes had no idea what he had done. With such a man in charge of the city, it was like leaving a wolf in charge of the sheep.

She instructed her maids to prepare her riding clothes for the following day. They looked at each other in wonder. *Had a queen ever ridden with the king in this manner to the summer palace?* Her thoughts tumbling, Esther listened half-heartedly to their excited whispers.

Later, her maids dressed her in a simple gown and Hegai soon appeared. He bowed and murmured, "The king awaits your company, majesty."

The next day dawned bright and clear, the warmth that heralded the coming spring already filling the air. Esther had dressed in her riding clothes, a silk mantle protecting her head from the sun and serving to partially hide her face. With her face thus obscured, none of her people would recognize her. For whatever reason Adonai led Mordecai to change her name, her identity must remain hidden still.

She observed the immense number of litters, servants, horses, and soldiers before her. It was overwhelming to see what preparations it took to move the king's household to another palace. Tents that would house the royal family when there were no accommodations during their journey were packed on wagons, along with rugs and all that was needed to furnish them.

Darius and Artaxerxes were mounted on fine stallions, awaiting the order to move. As she observed the princes, she realized they were older than she had assumed when she first met them. Darius was growing a beard and rode his horse with a regal bearing. Artaxerxes, only two years younger, had also grown into a handsome young man. She had thought of them as boys, but they were not children anymore.

As Xerxes helped Esther mount her mare, Farah, Haman approached with two of the king's advisors. As she settled into the saddle, he called out to Xerxes.

"A safe journey, my king. You may be assured all will be cared for to the best of my ability in your absence."

"I'm sure it will be, Haman. As we agreed, you will send me periodic reports."

"Of course, majesty." His words were smooth as silk, his posture was respectful, but his face belied his words. Xerxes nodded, distracted by one of the horses.

As soon as Xerxes turned away, Esther could see the gleam of triumph in Haman's eyes.

She looked around and was relieved to see the gold inlaid cart of Atossa. She had grown fond of the queen mother and would be glad for her company and wise advice. Darius and his brother rode behind Atossa's cart.

Artabanus, commander of the royal bodyguard, approached the king. He was a tall, almost handsome man with a rugged face, a man who had seen many battles. Although she rode beside Xerxes, Artabanus spoke to the king so quietly that Esther could not hear him. Xerxes glanced back at the men who composed his bodyguard. When he turned away, Esther was puzzled by the look on the commander's face. He almost looked angry. *Were there problems with their journey before it had even begun?* Artabanus motioned to the group of soldiers and then Xerxes gave the signal to move. The procession began to wend its way down the long ramp from the palace through the city and on toward the city gates. More than 3,000 of the king's immortals then joined them and brought up the rear of the procession; the rest remained to guard the city. Marching ahead of the immortals was the royal bodyguard, consisting of more than one hundred men.

As they rode, Esther wondered about Artabanus. She had only met him twice. He seemed to be a stern man, but was well-trusted by the king. Since the commander rode behind her, she would not see him again until they stopped at the first resting place. She turned her thoughts to the holiday ahead and tried to recall all that Hegai had told her about *Nowruz*, the Persian New Year.

"The name *Nowruz* means 'New Day,' majesty. It is a time of celebration not only for the Persian people, but for all races. The king will call for the satraps and noblemen from all of his provinces to come to Persepolis to celebrate. Winter is associated with the forces of evil and the people see spring as the rebirth of light. It celebrates the triumph of light over the dark, rejuvenating the world."

"Thank you, Hegai. I am grateful for your knowledge." She knew the king had assumed that since she lived in Susa before coming to the palace, she had celebrated the holiday before.

Hegai went on. "The celebration will be proceeded by *Chaharshanbe Suri*, a national holiday celebrating agriculture. It lasts thirteen days and includes a city-wide picnic where everyone, including the royal family, go out to enjoy nature. The people give each other gifts and visit friends and family."

As she rode by her husband's side, she felt a sense of elation and expectation. She was anxious to see the city of Persepolis.

Xerxes suddenly commented on the coming festival. "The priests have calculated the day for *Nowruz*. You shall enjoy the celebration, my queen. There will be feasting and entertainment. I look forward to sharing this with you."

Esther, remembering the feast before the Greek-Persian war, was not sure she would enjoy this occasion. It was during the six-month-long feast a few years earlier that the king had called for Vashti to appear before his drunken guests and she had been banished for refusing. Esther smiled and nodded as she listened to Xerxes, but she knew she tread a narrow path. Yes, she was beloved now…but her capricious husband could change her status at any moment.

34

*E*sther had ridden for several hours. She was amazed at the smoothness of the road, which had been built by Xerxes' father, Darius the Great. In villages and towns, the people came out to cheer the king and his entourage as they passed through. Sometimes, the whole company stopped when a messenger from one of the provinces brought news to the king.

When they stopped the first night, Xerxes put a hand on her shoulder. "Leave me for a time so your servants can refresh you, but return to me after sunset." A slight smile played about his lips. "I will tell you more about Persepolis."

She felt like a proper wife then, being able to spend the night with her husband. She bowed her head. "Yes, my lord."

He studied her face a moment. "You are young, my queen, but you are wise. You invigorate me." He turned away to speak with one of his advisors and she puzzled over his statement. So many times, she wondered what he was thinking...

Xerxes told her that more than twenty *chaparkhanehs*, or rest stations, were spread along the 600-kilometer route from Susa to

Persepolis, roughly the same distance apart, and they would spend several nights in these crowded quarters. She stayed with Xerxes that night, but the rest of the royal family, including Atossa, Darius and Artaxerxes, were put up in elaborate tents outside.

The next morning, Xerxes grinned at her. "We will stop for the night at a fortress built along the way by my father. It has been used for military purposes and to supply travelers along the route."

Esther noted that the guards, who maintained order along their way, went before the king to notify each of the rest stations of his approach.

They passed through a mountainous region with difficult terrain. The north branch of the road took them along the Shirin River as the sun beat down on the huge retinue.

When they stopped a few nights at smaller rest stations, Xerxes planned to meet with his officers and advisors in his tent, so she knew he might not call for her.

She stood and watched in amazement at the speed with which the traveling tent city rose up on bare ground. Xerxes' tent was elaborate, befitting a reigning monarch. Esther and her maids had a tent that was almost as large, furnished with bedding and soft Persian rugs. She was weary from the long day of riding, but Mamisa rubbed some juniper oil into her tense back muscles, which seemed to help.

Other than the actual traveling, this journey was not going to be a hardship for her. She knew the king toured his kingdom often, in part to take care of matters requiring his attention. But mostly, she had learned, the Persians were nomadic people at heart and Xerxes became restless after too many months in the palace.

Darius, Artaxerxes, and Atossa, whose tents had been set up nearby, joined Esther and Xerxes for meals. Esther was glad to have some time to talk to them on the journey.

Atossa usually left them after the evening meal to retire for the night. Esther could see that though the queen mother had made this trip many times, she was showing signs of great weariness.

This evening, Darius addressed her. "Did you see the falcon that flew over our heads earlier today? I'd like to train one to hunt for me."

"Yes, I did see him." She smiled. "He seemed to be looking us over."

Darius and Artaxerxes both laughed. The princes seemed to be relaxed, enjoying their journey. As she listened to the conversation between them and Xerxes, Esther felt the sense of family that she had missed. Her time with Mordecai and Jerusha seemed so long ago.

Her musings were interrupted when Atossa suddenly rose from her cushion. It seemed to take great effort. With the assistance of her servants, she nodded to them and left for her own quarters. Esther looked after her with concern, as did Xerxes. But the princes, absorbed in a conversation about falcons, did not seem to notice.

Today as the sun was going down, they approached the fortress and Esther marveled at the massive walls that surrounded it. A horn sounded somewhere from within and the huge gates opened for the king. Xerxes helped her off of her horse, sensing her weariness, and the animals were given over to the servants' care.

Atossa, also weary from the long journey, merely nodded to Esther and her son as she was led away to a small apartment reserved for her. The crown prince and his brother were housed with their servants nearby.

Xerxes led Esther to a large, sumptuous apartment that was obviously reserved for him, with an ornate, canopied bed, thick rugs, and tapestries on the walls. She wandered over to the window and looked out over a lovely valley. She turned back to smile at him.

"Your quarters are comfortable, my lord. Where shall I be staying with my maidens?"

"Your maidens have been taken to an apartment that is part of the women's quarters. You will wish to refresh yourself and my servant will take you there. Then I wish you to return to me."

She went into his arms, her eyes shining. "I am most the most fortunate of women, my lord."

He laughed. "Go, beloved. I will call for you at a later time."

The servant bowed and escorted Esther to an apartment, obviously reserved for her.

Her maids brought in jugs of water and she was happy to wash off the dust of the day. Refreshed and dressed in a simple gown, she silently thanked Adonai for all she was privileged to experience. Sometimes, she thought of the title, "queen of Persia" and wondered what her friends in Susa would say if they could see her now and know who the new queen truly was.

When she was again with Xerxes, they shared a meal together. He put an arm around her waist as they walked over and looked out the open window. The shadows had begun to creep down the hills and into the valley.

"Tomorrow we will again travel early. The next accommodations are like the smaller ones where we first stopped." He paused. "It is good to have you ride with me."

The softness of his voice touched her. Her husband was a complex man, ruling over a huge kingdom that required his diligence at all hours of the day and night. He could be ruthless...and yet he had been so gentle with her. Xerxes was not the Jewish husband she had dreamed of as a young girl; she still could not explain the love she had found so unexpectedly in the arms of this pagan king. She didn't understand the direction her life had taken, but over and over, Adonai had comforted her and given her peace. She served at His will and knew she had to trust Him, whatever His plan for her.

⟜

The next morning, Esther slipped away to her quarters and her maids dressed her for the day's travel. She quickly joined her husband in the open courtyard, where their horses were ready for them. When she saw Atossa being led toward her litter, Esther approached her.

"My lady, were you able to rest? We have had many long days."

Atossa smiled at her. "I have made this journey many times with my husband." She sighed. "Perhaps my age is catching up with me." She put a hand on Esther's arm and Esther led her to the closed cart, then watched as the queen mother's servants made sure she was comfortable.

"Have you seen your grandsons, my lady?"

Atossa smiled indulgently. "They joined me for the evening meal last night. They are faring well."

Esther wondered if Xerxes made any effort to speak to his sons on days when they did not share meals. It seemed that Persian kings left the upbringing of their children to servants. Jewish fathers openly demonstrated their love for their sons, spending time with them to teach them the ways of the Torah and helping them with Hebrew school, making sure they knew the prayers and customs of their people. She had once seen Artaxerses watching his father with a look of deep longing on his face.

Xerxes approached his mother and spoke briefly to her, then turned and helped Esther mount her horse.

As they left the fortress and began to ride, Esther pondered the few moments with Atossa. Something was not right. There were dark circles under Atossa's eyes and she wondered if the queen mother was ill. Xerxes looked over at her. "You are troubled over something?"

"I worry about your mother, my lord. She does not seem well."

"How is it that you see this?"

"Women sense things, my lord. There are dark circles under her eyes and she looks weary. She only says she is feeling her age."

He was silent for a moment. "She would not complain if she were ill. She is a strong woman. I will speak with her at the next *chaparkhaneh*."

When the ensemble stopped to rest the horses and take some refreshment, Esther walked over and sat under the shade of a tree while her maids brought some fruit, bread, and wine. She looked around for Xerxes and saw him talking to one of the servants, an older man, very dignified with white hair and a beard.

The two men conversed for a few moments before walking in the direction of Atossa's litter.

Hathach approached her. She had not seen him since they left Susa and she was glad to see his familiar face. "Your majesty is well?"

"I am well, Hathach. I did not know you were with the company."

"I go where my queen goes, majesty. You may not see me, but I am there."

She smiled at him. "I feel protected when you are near, Hathach." She looked over toward Atossa's litter. "Who is the man with the king?"

"He is a Greek physician, majesty. He returned with the king after the royal physician defected to Greece. His name is Marcos."

"I do not wish to intrude, but is the queen mother unwell?"

"The king wishes to have Marcos examine her. Her heart is not strong."

Esther looked over at them again. "I pray he can help her." Atossa had been her ally and friend. *Where would she be without her counsel?*

As Xerxes approached her, Esther stood up. "Your mother is well, my lord?"

"My physician has given her some herbs that he says will help her. We resume our travels."

The days seemed to run into each other as they went from way station to way station. The two princes now rode on either side of Atossa's cart and Xerxes seemed to be pushing the pace of their travel. He told Esther he was anxious to reach the palace in Persepolis. He checked on Atossa each time they stopped to rest; Esther made it a point to talk with her as well.

Atossa put a hand on Esther's arm. "I see the concern in your eyes, my daughter. It comforts me. Do not worry. I shall get to Persepolis. I have more comfortable quarters there." She glanced down at Esther's abdomen. "No sign of a child?"

Esther hung her head. "No, majesty, though I have prayed diligently. I do not understand."

"I will have Marcos examine you when we reach Persepolis. Perhaps among his herbs and potions, there is one that will help you."

Esther did not relish being examined by a strange man, doctor or no doctor, but she knew better than to protest. Perhaps this Marcos did have something that would help her.

Messengers continued to bring Xerxes news from different parts of his kingdom and couriers were sent with his answers. Esther again marveled at the immense responsibility the king carried and how seriously he took his duties, for no matter where he went, he kept his finger on the pulse of his kingdom. Many times, she sensed his weariness and sang to him to ease his burden. She was still finding her place of authority and as each day and month passed, she felt stronger in her role as queen. She would be there when he needed her, listen to his concerns regarding the kingdom, and not complain when he was occupied elsewhere.

Several times on the journey, she thought of Crown Prince Darius. His mother was taken away, but at least he still had his grandmother. Atossa was fond of both princes and made sure their tutor was diligent in teaching them. They studied geography, art, music, mathematics, and the history of their country. Should anything happen to Xerxes, Darius must be prepared to step into the role he'd been groomed for.

Then a thought crossed her mind. *If something did happen to Xerxes, what was her role? What would happen to her?* A cold shiver of fear passed down her back and she banished those thoughts from her mind, concentrating instead on the scenery.

35

*E*sther's excitement rose as they approached Persepolis. The city was set on a huge terrace against a mountain. They had passed small villages, farms, vineyards, many orchards, and other signs of prosperity as they neared the city.

Xerxes pointed ahead. "The mountain is called Rahmat. To the left is the Pulvar River. At this time of year, it's just a stream, but it flows into the larger Kur River. My grandfather chose this site for a palace, but my father built the terrace and the palaces you see before you."

She nodded. "It is magnificent, my lord."

They had paused the caravan and as Esther glanced at her husband's face, she saw pride as he contemplated the city before him.

"I understood that your father used Persepolis as his capital city. Why was it changed?"

"As you can see, it is in a more remote area, not convenient for communication with the rest of the kingdom. I find Susa more to my liking."

He leaned toward her, pointing ahead with his finger. "There is the *Apadana* and the Counsel Hall, the Triple Gate, and, just inside, the main imperial treasury."

People had gathered on the sides of the roadway to welcome the king to the city. Riding at the king's side, she saw the uplifted eyebrows and faces open with curiosity. It was the people's first glimpse of their new queen and their eyes followed her as she rode past.

They stopped at the base of a magnificent stairway of low terraces that graduated to the entrance of the palace above. Xerxes dismounted and a servant quickly came forward to help Esther. The king took her elbow and they began to ascend the stairs. Atossa was a short distance behind them, walking regally with a servant on either side of her. Darius and Artaxerxes followed behind her. Esther noticed that the physician, Marcos, was also following closely behind.

As they began the gradual ascent up the stairway to the city, there were almost more steps than she could count. It took all of her strength after the journey of the day to climb before stopping to rest in a small yard in the northeastern side of the terrace. Opposite them was the Gate of All Nations, which her tutor had told her about.

Esther looked around and realized Atossa was not with them. She had evidently gone directly to her quarters. The princes had most likely been led away also. She resolved to call on Atossa as quickly as possible. She also hoped to find a time to speak with Darius and Artaxerxes.

Followed by their servants, Esther and Xerxes entered a grand hall with four columns, its entrance on the western wall. Two more doors opened to the south and the *Apadana*, the palace where the king held official audiences. The other opened to a long road leading to the east. The wooden doors were covered with sheets of gold. Large statues stood by the western threshold—a pair of winged bulls with the heads of distinctly Persian men. These immense statutes were obviously to meant to evoke the strength of the Persian Empire. Xerxes' name was written several languages over the entrances, leaving no doubt about the ruler who ordered the hall be built.

The buildings appeared to be grey limestone. Major tunnels had been dug beneath them for the disposal of sewage, while a large elevated tank for storing water was carved at the eastern foot of the mountain. The last few weeks in Susa, at her request, her tutor had imparted all of his knowledge about Persepolis. It helped her appreciate this beautiful city even more. When she climbed the staircase, Esther saw carvings in stone, many representing the Zoroastrianism symbols for *Nowruz* and another representing a group of Armenians, famous for their wine, bringing that gift to the king. Stone lotus flowers were interspersed between reliefs of people from across the empire in their traditional dress. There was even a relief of Xerxes himself, in minute detail.

They entered the Gate of All Nations. "Our quarters are in the Hadish Palace." The king pointed to another large building. "I keep the archives there."

"How many buildings make up the palace grounds, my lord?"

He grinned at her. "You have insatiable curiosity, my queen. I must not let it go unanswered." He glanced at the structure before him. "We entered on the great stairway, which I finished for my father."

Esther's tutor had drawn a crude map of the complex for her to study. There were three general groupings—the treasury, the reception halls, and the quarters for the military, with occasional houses for the king. He had described the Great Stairway, the Gate of All Nations, the Apadana—often called the Hall of a Hundred Columns—the Tripylon Hall, the Tachara, the Hadish Palace, the Imperial Treasury, the royal stables, and the housing for the king's chariots.

Xerxes took Esther into the Apadana Palace. "I had it completed, but it was begun by my father over thirty years ago." He gestured at the columns. "There are seventy-two of them."

From the size of the columns, she realized they carried the weight of the enormous ceiling. Each column had a human or animal figure sculpted at the top, including two-headed lions, eagles, and cows, a Persian symbol of fertility. The columns were joined by oak and cedar beams that Xerxes told her were imported from Lebanon. The walls were finished with greenish stucco.

Then, Xerxes led her to the Tachara, the winter palace his father had started in the compound.

"My father could not finish so I had it finished."

"This is where you will reside?"

He glanced at her a moment before responding. "Yes, these are my quarters."

She kept her tone light. "It is beautiful, my lord."

A slight smile played about his lips. "You will find your quarters well to your liking."

She turned her attention to admire the bas reliefs carved into the door frames. Royal inscriptions were carved into the walls, doorways, and window frames, even on the doorknobs. Window spaces reflected the light off the highly polished stonework within the room. Colorful Persian carpets were placed strategically on the marble tiled floor.

"Come, I've something else to show you." He took her arm and led her to an ornate door, which opened to reveal a beautiful garden. There were thousands of plants and many trees. Among them, Esther recognized mulberry, olive, and date.

"Oh, my lord, the garden is beautiful. I spend much of my time in the garden near my quarters in Susa." She turned to him, delighted that he shared this with her.

He put an arm around her and drew her close. "There is a garden next to your quarters, beloved. I made sure it was ready for you." Leaning down, he kissed her. "You are like a beautiful flower in my garden. I am most fortunate."

A servant interrupted their quiet moment with news. Xerxes reluctantly released her and sent her to her quarters as he headed for a meeting with his advisors. "There is so much I want to show you, but duty calls. Your maids have prepared your quarters by now. Go and rest."

A servant stepped forward and bowing his head, he swept one arm indicating she was to follow him. As they exited, she saw Hathach waiting faithfully for her. He followed them to the queen's quarters and took up his post outside. Two guards were also posted nearby.

Yasmin spoke up. "My lady, we have waited for you. Are these not fine quarters?"

Esther nodded, finding her apartment quite to her liking. The stone floor was covered with large, soft rugs that invited bare feet to sink into them. Colorful tapestries hung on the walls. The bed was draped with silken fabric and held an intricately embroidered coverlet and multiple cushions. Her maidens had emptied the trunks and put her clothes in a carved wooden cupboard. As she looked around, she realized that Vashti had probably stayed here in the past. *Did Xerxes ever think of Vashti when he came to Persepolis?* A tinge of jealousy raised its head and she brushed it away. She was here now, beloved of her husband, and this was her life. She had no guarantee how long it would last, but Adonai was with her and she could only trust Him for her future.

Amireh and Parisa helped her out of her riding clothes, still a little dusty despite her long walk with Xerxes. Esther was delighted to find the bathing pool was heated by a fire underneath. As she stepped down into the warm water, she sighed and let the weariness of the day begin to fade away. She gave herself into the care of her maids, bathed, and dressed in a soft tunic.

She would be ready for Xerxes' summons, if he needed her. While she waited, she lay down on the bed. As Yasmin softly played her harp, Esther drifted off to sleep.

36

The balcony outside the king's quarters was so high, they had a magnificent view of the city. The sun was going down and the sky was glorious in shades of pink, orange, and gold.

Esther sighed, leaning against him. "I never get tired of seeing the sunset—or the sunrise, for that matter. The colors are so beautiful."

"I've never paid much attention. There was always something to do and someone needing me for one matter or another. It is through your eyes that I see so much more than I did before, my love."

She looked out over Persepolis. *Chaharshanbe Suri* had begun. "It is good the people can celebrate the goodness of God and the prosperity of the New Year." Xerxes did not comment on her reference to God, perhaps thinking she meant the god of the Zoroastrians. She turned to him. "I see that many nobles from your kingdom are arriving."

"It is not a religious holiday, so those who do not share each other's faith feel free to take part. You will have an opportunity to meet my brother, Hystaspes. He arrives from Bactria, where he is the governor. It is a crucial province in the kingdom."

"Do you not have other brothers?"

He nodded. "My brother Achaemenes was satrap of Egypt. There was a rebellion and he was killed. Masistes served in the army and was killed in Greece."

She looked up at him. "I'm sorry."

"It is the will of the gods." He looked off into the distance.

She decided to change the subject. "The officials bring you many gifts, my lord."

"True. I add to my treasury." Somehow, his voice sounded cynical and she decided to remain silent for a while. She glanced at his face. "You are weary, my lord. Shall I return to my quarters?"

He seemed relieved that she had discerned his mood. "I have much on my mind tonight." He leaned down and kissed her on the forehead. "Sleep well."

She knew Xerxes needed to be alone from time to time. She put her hand on his cheek, then turned and left him.

Hathach was waiting. "You are troubled, my queen?"

"The king is weary. He has much on his mind."

He did not answer, but walked with her to her quarters. Strange that she should feel relieved, but she realized she too was still very weary from their long journey.

After thirteen days of celebration, the end of the festival of *Chaharshanbe Suri* came. This day, *Sizdah Bedar*, was a national day of picnicking. Esther observed the people going out of the city to enjoy nature and the beauty of the revitalized world around them. They took baskets of bread, fruit, wine, and many dishes of various favorite foods. Rugs were placed on grassy areas and the women cooked kabobs over small open fires. Every family took bunches of bean sprouts, representing embodied ailments and misfortunes, to throw into the river. Esther was told it symbolized all of the unlucky and inauspicious thoughts, feelings, and happenings that had been looming over the home. Families would return home refreshed and content.

As Esther thought of these things, she wished she had some bean sprouts from the palace to toss into the river. Perhaps it would help dissipate all of the negative thoughts she had about Haman and what manipulative schemes he might be hatching in the kingdom while they were gone. She also thought about Mordecai. *How was he? Were the Jews in Susa suffering under the king's absence?*

Xerxes was giving a banquet for his visiting satraps and officials. As Esther met Hystaspes and he bowed to her, she could see the family resemblance.

"Greetings from the province of Bactria, majesty. It is good to finally meet you in person. You exceed all I have heard of the king's beautiful queen."

Xerxes moved closer to her side. "Have you paid respects to our mother?"

A small smile played around his brother's lips. "Of course." He looked past the king. "She comes even now."

Escorted into the hall by Darius and Artaxerxes, Atossa seemed to have rallied. She smiled proudly at her two sons, who bowed their heads to her. Atossa turned to Esther. "I am feeling much better now." She nodded to her grandsons and then gave her arm to Hystaspes, who led her to her seat at the table.

They were now in the thirteen days of *Nowruz* and Xerxes was in a good mood, celebrating the prosperity of his vast kingdom and the prospect of a new year. The second day, Esther would entertain the wives of the officials who had come with their husbands. She could not help but think of Vashti. *Would Xerxes drink too much wine and then call for her to present her to his guests?* If so, she would not follow in Vashti's footsteps and refuse. But then again, she reasoned, perhaps the king had learned something from that incident.

37

*E*sther visited Atossa over the next few days, sometimes alone and sometimes with Hystaspes and Xerxes. While neither brother spoke of it, the queen mother's color after the night of the banquet was not good. She usually greeted Esther sitting in an ornate chair, but this time, Atossa was in her bed. Her face was pale. She turned her head and smiled at Esther. Then she turned to the doctor with exasperation.

"This physician will not let me rise." She indicated the man standing on the far side of the bed.

"My lady, you need rest. Too much company is hard on you."

Atossa huffed. "Leave us for a while. I will have company when I wish it."

Esther took Atossa's hand. It felt frail and the veins were clearly showing. "How are you feeling?"

"As well as can be expected." She leaned closer to Esther. "What word do you hear from Susa?"

She knew Atossa was asking about Haman. "All is well...or so the king has been informed. There was a minor rebellion, but it was handled."

Atossa sniffed. "I can imagine how. Be very aware of that man, Esther. He has the king's signet ring, but I fear he will not use it for good."

She sighed and then contemplated Esther. "You shall not bear him a child. I know that now. I do not know the reason, but it is not important. Listen to me carefully. You must cultivate the crown prince—and his brother. They are lonely and vulnerable. They need a mother's touch. You are not Vashti, but you are kind, tactful, and intelligent. You will know how to approach them. And it is for your own good as well. Be kind to the crown prince, for one day he will be king and your future may hang in the balance of how he sees you."

Her eyes narrowed and she searched Esther's face. "You are happy with my son?"

"I am happy, my lady. He is a complex man, but a lesser man could not rule a kingdom such as this."

"I believe the king still grieves for Memucan."

"I still do not understand his cousin's motive, my lady. He was not in line for the throne. Why did he plot to poison Xerxes?"

"I'm not sure. Either he was clearing the way for Prince Darius, whom he thought he could manipulate as regent, or someone else was involved. I'm afraid we will never know."

The door suddenly opened; Xerxes and Hystaspes strode into the room. The king's face softened when he saw Esther sitting by the side of Atossa's bed.

"How are you feeling, Mother?"

She put out a hand and he grasped it in his own. "As well as can be expected, my son. My heart is not strong and your physician has probably told you. The journey was hard on me this time."

Hystaspes leaned toward her. "What can we do for you?"

"Nothing. All this fuss wearies me. I will soon join my ancestors."

At her words, a look of pain crossed Xerxes' face. "You will not return to Susa with us?" It was more a statement than a question.

"The tomb of your father is nearby in Naqsh-a Rostam. I wish to be buried with him there."

"Do not speak of death! You are not yet an old woman." Xerxes' eyes were dark with emotion. "What would we do without your wise counsel?"

Atossa huffed. "Nonsense! You have a dozen advisors and you seldom listen to me. If you had, you would not have gone off to fight Greece. I tried to discourage you, but you wanted to avenge your father. At a great cost of men and fortune, you returned home in defeat."

Esther's eyes widened as she listened to this exchange in amazement. No one could talk to the king like that…but he heard the words from his mother without comment or protest.

Atossa's face suddenly contorted in pain and she grabbed at her chest.

"Guards, send for the physician!" Xerxes rose and shouted at the door, where he knew the guards would hear him.

The physician, Marcos, had evidently been nearby, for in moments, he was in the room. As Esther, Xerxes, and Hystaspes stepped away, he immediately examined his patient.

Atossa's face relaxed finally, but the spasm had taken its toll on her. The physician turned to the king. "Majesty, she must rest. I will give her a potion of herbs that will quiet the spasms, but she is gravely ill."

"I am to be notified if there is any change. Any change at all."

Marcos bowed. "Yes, majesty, I will keep you apprised and send a messenger to you immediately."

Xerxes took Esther's hand and, nodding to his brother, led her from the room.

Esther once again stood on the king's balcony, where they could see the lights of small fires here and there. The holiday was over; the city below them was quiet and peaceful.

Xerxes stood beside her, but his mind was far away. He gave vague answers when she attempted to make light conversation with him.

Atossa had grown weaker by the day. Finally, she brought up what she knew was foremost on his mind. "You are concerned for your mother, my lord?"

"The physician says her time is short. Hystaspes is delaying his journey home so he can be with her."

There was a knock on the door and when Xerxes answered it, a servant bowed. "The physician calls for you, majesty. It is urgent."

Esther and Xerxes hurried down the halls and met Hystaspes at the door to Atossa's chamber.

"I was summoned also," he murmured.

When they entered the room Atossa lay still on her bed. Darius and Artaxerses stood by her bedside, their eyes wet with tears. For a moment, Esther thought the queen mother had already left them. When they stood by her bedside, she opened her eyes.

"You will place my estuary in the tomb of your father. We have been parted these years and I wish to rejoin him."

Xerxes bit his lip. "It shall be done."

Hystaspes knelt by the side of the bed. "I have missed your company. Will you leave me so soon?"

She reached out a hand and touched his cheek. "I was blessed with four sons. I miss my daughters, but that is what we must contend with. They are far away with their husbands. There is no time to bring them here. You will send word of my death to them?"

Xerxes nodded. "Yes. Messengers will take them the news."

Esther looked at her husband through the tears, which ran unbidden down her cheeks. His face was almost forlorn. For a moment, he was not the king of a mighty empire; he was just a son watching his mother die. His and Hystaspes' eyes were moist.

Now she marveled at the frail woman in the bed. Atossa had ruled with her husband, Darius, and borne him sons and daughters. Two sons had died and her daughters had been given in marriage to form alliances with other countries. Many times, Atossa had ridden with her servants and private guard to oversee her lands and estates. A strong and proud woman, she was revered by her people. Esther could not imagine the palace in Susa without her.

Atossa turned her head and reached for Xerxes' hand. "You carry a great burden, my son. Beware of those around you who do not have your best interests at heart. You have dealt with one traitor, but there will be others." Her voice softened. "Never forget, the best kings rule with compassion. You have a queen who loves you and is loyal. Honor her."

She turned to Hystaspes. "Honor your brother for he is your king. Your father would be proud of both of you. I have loved you both."

She closed her eyes, gave a deep sigh…and was gone.

Darius and Artaxerxes cried out and knelt to put their heads on the bed near their grandmother. Xerxes looked down at them for a moment, hesitating, then quietly put a hand on each of their shoulders. He was as comforting as he could be for them; for that, Esther silently thanked Adonai.

The king called for the servants who waited outside the door. "Prepare her majesty for the Tower of Silence…and notify the priests."

Darius and Artaxerxes rose slowly and faced her. "I am sorry. I loved her, too," she murmured. The king and his brother left the room with the princes following them. Esther trailed behind the men. When they had all left the chamber, one of the eunuchs walked with the princes back to their quarters. Darius walked quickly, but Artaxerxes turned back briefly to give Esther an anguished look.

Hystaspes clenched his jaw. "In the morning..." He turned quickly away toward his quarters.

Xerxes followed his figure for a few moments and then faced Esther. "I would be alone, beloved. You will join me in the morning."

"As you wish, my lord. You will be in my prayers."

"Prayers." He considered that a moment. "Yes." He turned away and left her standing by her faithful Hathach.

She longed to comfort her husband in his grief, but she knew he had to handle his emotions in his own way, as did his brother. Reluctantly, she nodded to Hathach and he escorted her in silence to her quarters. Once there, her maids gave her privacy as she gave in to her emotions and wept for the courageous woman she had come to know and love.

$\mathcal{X}$erxes and Hystaspes met her at the entrance to the palace. Both looked haggard and merely nodded to each other. The young princes followed with their servants. The family slowly walked down the graduated steps, followed by the palace officials, servants, and eunuchs. Esther glanced at Artaxerxes, whom she sensed was friendly toward her, and he returned a pain-filled glance. Darius looked away, preferring to keep his emotions to himself. She turned back to observe her husband and focus her thoughts on what was to come next.

Four Zoroastrian priests came from the town mortuary to meet them. Dressed in white, they carried a half shell of metal that held the shrouded body of Atossa. As the priests moved out, Xerxes, Hystaspes, and Esther walked slowly behind them. At the edge of the city, they reached a tall, rounded building: the *Drakma*, the Tower of Silence.

Walking beside her husband, Esther had many conflict-ing thoughts. Her tutor had told her about the *Drakma* and the Zoroastrian burial practices. She had to steel herself to prevent her face from showing her revulsion at what was to come. Her husband's religion forbid the body to come in contact with soil, water, or fire. Zoroastrians believed that burying the body as her people did, burning it on a funeral pyre, or sending it adrift on the sea were all practices that would pollute the sacred elements.

At the door to the *Drakma*, Atossa's body was placed on a platform and the head priest recited a long prayer for her departed soul. Two more men, the *salars*, also dressed in white, joined the priests and four men carried the body into the tower. As a member of the royal family, Atossa's body would not be placed in the upper circle with others, but would be laid in an indentation at the top of the tower, open to the sun. Her shroud would be removed and her naked body would remain for four days while the birds of prey consumed her flesh. The hot sun also hastened the drying of the exposed bones. After four days, when her soul had ascended up to heaven, her bones would be gathered into an ossuary and placed in the tomb of her husband, Darius the Great.

Esther felt almost nauseous at the thought of what was going to happen to this great woman's body. Her own people buried the deceased immediately—usually the same day—and would never leave the body exposed to that kind of desecration. Yet, as she considered these things, Esther knew she could never voice such thoughts to her husband. She could not question the beliefs and customs of his people. She sighed inwardly. She could only do her best to support him in the loss of his mother.

During the four days they waited to retrieve the bones of Atossa, Xerxes did not call for her. He had withdrawn to the *Tripylon*, the private room for the king and his counselors, where they discussed plans for the empire, projects the king wanted to complete, new sea routes, and other business brought before him.

The sweeping empire of Persia could not come to a halt over the death of the queen mother.

Today, as she gave herself to the ministrations and fussing of her maids, she considered the events she had witnessed. She gave a slight shudder as she thought of Atossa's body, now open to the sun...and the birds circling overhead.

39

*E*sther sat in the small garden where they had first stopped when they climbed the steps to the palace compound. She wanted to walk and Hathach had followed at a discreet distance, keeping his usual watchful eye on his mistress. She heard footsteps on the stones and looked up to see Darius and Artaxerxes approaching with their tutor. *What fine young men they had grown to be.* She smiled up at them and waited to find out the reason for their company.

Artaxerxes spoke first. "We are tired of our quarters and there is little to do besides study." He gave the tutor a quick look.

The tutor seemed uncomfortable. "My lady, forgive us for disturbing you. They said you tell stories and persuaded me to help find you."

She smiled at them. "I'm glad you did. I was feeling a little bored, too. Come, join me." She turned to Darius, who remained silent. "Did you wish to hear a particular story?"

Artaxerxes glanced at his brother. "We would like to hear a story about a battle."

David and Goliath immediately came to mind. The princes were trained for battle. That story might appeal to them. She considered how much of the story she could tell.

"Ah, well, I do know a story about a battle that you might enjoy hearing. It was told me a long time ago."

The princes gingerly sat down on a nearby bench and waited. Their tutor also seemed eager to hear the story.

"Once, there was a young man named David, who was the youngest of his father's seven sons. His job was to tend the sheep. Their king was out fighting a battle with the forces of one of their enemies and David was sent by his father to take food for his brothers and see how the battle was going. When he arrived, the king's men were on one hill and the enemy's forces were on another hill, with a valley in between them. Standing in front of the enemy was the biggest man David had ever seen—a giant, over nine feet tall..."

Darius interrupted. "I've never seen a giant and I don't believe there are any."

"Of course, your highness, but remember, this is a story."

He frowned, but sat back and waited for Esther to continue.

"The giant's name was Goliath. His spear was as thick as a young tree and his armor weighed more than most strong men. He shouted and jeered at the king's army, but they were silent..."

Darius frowned. "Were they afraid? My father's army would not be afraid."

Esther sighed. "Yes, I think they were. The giant was very intimidating."

She went on, "The giant had railed at them for forty days, 'Why don't you come out to fight? Choose one man to fight me. If he kills me, we will be your slaves, but if I kill him, you will all be our slaves!'"

Artaxerxes asked, "Didn't the king's army have a champion to fight him?"

She leaned forward. "I'm coming to that.... So David listened to the giant make fun of the God of his people and asked, 'Hasn't anyone offered to fight against this man who makes fun of our God?' But David's brothers jeered at him. 'Aren't you supposed to be tending the sheep?' they asked. 'Go home. You just want to see the battle.'

"But David persisted. He asked a soldier, 'What will the king give to the man who fights this Goliath who defies us and mocks our God?' And he learned that the king would give one of his daughters in marriage to that champion and the man's family would be exempt from paying taxes.

"And David said, 'Then I will go fight this giant.' He ignored his brothers and went to the king. 'No one should lose heart because of this giant,' he told the king. 'Let me fight him for our army.'

"The king said in reply, 'You are only a boy. How will you fight him?' And David said, 'I have killed a bear and a lion with my sling when I was tending sheep for my father. Our God will give me strength to fight this man.'

"Since no other man had come forth to fight the giant, the king decided to let David try. 'Go then,' the king said. 'May our God be with you.' He tried to give David his armor and weapon to fight Goliath, but they were too big. David instead gathered five smooth stones from a nearby stream and started down into the valley toward the giant.

"Now the giant was insulted that this young boy had been sent out to fight him. Seeing David with his sling, he shouted, 'Am I a dog? Is that why you're coming at me with sticks?' And he cursed David by his God and told him that he would feed his flesh to birds and wild animals.

"But David replied, 'You come at me with a sword, a spear, and a javelin, but I come at you in the name of our God, who will hand you over to me. I will slay you and lop off your head.' And David took one of the stones from his shepherd's pouch, put it in his sling, and hurled it at the giant. The stone struck the giant in the forehead and he fell face down on the ground. David took the giant's sword and quickly cut off his head. When the enemy saw their champion was dead, they ran away. And the king's soldiers gave a great shout, ran after them, and killed many of their foes."

Darius nodded. "That was a good story."

Artaxerxes asked, "What happened to David then?"

"The king took him into the palace to serve him and eventually gave him one of his daughters as his wife."

Esther had been absorbed in telling the story and was suddenly aware of another person nearby. Xerxes leaned against the wall, listening. A smile played around his lips. "You may leave us." He gestured to the tutor to take his sons away.

The princes bowed, a little chagrined at having their father catch them listening to a story like little children. They bowed to Esther and quickly returned to the palace.

"I've told stories to the royal children. The princes have joined us from time to time, perhaps to get away from their tutor. They listened, perhaps reluctantly."

He shrugged. "I'm afraid I am guilty of enjoying your stories also." He looked in the direction his sons had gone. "There is much for them to learn. I have taken them hunting and they have had lessons in battle tactics, but sometimes it is good to get away from duties."

She detected a hint of wistfulness in his voice. His vast empire presented challenges for him day and night. Yet perhaps inside every tough soldier or king, there was a little boy who still loved stories.

40

The king had been moody since his mother's death. On the days he was too busy with affairs of the kingdom, he was just tired. Other days, he brooded over the loss of Atossa. Her bones had finally been retrieved and placed in an ossuary. Esther waited to see what the next step entailed.

That evening, Xerxes was in one of his moods when he sent a short, terse message to her. "Tomorrow, you will accompany me to *Naqsh-e-Rustam*, where the bones of my mother are to be placed according to her wishes. We will leave at dawn. Be ready."

She dreaded the journey to dispose of Atossa's remains. Hegai informed her that the tomb at *Naqsh-e-Rustam*, the royal family's burial place, was about five kilometers northwest of Persepolis.

At dawn, Esther was ready in her riding clothes. This time, a cape of gold-embroidered fabric was draped about her shoulders, denoting her rank, and she wore a small crown on her head. A sheer veil covered the lower half of her face for propriety. She mounted Farah and patted her mare on the withers. The horse tossed her head, seeming eager to set off.

Xerxes did not speak and she realized he was keeping his emotions under control. Darius and Artaxerxes were also mounted and waiting. A contingency of troops joined them, along with a few servants who had been chosen for the task of placing the ossuary in the tomb. They carried a ladder of some sorts and while Esther wondered about it, she remained silent, watching her husband for the signal to ride. An ornate cart was brought out, encrusted with precious stones. It held Atossa's ossuary.

Xerxes glanced back at the assembled group and Artabanus gave the signal to move forward. The soldiers marched stoically behind the royal family. Although Esther wanted to speak to Xerxes, she felt a check in her spirit and rode silently beside him, inwardly praying for this day, this time, and the task ahead.

After several kilometers, the form of a mountain loomed ahead of them. As they drew closer, Esther could see that several caves had been carved in the edifice and barred doors were placed at each of the openings. The caves were several feet off the ground and she then understood the reason for the ladder.

The king signaled a halt at the base of the monument and a Zoroastrian priest appeared from somewhere in the group. As the ossuary of Atossa was removed from the cart, Xerxes, Esther, Darius, and Artaxerxes dismounted and waited while the servants placed a ladder in front of one of the caves. One came to Xerxes and bowed before the king, who produced a large iron key, which he handed to the servant.

"It is the tomb of your father, my lord?" She spoke softly. He nodded and turned back to face the tomb.

After the priest had prayed over the ossuary, the servants placed the ladder against the face of the rock and climbed up. One used the large key to open the iron door of the tomb. Two others carried the ossuary up the ladder and entered the opening, depositing their charge inside. When they came out, the iron door was again locked. When the servants were on the ground, the ladder was removed. One came before Xerxes once more, bowed deeply, and returned the key to him.

Esther glanced back at the two princes; their faces were as stoic as their father's. She wanted to comfort them, but felt the need to wait.

When they had returned to the palace and dismounted, the princes turned to their father.

"You did well, my sons." It was enough. They nodded and returned to their quarters.

Xerxes turned to Esther. "You are a comfort to me, beloved. Even without speech, you give me strength." His eyes were warm as he looked down at her face. "Come to me this evening after the sun has gone down."

"Yes, my lord." She returned to her chambers and found her maidens eager to hear about everything that had occurred that morning.

"The queen mother is now with her husband. It is good."

They commented among themselves and Esther listened absentmindedly. She looked forward to a bath after the dusty ride and a time of rest.

⌒

Later that evening, Esther and Xerxes talked quietly and he spoke of returning to Susa. "I have spoken to Artabanus. He agrees I've been away long enough. The news from Haman is that all is well, but I hear news of other things, too."

"It is cause for concern, my lord?" She had been wondering how the palace had fared with Haman in charge. She remembered the faces of some of the servants as they went about the palace, fearing to say anything against the prime minister that might be overheard.

Xerxes' brow furrowed. "I am uncertain. I just feel the need to return."

Esther touched his cheek. "Your instincts have served you well in the past."

He took a breath and let it out slowly. "Perhaps that is so. Persepolis has always been a celebration city, but this time, it has brought sadness."

Esther was silent for a moment. "Would it help you to talk about your mother, my husband? To tell me about Atossa's life story?"

Xerxes looked toward the window for a long moment. "I think it may help. You see, my love, my mother was a strong woman and made the best of her life. She was married twice, to seal an alliance. And widowed twice. Once, she was imprisoned in the *haremsara*..." He paused so long, she wondered if he was thinking of Vashti, but he began to speak again.

"She was the daughter of my grandfather Cyrus and when my father became king, he married her to seal the kingship. It worked well. She was revered by the people and ruled with him as an equal. She bore him my three brothers and me, along with two daughters."

To Esther, it seemed to be a very condensed version of Atossa's life, but she had learned that men were not as interested in details as women. Under the circumstances, it was a lot for him to tell her. Fortunately, she had learned much about Atossa on the many occasions she visited with her.

"My mother had estates of her own and much land. She traveled many times to inspect her properties."

"Yes, she told me that. I admired her very much," Esther murmured.

He was quiet for a moment. Then he cleared his throat. "You have no property of your own as queen. I have decided to give you one of my mother's estates, with adjoining lands and a town."

Feeling overwhelmed by his offer, Esther searched his face. "You wish to give me an estate and town? Where is it?"

"It's in Ecbatana, a beautiful city on the side of a mountain in the Awan region, a day's ride from here. I will have the decree drawn up when we return to Susa."

"You are most generous, my lord. I would be honored to have one of Atossa's estates, but..."

"If you are thinking of the crown prince and Artexerxes, they will receive the rest of my mother's properties. And Darius will acquire my holdings when he becomes king."

"And Artaxerxes?"

"He also will have lands of his own, when he is old enough to marry and take possession of them."

"Then thank you, my lord. I will be delighted to look after this estate." She leaned over and kissed him on the cheek.

He smiled, pleased. "So are you ready to make the journey back to Susa?"

"I will go where you go. You have a great task to oversee your kingdom. It is not easy, with intrigue everywhere and having to trust the people around you, never knowing where danger might lie. I would take some of the worry from your brow and soothe you with my songs. I cannot give you advice for that is the task of your counselors. I can only give you my love and what strength I can impart."

He'd listened to her words and gathered her to himself. "It is enough," he murmured.

41

A week later, after many preparations, the king's household and family left for Susa, along with the contingent of immortals. She had noted that everywhere the king went, Artabanus was not far away. He took his task seriously and Esther felt the king was well-protected.

Looking back at the curtained carriages of his concubines, Esther wondered if any of them visited her husband during the times he did not call for her. A pang of jealousy touched her, but she ignored it, remembering Atossa's words of advice.

As they left Persepolis, the people lined the streets and cheered the king as he passed, bowing their heads in respect.

On this journey back to Susa, Esther now knew what to expect and made the best of each of the accommodations. Once again, the fortress provided the most respite halfway between Persepolis and Susa. They made good time and she felt the king was pushing them to go as far as possible each day.

The young princes joined them for meals and Xerxes quizzed them on their studies. Then he made an unexpected announcement. "It is time for you to have apartments of your own. I will have arrangements made."

The faces of both young men lit up. Their father had acknowledged that they were no longer children. Darius seemed to sit up a little taller, perhaps knowing he was next in line for the throne when his father died.

It was not unnoticed by Xerxes. "I plan to go boar hunting when we return. You both shall accompany me." He turned to Esther. "And you, my queen? You have become quite proficient with a bow and arrow."

"If your majesty permits, I prefer to remain at home. Boar hunting is for men."

Xerxes burst out laughing. "We shall bring you a fine boar for our table."

The two princes, used to seeing their father in a sterner mood, were startled but their faces showed they were pleased. Esther heard Atossa's words of advice in her mind. *Be kind to the crown prince, for one day he will be king and your future may hang in the balance of how he sees you. If you survive Xerxes, Darius will be the one to decide what happens to you.*

A little over three weeks later, they at last entered the city of Susa. Once again, the people waved and cheered their king's return. Esther looked for Mordecai among the throng. Although they were only able to communicate through messengers, she still had missed him greatly. She scanned the crowd and there he was, standing tall against one of the buildings so she could see him. Tears ran down his face as he lifted one hand in greeting, not to the king, but to the daughter he'd raised so lovingly. She could only nod her head as their eyes met and held for a long moment. In her heart, she longed to jump off Farah and run into his arms.

She looked back as long as she was able and then turned as they entered the palace gates.

Haman and the king's other advisors who had remained behind were there to greet them.

Haman bowed. "It is good you have returned, majesty. All is well, but we have missed you here." He bowed to Esther. "And you also, my lady."

Artabanus dismissed the contingency of immortals. With a curt nod to Esther and a deeper bow to his king, he assigned ten men to remain with Xerxes and strode quickly away.

The king only briefly acknowledged him and turned to clap Haman on the shoulder. "I am glad to hear that." He turned to the other advisors. "I will refresh myself and then meet you to discuss current matters."

They bowed. "Yes, majesty."

Haman almost strutted into the palace. He did not see the looks of anger and resentment on the faces of his peers.

Xerxes turned to Esther. "Rest yourself. It has been a long journey." He entered the palace and turned toward his quarters.

She turned to talk to Darius and Artaxerxes, but they were intent on watching their father, so she headed toward her own quarters, Hethach and her maidens close behind.

Hegai greeted her warmly as she appeared. "You had a safe journey, my lady? We are all sorry about the queen mother. Everyone thought well of her."

"Yes, I will miss her very much. The journey was a long one, but without incident. How have you fared in the palace while we were gone?"

Hegai looked around cautiously. Seeing her maidens occupied with putting away all of the clothes and other belongings, he murmured under his breath. "It is not good, my lady. Fear permeates the palace like a bad odor. Bearable, but unpleasant."

Hegai and Esther shared a mutual dislike of Haman but were careful to couch their words. This was the closest Hegai had come to naming Haman.

She changed the subject, raising her voice slightly in case anyone was listening. "Prince Darius and Prince Artaxerxes handled the death of their grandmother well. I believe the king plans to spend more time with them."

Hegai nodded. "That is good. Darius is impulsive, like his father. Artaxerxes is more thoughtful in what he says and does. They were close to Atossa."

When Hegai left, her maids helped her bathe and dress again. She was weary from long days of riding and realized her horse might be tired, too. Perhaps Farah wouldn't mind if she stayed in the stables for a while and could get her fill of grain and hay. If Xerxes wanted to go boar hunting with his sons, Esther was more than happy to remain in the palace.

That evening as she spoke with Xerxes, she considered for a moment how to bring up the topic of Haman. When he mentioned the need to meet with his advisors again in the morning, she took that as her opportunity. "Has your prime minister done well in your absence, my lord?"

"Haman seems capable and I have liked his advice on several matters. And it was Haman who suspected Memucan. My other advisors seem to dislike Haman. I'm not sure why. Jealousy perhaps. Carshena, Shethat, and Admatha are more open with their contempt. Tarshish, Meres, and Marsena, who came with us to Persepolis, are more subtle, but still obvious."

So there was unrest among the advisors. *How much could she say to the king about what was going on in the palace? Was her husband unaware of the murmuring of the servants? If she mentioned anything to Xerxes, would he ask Haman about it and thus stir up more trouble?* Wisely, she decided to keep her thoughts to herself and be more observant whenever she saw Haman.

She changed her tactic. "Is Haman a wealthy man? I know so little about him. He seems to be very prosperous."

Xerxes shrugged and reached for a cluster of grapes. "He calls himself Prince Haman. It seems that his great-great-grand-father—oh, several generations back—was a king. He does have some riches and brags much about his ten sons. He has given me sound advice on many occasions."

Esther felt a jolt to her stomach. *So Haman was descended from Agag?* Mordecai had told her that the prophet Samuel had hacked the Amalekite king to death after the rest of his army was slain. But the queen had escaped—and she was with child. Haman could well be her progeny.

She wished she could warn her husband about Haman, but suspected he would not listen...and might even resent her inter-fering. She could only watch and listen.

They stood on the balcony of the king's chambers, quietly enjoying the peacefulness of the evening. The night was cooler and the air had a crisp smell to it.

"Autumn is coming," she murmured, drawing her shawl around her. There were so many pressing matters lately, Xerxes had only called her twice in the last two weeks. In the silence, she sensed her husband had many things on his mind. His days were long and full of the affairs of his immense empire. She considered Haman and couldn't help but wonder what his ultimate plan was. He had arrived out of nowhere, ingratiated himself to the king, and now held a position second in command to the king himself.

She recalled Atossa's words of wisdom during one of their con-versations: "An ambitious man is never satisfied until he reaches his ultimate goal." *But what was Haman's goal?*

42

After Xerxes arranged to leave the palace for several weeks on matters of the empire, Esther decided to visit the estate of Atossa that he had given to her. Xerxes assigned a guard to accompany her and she felt overwhelmed to see over thirty immortals among her traveling companions. Riding Farah, with her maids in two wagons with silk coverings behind her, she spoke briefly with Artabanus.

"The king wishes you to be well protected, majesty."

"Thank you, Artabanus. I will feel safe with your men surrounding me."

He bowed and nodded to the men as the entourage left the palace and made their way through the city. A veil covered the lower half of her face and she nodded to the people who bowed their heads as she passed by. She did not see Mordecai until she was nearly out of Susa. He seemed out of breath as he stood by the city gate and nodded to her. She fought the urge to stop and speak with him, knowing it could not be, and continued on her way.

Hegai had left the chamberlain eunuch Aspamitras in charge of the harem so that both he and Hathach could accompany Esther. Hegai knew the way, having made the trip with Atossa several times.

They rode for most of the day and finally came to a road off to one side that led through a grove of trees. When they rounded a bend, Esther stopped her horse and looked on in amazement. The great house, set on a knoll overlooking the valley they had just ridden through, was almost the size of a small castle.

She turned to Hegai. "This is the estate of Atossa?"

"Yes, my lady. It is delightful, is it not? She had other estates, but they are farther away."

She could only nod and pressed Farah onward. The leader of the group of immortals gave orders to the men to disperse to their quarters behind the house.

Esther dismounted and walked to the large, iron double doors, which opened before her. A male servant bowed.

"Welcome, mistress. I am Jabbar, steward of the house. We have been expecting you. His majesty sent word to prepare for your arrival."

Two female servants bowed to her and Jabbar introduced them. "This is Dilshad and Shokufeh, mistress. They are at your disposal."

Esther smiled. "Thank you, Jabbar. I have also brought my own maidens with me, so I will be well cared for indeed."

Her maids shyly looked around the estate as the men began to bring in boxes and baskets from the wagons. Jabbar indicated they should follow him. "Let me show you to your quarters, my lady."

Atossa's former quarters had been dusted and swept. The murals on the walls, the gold bedstead, and the thick carpets decorated with woven birds and flowers all spoke of the wealth and opulence of the queen mother. There were fresh flowers in a vase by the window and their fragrance lingered in the room.

"I will leave you to rest, my lady, and when you are ready, I shall be delighted to show you the estate. Her majesty, the queen mother, also owned the town that is over the hill. You may wish to see it in the next day or so. The fields are ripe with grain and your purser will inform you of the rents and monies that are due you each month."

Esther almost could not speak, trying to process all that Jabbar told her. She smiled and nodded. "Thank you, Jabbar. I will call for you soon."

When he left them, her maids began to chatter excitedly.

"How good the king is to you, mistress!"

"The house is beautiful. Will we be able to go with you to see the rest of it?"

"You are most fortunate, mistress, that the king delights in you."

Razak spoke up, perhaps saying what was on all of their minds. "There are sure to be lovely gardens with more flowers such as these. Wouldn't it be wonderful to wander among them, mistress?"

They opened a door and found another room with a small pool for bathing. Esther was more than happy to wash off the dust of the day's travel.

⟅⟆

When she had rested, Jabbar returned at her summons and escorted her to the dining hall. She could not insult his office by having her maids join her at the huge table, so with a sigh, she ate alone. He had directed her maids to another part of the house to eat their meal with the rest of the staff.

After the evening meal, Esther chose to retire for the night with the promise of a tour of the rest of the house and lands in the morning. Climbing into the huge bed, she lay awake for a long time, considering where she had come in the last few years—from a simple Jewish girl, contemplating a possible marriage to the rabbi's son, her capture and months in the harem, her night with the king, and the startling words that would make her queen of the Persian Empire. Married to the most powerful man in the world who, wonder of wonders, loved her. It sometimes seemed to her that it was all a dream and she would wake up one day. Adonai had blessed her in many ways. She did not understand why she was not a mother, but Adonai was omniscient. She had trusted Him all of her days and He had given her peace. She did not need to understand. She only needed to be thankful for all that had brought her to this place in her life.

When her maids were settled in a nearby room, she closed her eyes and gave herself to sleep.

The morning dawned crisp and clear. Esther woke to the muted sounds of her maids preparing her clothes for the day and setting a tray with some fresh bread, fruit, and a cup of wine on her small table. Looking around the beautiful room, she decided she would take her meals here, where she had company, instead of the large dining hall. She smiled to herself. Maybe one day she could have a banquet there. The area could seat thirty or more people. Then she thought of the woman who had occupied this room before her. How she missed the times she spent with the queen mother! Atossa had been her only female friend in the palace besides her maids.

When she descended the steps from the upper wing of the house, Jabbar was waiting. With a smile, he bowed and swept his hand before her. "Good morning, majesty. I trust you slept well. Are you ready to review your property?"

"I am ready, Jabbar. My maids will remain here and I do not need the entire company of my bodyguard. Perhaps just three or four?"

"That is well, majesty. It shall be arranged. The people of the town have been notified of your coming."

"Thank you. Let us visit the people first. I can see the rest of the house and the grounds when I return."

He bowed again. "As you wish, majesty."

A strange feeling came over her and Esther felt older than she was. Inside, she was still Hadassah, but she must portray herself as a queen at all times outside her own chamber. Sometimes, the burden felt heavy. Her husband had been so attentive...and she felt suddenly bereft. *If something happened to Xerxes, what would she do?* But she put these negative thoughts aside, smiled at Jabbar, and went outside to greet the remnants of her bodyguard.

There were four guards waiting for her, each looking like the strongest soldiers in the army. Xerxes had sent his very best men to protect her. She drew herself up and inclined her head slightly. The men touched their fists to their chests in respect and waited until she had mounted her horse.

The town was a good size, but not as large as some of the ones she had seen on the journey between Susa and Persepolis. The people seemed friendly and curious about the new owner of the estate and their lands. She saw fields ripe for harvest and looked forward to meeting her overseer to find out what rents and monies would be put in her account with the bankers for her. She didn't have to wait long. A distinguished-looking older man emerged from one of the buildings. As she studied his face, she realized he was a Jew—and she thought she had seen him somewhere before. *Had he been one of Mordecai's colleagues?*

He spoke to her in Aramaic. "My lady, I am Nahor, your overseer. I served the queen mother for over fifteen years and now, I am at your service."

As Nahor glanced up at her, a puzzled look came to his face, but he promptly regained his dignified composure. Somehow, she sensed that he knew her secret. *Had they indeed met in the past or did he recognize their common heritage?* She felt ill at ease, but Nahor's warm, brief smile told her he would not say a word. He was all business from that moment on.

A groomsman took Esther's horse and Nahor led her into the building, where servants worked at tables with scrolls, marking figures in columns. They stood and bowed low before her.

As he went over the accounts, Esther was amazed at the amount of funds generated by the estate. She was also glad Abba had shown her how to read figures and read and speak Aramaic fluently.

When she left, Nahor bowed low again and promised to meet with her again before she returned to Susa.

The house that had belonged to Atossa was sumptuous but comfortable. The queen mother had added many touches that made it seem very livable. The atmosphere was peaceful; the servants were good-natured and she suspected they were pleased that their new mistress had come for a visit. As she walked in the garden and noted the variety of trees and flowers, she felt she was at home.

Would she ever live here though? Esther sat on a stone bench and pondered the thought. As long as she was in the king's good graces, she had her quarters in the palace. *If she ever fell out of favor, would she be banished to the haremsara as Vashti was? Or could she come here? If the king died, what would happen to her?*

She shook her head as if to disperse the troublesome thoughts. Only Adonai knew her future and He would reveal it in His good time. She bowed her head and prayed silently for wisdom in the months and years to come.

43

When at last she returned to Susa, she barely had time to bathe and change before Xerxes sent for her. He gathered her in his arms and his voice was almost wistful. "I missed you. How did you find the estate?"

She smiled up at him. "Beautiful. The building and grounds were extremely pleasant and the staff very efficient. The overseer, Nahor, was most helpful. He was with your mother many years."

"He was indeed. She depended on him and he proved to be an honest and trustworthy servant."

He bent his head to kiss her. "I did miss you, beloved," he murmured, his voice husky.

The next two years passed quickly. She went on several hunting trips with the king and the princes, once again showing her prowess with the bow and arrow. They had gone each year to Persepolis for the New Year and the summer, but it didn't seem the same without Atossa. Esther still felt a chill up her spine when she thought about Atossa's burial.

She did not have the dear woman to share her sorrow that she still remained childless. Thankfully, Xerxes did not bring up the subject. Esther wondered if it mattered to him or if his earlier words of not needing more children still held true.

One day after they had once again returned from Persepolis, it occurred to her that several days had passed and Xerxes had not called for her. She tried not to give the matter much thought because Xerxes sometimes was occupied with matters of the empire for days.

Two weeks went by. Finally, when nearly a month had gone by, Esther began to wonder if somehow she had incurred the king's anger or was out of favor for some reason. Her maids whispered among themselves and Esther spent time in the garden, but evening after evening passed and there was no word from her husband.

She questioned Hegai, but his answers were evasive. The king had gone on several hunting trips, taking Darius and Artaxerxes with him. One trip for some elusive game took him out of the palace for a week—but that did not account for the long days with no word from him.

Esther finally confronted Hegai. "Tell me what occupies the king and do not lie to me."

He sighed. "Haman brought a woman to the palace. He thought her dancing would please the king. She is very beautiful."

Esther fought down the disappointment and the pang of jealousy. "And her dancing was enticing?" Her mind turned. *Haman brought her?*

Hegai looked chagrined. "The king was…ah, intrigued by her."

Esther looked him in the eye. "Evidently. She was willing?"

Hegai sighed again and looked down at the floor. "She has occupied the king for several weeks."

She felt anger rise within her. "Why have I heard nothing of this?"

He looked up at her with sad eyes. "I'm sorry, majesty, but we were ordered to remain quiet by Haman. Speak of this to no one, I beg you, my lady, or you will bring trouble on all of us."

Esther felt like a knife had been driven into her heart. She knew her husband would see other women in his harem, but had steeled herself to be the wife Atossa said she must be. In their time together, she felt sure that Xerxes loved her. *It could not have been a sham...or was it?*

"Thank you, Hegai. I will discuss this with no one else."

She went out into the garden to her private place in the shadows. She felt betrayed, but she could not confront her betrayer. Tears ran down her cheeks, but she wept silently. Then as reason began to enter her thoughts, she considered the situation again. This was Haman's doing. *What was he up to? What purpose would this serve? Was he trying to find someone to take her place, have her exiled like Vashti?* Dreadful possibilities filled her head and she began to pray for wisdom. Never before had she sensed such danger.

44

*M*ordecai watched Hadassah return from visiting the estate Xerxes had given her. She always saw and acknowledged him, but never stopped to speak. She appeared well and rode her horse like she had been born to it. He felt great pride, but also great sorrow. *What was her life like in the palace? Was the king still kind to her?* He needed to know how she fared. He knew she still had not borne Xerxes a child and he wondered how that had affected the king. With Haman's spies in the palace, he had to be extremely careful of any messages he sent to her through Hathach, confining them strictly to spoken words, not written scrolls as he had been able to do in the past.

He still missed Hadassah greatly and longed to talk with her directly.

Another concern troubled Mordecai. The last time Haman rode out from the palace, the people bowed as they had been commanded to do. But Mordecai could not bring himself to bow to the hated Amalakite, no matter how persuasive his friends were. Officials at the gate noticed this one day and asked him why he disobeyed the king's command. And evidently, this bit of information had been relayed to Haman. Usually, the prime minister passed by and did not see Mordecai, occupied as he was with the fawning of the king's subjects. This time, however, Haman looked directly at him. When he saw for himself that Mordecai was not giving him the obeisance he craved, his face reddened with anger. Haman spoke to one of his men, who looked over at Mordecai, and then turned back to Haman to make some reply.

Mordecai's friend Amos had pulled him into the shadows, but it was too late. His enemy had seen his defiance. He sighed. Haman would not let this go. There would be repercussions.

When he left his house the next day, one of his neighbors hurried up to him in great distress. "Have you seen the king's edict?"

He shook his head. "What is it now?"

"Come see!" his neighbor urged him. They hurried to the marketplace, where the king's edict had been posted. The city of Susa was in mass confusion. All around him, the Jewish people were weeping and tearing their clothes. Mordecai read the king's decree:

On March 7th of the coming year, all Jews must be killed. Men, women and children are to be slaughtered and annihilated on a single day. The property of the Jews will be given to those who kill them.

By order of King Xerxes

Amos came over. "My friend in the palace says Haman offered the king 10,000 sacks of silver to issue the decree!"

Mordecai stared at the document in disbelief. *How could the king do such a thing? And what about Hadassah?* Queen or not, it was her death warrant also. He tore his clothes in anguish, went home, and put on burlap and ashes as others had already done. Then he went about the city, crying and wailing in bitterness of soul.

⁓

As soon as he heard the news, Hathach went immediately to Esther. He was frowning and his brows creased with his look of concern. "My lady, there is word that Mordecai the Jew who sits at the king's gate is moaning in sackcloth and ashes. The rest of the city also is in an uproar."

"What? Why would he do this?" Esther was perplexed. "Send him clothing to replace the sackcloth. He cannot go about like that and serve in the king's treasury."

She waited anxiously for her servant's return, but when Hathach came back, he shook his head. "He will not accept the clothing, my lady. He says he is in mourning."

"Go back and find out what is troubling him and why he is in mourning."

It seemed like a very long time before Hathach returned again. In his hand, he had a copy of the king's decree for Mordecai had asked him to explain it to her. "Forgive me, my lady, but Mordecai told me that he *directs* you to go to the king to beg for mercy and plead for your people."

Esther's maids listened to Hathach with growing alarm. They looked at Hathach and back at Esther, murmuring among themselves. The queen was a Jew?

Esther was distraught. *What could she do?* "Go and tell Mordecai this: all of the king's officials and even the people in the provinces know that anyone who appears before the king in his inner court without first being invited is doomed to die unless the king holds out his golden scepter. And the king has not called for me to come to him for over thirty days."

Hathach hurried to give her message to Mordecai and Esther waited anxiously for his reply. When Hathach returned yet again, he recited Mordecai's message:

"Your majesty, do not think for a moment that because you're in the palace you will escape when all other Jews are killed. If you keep quiet at a time like this, deliverance and relief for the Jews will arise from some other place, but you and your relatives will die. Who knows if perhaps you were made queen for just such a time as this?"

Esther felt as though a bolt of lightning had gone through her heart. Mordecai was right. Suddenly she knew what she must do.

"Send this message to Mordecai: 'Go and gather together all the Jews of Susa and fast for me. Pray diligently. Do not eat or drink for three days, night or day. My maids and I will do the same. And then, though it is against the law, I will go in to see the king. If I must die, I must die.'"

When Hathach had gone, Esther turned to her maids who watched her with anxious faces. "As you have heard, I am indeed a Jew. Chosen by my God, Adonai, to be queen of Persia among all the other maidens."

They fell at her feet, weeping, and Nadia spoke for all of them. "Nothing must happen to you. We will do whatever you wish us to do. You must save your people."

With tears in her eyes, Esther gathered them all to herself and they wept together. Then she drew herself up. "What I ask is that you fast and pray with me for three days, no food or drink. At the end of that time, you will prepare me in my finest clothing to go before the king."

They all agreed and Esther informed Hegai that they would not be taking meals for three days. He studied her drawn face and nodded. "I understand, my lady, for I know more than you believe. I felt you were the one from the time you entered the palace."

"You have my gratitude and thanks, Hegai, for your kindness and loyalty."

"I will also fast and pray for you, my lady."

Overcome with emotion, she could only put a hand on his arm in response.

He closed the door to her quarters as Esther and her maidens got on their knees to beseech God for the Jewish people. They took turns walking in the garden, praying quietly throughout the day. They prayed before they slept and then again in the morning. Most of the young women had never fasted in their life, but so great was their love for Esther that they willingly prayed to her God to save her and her people.

Before they knew it, the end of the third day came. Esther would go before the king. Her maids did her hair and applied a small amount of makeup. She put on her royal robes and the lapis lazuli jewelry. A crown was placed upon her head.

When they were finished, Amirah exclaimed, "Oh, majesty, you are so beautiful. How can the king resist your plea? We will wait anxiously for news."

Nadia made a minor adjustment to her robes. "May your God go with you, majesty."

Parisa opened the door to admit Hegai and when he saw her, his eyes widened. "My lady, you are magnificent."

"Hegai, I am trusting that I will be successful. Please immediately prepare a banquet for the king. All of his favorite foods."

"Yes, majesty, it shall be done."

With her head held high and trusting in her God, Esther slowly followed Hegai to the king's court. Then Hegai waited and Esther, taking a deep breath, stepped into the inner court.

Xerxes was deep in conversation with his advisors, but she did not see Haman. If he had left Susa, her plan would not work. One of the king's advisors saw her and gasped. "Majesty! The queen!"

The king looked up, completely startled to see Esther standing in the inner court. Before the immortals who stood by him could draw their swords, he picked up the golden scepter that lay across his lap and quickly extended it to Esther.

She gracefully moved forward and with a deep bow, touched the end of the scepter. As she looked at Xerxes, she thought he looked a little chagrined, but his eyes softened.

"What is it you want, Queen Esther? What is your request? I will give it to you, even if it is half the kingdom."

She had not expected him to be so repentant for forgetting her for so long as to offer her that much, but she just smiled at him. "If it please the king, let the king and Haman come today to a banquet I have prepared for the king."

The king turned to his attendants, almost eagerly, and said, "Tell Haman to come today to a banquet as Queen Esther has requested."

He was in Susa after all. "Thank you, your majesty." She bowed low and with another loving smile, Esther returned to her quarters to make sure the banquet was ready.

⟡

As the king and Haman arrived, Haman could hardly hide his arrogance. He almost swaggered to his couch. The banquet went well. Both Xerxes and Haman complimented Esther on the meal and she could tell her enemy was pleased to be the only advisor asked to join the king. His chest was almost puffed up with his own importance.

As she served the wine, Xerxes smiled at her. "Now, tell me what you really want. What is your request? I will give it to you, even if it is half the kingdom."

Esther was not yet ready to reveal her plan, so she answered, "This is my request and my deepest wish. If I have found favor with the king, and if it pleases the king to grant my request and do what I ask, please come with Haman tomorrow to the banquet I will prepare for you. Then I will explain what this is all about."

The king studied her face and a slight smile played around his mouth. "I am intrigued. As you wish, my queen. Tomorrow then."

Haman was almost beside himself with glee—a second invitation from the queen! He bowed low, his eyes glittering. "Tomorrow, your majesty."

She smiled at him. No doubt he was heading to his home to brag about this recent honor. With a wife and ten sons, he had many to hear his boasting.

When they had gone, Esther breathed a sigh of relief. It was going well so far, but with much prayer and Adonai's blessing, tomorrow would bring her plans to fruition.

45

After Esther's last message to him, Mordecai had gone to the synagogue at once, quietly sending out word for all of the Jews to meet him there. When he reached the synagogue, he waited until the room was full. Many still wore sackcloth and showed signs of weeping, with ashes on their heads. Out of respect for Mordecai, they had dutifully come to see why he had called them together.

He looked out at the faces of his people and lifted his voice. "My friends, I have news that there is hope for us. I have kept my silence in obedience to Adonai, who knows our way when we do not and has put in place our possible deliverance in a way we cannot imagine. I could not tell you before, partly to ensure her safety in the palace, but the time has come when I am permitted to reveal this to you."

Puzzled murmurings went through the crowd. "What is it you are now allowed to tell us?" one man called out.

"When the young maidens of Susa were captured and taken to the palace, as you know, my Hadassah was among them. The Most

High told me not to have her reveal her identity as a Jew and said she was to take the name of Esther instead for her safety."

There were gasps and excited whispers then. The rabbi, who was standing beside Mordecai, turned to him. "Esther is the name of our queen," he said pointedly.

"Yes, that is the name of our queen. My Hadassah is Queen Esther."

The people looked at him with astonished faces and the room grew noisier still, the chatter reaching a crescendo. *Hadassah was queen of Persia?*

Amos stepped forward and cleared his throat. Conversations stilled. "This is overwhelming news, Mordecai, but how can she help us? She too is a Jew and will perish with us." Others began murmuring again.

Mordecai nodded and put up a hand for silence. "As you know, the law says no one can enter the inner court of the king without being invited. It means instant death. Esther has asked every Jew in Susa to fast and pray for her. No food or drink for three days. She and her maids will fast also. At the end of three days, she will take her life in her hands and go before the king. If he does not extend the golden scepter to her, his immortals will kill her."

Another gasp from the crowd and Mordecai spoke up again. "As I told Esther, perhaps it was the plan of our God to place her in the position of queen for such a time as this. Did our God not know this was coming?"

All around him, people nodded their heads and their countenances were lifted by a ray of hope for their families.

The rabbi looked over his congregation. "I and my family will do as Mordecai and the queen have asked. We will fast for three days and pray for our deliverance. Who will join me?"

Every person agreed and hurried home to tell their families what they must do. As Mordecai left to go to his own home to pray, Shamir approached him.

"It is hard to believe that Hadassah is queen of Persia. As you said, perhaps it was for such a time as this." He put a hand on Mordecai's shoulder and then turned away. For a moment, Mordecai watched the young man walk away, his shoulders slumped. Shamir could have been Hadassah's husband, the father of her children. He shrugged. Who can fathom the mind of God?

The next morning, Mordecai sensed unrest in his spirit. Trusting in Adonai, he started toward the palace gate. A crowd gathered in front of Haman's imposing house, which stopped him on his way. In the courtyard, a spiked pole had been erected, nearly seventy-five feet high. *Someone was going to die, but who?* Suddenly, he had a cold knot in the pit of his stomach. Glancing back at the pole, he hurried on to the king's gate.

Some of the elders joined him and they talked quietly. Every Jew in Susa had been notified of the need for fasting and prayer and they had complied with Mordecai's request. It was the only hope they had.

Amos shook his head. "And to think it has been Hadassah all these years. It must have been difficult, my friend, to keep silent, knowing who she was."

Mordecai stroked his beard, looking toward the palace. "I have been on the verge of blurting it out several times. I have missed her so! We have only been able to communicate by message." He looked toward the direction Hathach usually came, but no one appeared. He did not know if Esther was successful in her appeal to the king. The silence was almost unbearable.

As they were speaking, he glanced up and saw Haman coming toward him. A servant was carrying some garments and Haman was leading the king's white horse, with the royal emblem hanging on the horse's forehead. Mordecai stood apprehensively, waiting for Haman to speak.

The man's eyes flashed with hatred, but the words that came out of his mouth nearly caused Mordecai to take a step backward. *Was he hearing the Amalekite correctly?*

With clenched teeth, Haman recited in a monotone: "The king regrets that he did not acknowledge your service to him in the matter of the king's guards. He wishes to honor you. You are to put on the king's robe that he himself has worn and mount his horse. I am to lead you through the streets to proclaim that this is what is done for the man the king chooses to honor."

The king wanted to honor him? Too astonished to speak, Mordecai obediently put on the king's robe and mounted the king's horse. The synagogue elders stood without speaking, trying to comprehend what they were witnessing. No one uttered a word as Haman began to lead the horse toward the city. They passed through the streets as Haman loudly proclaimed, "This is what the king does for someone he wishes to honor!"

Mordecai watched as Susa's citizens gave Haman astonished looks or smirks. Some put their hands over their mouths to muffle their laughter. Unsure of what this strange procession meant, no one bowed to Haman. They knew who he was—and hated him. Some also knew that Mordecai was a Jew who worked in the king's treasury. Even his fellow Jews watched him, their eyes wide as he and Haman passed them.

When Haman had done his duty to the king, he led the horse back to the king's gate as fast as he could walk. Throwing the reins to the waiting servant, he glared at Mordecai and stalked off. Everyone had seen his humiliation.

Mordecai gave the king's robe back to the servant and another servant led the horse away. When they had gone, Mordecai sank down on a stone bench outside the gate. Amos and the other elders went to him quickly, having gone into the city to witness the spectacle.

"I've never seen anything like it," one murmured. "What did you do for the king to honor you in that way—and by Haman, of all people?"

Mordecai was still overwhelmed by what had just happened. *What could it mean?* He stroked his beard thoughtfully. "Perhaps our God has a sense of humor," was all he could say.

46

*W*hen word got back to Esther about what Haman had done for Mordecai, she too was astonished. She quickly called for Hegai.

"Hegai, I've just learned what Haman did for Mordecai the Jew. Please tell me how this came about. Why would Haman do such a thing?"

The eunuch chuckled. "It is ironic, is it not? Majesty, the king could not sleep last night and called for one of the scribes to read from the history of his reign, perhaps thinking it would lull him to sleep. The passage the scribe happened to read was related to the occasion when Mordecai discovered the plot by the king's personal guards who stood at the door to his chambers. They were going to poison him, as you recall."

"Yes, I remember. He overheard them in the marketplace and sent me a message. In turn, I informed the king."

"And saved the king's life. The king wanted to know how Mordecai had been honored for this. When the scribe told him nothing had been done, the king immediately asked who of his officials were in the outer court waiting to see him and was told Haman was there." Hegai shook his head. "The king asked him what he would suggest to do for a man the king chooses to honor. The horse and robe and declaration was Haman's idea."

"But Haman hates Mordecai." Esther was bewildered.

"True, majesty, but I believe Haman was possibly thinking the king wanted to honor him. He expected to be the rider on the horse."

"So he outlined all these honors, thinking the king was going to do that for him?"

"I believe so. It must have been a shock, but Haman was duty bound to honor the king's command."

Knowing they shared a mutual dislike of Haman, Esther found herself suppressing a smile.

From Hegai's expression, he too was holding in his mirth. "I must return to my duties, majesty."

When he had gone, Esther shook her head in wonder. *How strange that the king chose now to honor her cousin for a deed done so long ago.* It was beyond her understanding. She could only marvel at the ways of Adonai. *What was the reason for this strange occurrence?* Then she considered the banquet she was planning for that evening and felt peace settle over her spirit. She felt Adonai approved of her plan.

After they enjoyed another fine meal and Xerxes had patiently waited to hear Esther's request, she poured choice wine for him and Haman, sat back, and gave her husband a radiant smile. The time had come.

He sat back. "Tell me what you want, Queen Esther. What is your request? I will give it to you, even if it is half the kingdom."

She took a quick breath and knelt before him. "If I have found favor with the king and if it pleases the king to grant my request, I ask that my life and the lives of my people be spared. For my people and I have been sold to those who would kill, slaughter, and annihilate us. If we had merely been sold as slaves, I could remain quiet, for that would be too trivial a matter to warrant disturbing you, oh my king." She sat up.

Anger flashed from the king's eyes. "Who would do such a thing?" he demanded. "Who would be so presumptuous as to touch you?"

Esther turned and pointed to their guest. "This wicked Haman is our adversary and our enemy."

Haman grew pale with fright before them. "You are a Jew?"

The king looked at Haman and then at Esther. He jumped to his feet in a rage, stalking out to the palace garden.

Esther knew Xerxes could not punish Haman for a decree that he himself had signed. *What would he do? Was he angry she had hidden her lineage?"*

Haman remained where he was, quaking, to plead with Esther for his life. She knew the king intended to kill him. "Forgive me, majesty, I did not know. Tell the king I did not know." In despair, he fell on the couch where Esther was reclining, just as the king returned from the palace garden.

The king jerked him up from the floor. "Would you even assault my queen right here in the palace, before my very eyes?!" He turned toward the entrance and bellowed, "Guards! Take him away." And Xerxes reached out and pulled his signet ring off of Haman's finger.

His attendants came quickly and covered Haman's face with a cloth bag, signaling his doom. Haman, for all his bravado, was whimpering like a child.

Harbona, one of the king's eunuchs, who had entered with the guards, spoke up. "Haman has set up a sharpened pole that stands seventy-five feet tall in his own courtyard. He intended to use it to impale Mordecai, the man who saved the king from assassination."

"Then impale Haman on it!" Xerxes roared.

For a brief moment, as Haman's cries died away, Esther felt sorry for him. As Atossa had told her years ago, a man who is too ambitious many times seals his own doom.

Xerxes turned to Esther, his brows furrowed. "Why did you not tell me you were Jewish? Haman did not state it was the Jews causing trouble in the kingdom, only a small group of people."

"It is true, my lord. Our numbers are small in Persia."

He gazed thoughtfully into her eyes. "You said you came from the lineage of a king."

"I did indeed, my lord. I am from the tribe of Benjamin and descended from Saul, the first king of Israel. My name is Esther, but my birth name was Hadassah."

"Hadassah." He said her name slowly and a slow smile spread across his face. "Hadassah. It suits you." He pulled her into his arms. "I have neglected you for…"

"I know, my lord, but I am grateful you chose to act on my behalf. I must also tell you one more thing. Mordecai—the man who saved your life and has been a faithful servant to you and your father before you—he is my cousin. He was like a father to me, raising me from childhood after my parents died."

The king shook his head. "Will you never cease to surprise me, my queen?" He turned to Harbona. "Bring in Mordecai the Jew who sits at the gate. At once."

⌒

Almost the entire city gathered outside Haman's home when word spread that Haman had been arrested by the king and was to die. The soldiers dragged Haman in his own gate and as the astonished crowd watched, he was impaled, howling on the very pole he had erected for Mordecai. The people were quiet as they watched their enemy struggle and finally hang limp in death.

Mordecai was among them. Haman has been dealt with, he thought, but what about the decree against the Jewish people? As he was still wondering, the soldiers came for him in the crowd and told him he was to see the king and queen at once.

"You must change your clothes. You may not go in to the king and queen in mourning."

Mordecai nodded and with the soldiers following behind him, he hurried home to change. *What had Esther accomplished?* He would soon know.

Dressed in appropriate clothing, he followed the soldiers and hurried into the palace.

When Mordecai entered the hall, he bowed low to the king and queen.

"Rise up." Esther went over, took him by the hand, and led him to Xerxes. "My lord, may I present Mordecai? This man raised me like a daughter when my parents died."

Xerxes studied Mordecai and finally nodded his head. "A man to be trusted." The king took his signet ring and placed it on Mordecai's finger. "I am pleased to make you my prime minister in the place of Haman and I am giving Esther—that is, Hadassah…" He gave Esther a half smile, "…the estate and property of Haman."

Esther turned to her cousin. "In turn, Abba, I appoint you to be the caretaker of that property."

Mordecai bowed low before the king. "May I be worthy of the great honor you have bestowed on me this day, majesty. I am your humble servant."

The king put a hand on Mordecai's shoulder. "I believe you will serve me well." Then he sighed. "There are matters I must return to. You may leave us and join my advisors in the morning."

When Mordecai had gone, Xerxes turned to Esther and his eyes were warm. "I welcome the opportunity to hear more of your secrets, my queen. Come."

As she walked with her husband toward his quarters, Esther felt relief and joy. She was still in his favor and while they had this night, there was one more request she must make of him.

Before he left, Esther glanced at Mordecai, who gave a slight nod. There was still the decree to deal with.

47

The next day, with Mordecai standing in the outer court, waiting, Esther once again entered the inner court, went to her knees before her husband and touched the golden scepter he held out to her. As her eyes watered with tears, she knew she somehow had to get the king to stop the evil plot devised by Haman.

Xerxes lifted her to her feet. "My queen, I have had Haman impaled on a pole for his crimes and have given his property to you to dispose of as you wish. And yet you weep. What is there that you still wish me to do for you?"

"If it please the king and if I have found favor with him and if he thinks it is right, let there be a decree that reverses the orders of Haman, son of Hammedatha the Agagite, who ordered the deaths of the Jews throughout the king's provinces. For how can I endure seeing my people and my family slaughtered?"

Xerxes gave a deep sigh. "Esther, the law of the Medes and Persians cannot be changed. But I give you permission to send any message that pleases you with the authority of my signet ring.

Remember that whatever has been decreed and sealed with my ring cannot be revoked."

Mordecai was then allowed to enter the inner court and told of the king's decision. Afterward, Mordecai called for the king's secretaries and dictated a new decree for them to write. The decree was sent to all of the Jewish communities in Persia as well as all of the highest officers, governors, and the nobles of all 127 provinces stretching from India to Ethiopia. In the scripts and languages of all of the empire's peoples, the decree was written in the name of King Xerxes and sealed with his signet ring. Mordecai sent the dispatches by dedicated messengers, who rode the fastest horses especially bred for the king's service.

The new decree gave the Jews in every city the authority to unite to defend themselves and their families any way they wished. They were allowed to slaughter their enemies and take their property. This was to go into effect the same day as the earlier decree of Haman.

Mordecai had left the king's presence wearing the royal robe of blue and white, a crown of gold, and a purple outer cloak of fine linen. The people of the city celebrated the new decree. The Jews were filled with gladness and joy and honored everywhere in the kingdom. A public celebration was also held. Mordecai was amazed that many people in Persia hastened to affiliate themselves with the Jews, fearing what might be in store for them otherwise.

When the fateful day arrived, the Jews took a stand against their enemies who had hoped to kill them and emerged victorious in every province. The nobles, the highest officers, the governors, and the royal officials who feared Mordecai's power as prime minister helped the Jewish communities in their battles. In the fortress of Susa, five hundred men were killed, including the ten sons of Haman. In her despair at the loss of her husband and her sons, Haman's wife took poison and killed herself.

Xerxes, listening to the reports from all over his kingdom, turned to Esther and frowned. "The Jews have taken no plunder. Why is this? They have vanquished their enemies."

"They did not fight for plunder, my lord. They only wished to protect and save their families."

He shook his head in disbelief. "The Jews have killed five hundred men in the city of Susa, along with Haman's ten sons. If they have done that here, what has happened in the rest of my provinces? Is there anything more you wish, Esther? Tell me and I will do it."

Was she asking too much? She faced him. "If it please the king, give the Jews in Susa permission to defend themselves one more day. The ten sons of Haman have been killed and the threat of his dynasty is ended, but others with ill will may still traverse your empire."

"It shall be done as you wish, my love." The order was given and three hundred more men were killed. Again, the Jews took no plunder.

On the third day, the slaughter was over. The Jews made it a day of feasting and celebration. Mordecai sent letters to all of the Jews in the 127 provinces, declaring an annual holiday. They were to rejoice, send portions of food to each other, and give gifts to the poor in memory of the defeat of their enemies. Haman had plotted to destroy them and had thrown *pur*—that is, cast lots—as he tried to crush and destroy them. Thus, the Festival of Purim was established and Esther put the full weight of her authority as queen behind the letter. The Jewish people decided that the Festival of Purim would never cease to be celebrated, nor would the memory of what happened ever die out among their descendants. Esther had other letters calling for peace and security sent to the Jews throughout the 127 provinces of Xerxes' empire.

Mordecai found favor with the rest of the king's advisors and under his leadership, there was peace in the kingdom and the Jews had respite from their enemies. The people of Susa, especially his own people, revered Mordecai.

The king's advisors, observing what had happened to Haman, were more than ready to work with Mordecai. Feeling he had the hand of his God upon him, they listened to his sage advice.

Only one seemed to not be pleased with the turn of events. Artabanus's expression of distaste when he encountered Mordecai concerned Esther. She didn't know the reason for his attitude, so she remained gracious to Artabanus when she encountered him in the palace. Yet there was something about him that gave her a sense of discomfort. She could not go to Xerxes just because she had a certain feeling. The palace had always been full of intrigue. She had learned to watch and listen as she moved about. Adonai would reveal the source of her unease in His time.

After Haman's death, the woman he had brought to the palace quickly left. Esther never did find out why he gave the woman to Xerxes in the first place. *As a gift—or as a spy?* Xerxes did not speak of her and Esther found herself once again in the king's good graces. She had risen in stature in his eyes for her boldness and the strength she showed in handling the crises with Haman. She sensed her husband rued his trust of the Amalekite and the fact that he had not seen Haman for what he was. He did not speak of Haman and she knew it was a subject best left closed.

One pleasurable evening, after they had dined together, she brought up a subject dear to her heart. "My lord, I pray that you are pleased with Mordecai. My people revere him for his wisdom. I know he will serve you well."

He gave her a brief smile. "For once, perhaps, I have made a wise decision."

Esther had to laugh. It was the closest Xerxes would come to admitting he had ever made a mistake. "Ah, my husband, your decisions are usually wise. No one else could manage this vast kingdom of yours so well."

He seemed pleased to hear those words of praise from her lips. They watched the sun go down, filling the sky with the vibrant colors of orange, gold, and rose. He slipped an arm around her waist. "Perhaps there is another wise decision I have made."

She turned in his arms. "And what is that, my lord?'

"To make you my queen." He reached for a small box on the table and handed it to her. When she opened it, a beautiful ruby pendant sparkled against the silk.

She gasped. "It is beautiful. Thank you, my lord."

"It is to celebrate the fifth anniversary of our marriage. I am indeed fortunate."

She had known it was their anniversary, but had not mentioned it, not wishing him to feel obligated to arrange any celebration.

"When we return from our hunting trip, I have arranged a banquet to commemorate the occasion with Darius, Artaxerxes, and the nobles of the city."

She went into his arms and laid her head against his chest. This complex man she had married never ceased to amaze her.

48

The next morning as she went to her quarters, followed by Hathach, to prepare for a hunting trip with Xerxes—the first one he was taking her on in many months—they suddenly came upon Artabanus in the corridor. The commander was deep in conversation with Aspamitras. Powerful among the eunuchs, perhaps because he was in charge of the king's finances, Aspamitras stayed in the background most of the time. In fact, Esther had never had occasion to speak with him.

The two seemed startled to see Esther so early in the morning, coming from the king's quarters. They stopped speaking, bowing in respect as she passed. She glanced at Hathach, but his face was expressionless. He looked the other way. Puzzled, and realizing she had interrupted their conversation, she only acknowledged them by inclining her head and continued to her quarters. She wondered if she should ask Xerxes to tell her about Aspamitras's role in the kingdom. When they had arrived at her quarters, she turned to Hathach.

"Do you know why Aspamitras is here?"

He looked behind them into the corridor, as if to make sure no one else was near.

He hesitated. "It is not unusual, my lady. He travels between Persepolis, Susa, and Babylon, in the course of his duties."

"Thank you, Hathach. Perhaps the king has sent for him for some reason."

"Perhaps, my lady." He seemed reluctant to say more. He bowed and left her, rather quickly. Esther watched him for a moment and then shrugged. There had been too much intrigue in the palace in past years. She might be reading something into what could be nothing at all.

When she was dressed for the hunting trip, she joined her husband in the front of the palace and mounted her horse. Her bow and quiver of arrows hung from the back of Farah's saddle. Darius and Artaxerxes were already mounted, along with the crown prince's bride, Artaynte, the daughter of the king's brother, Masistes. Darius and Artaynte were still on their *mah-e-asal* after an elaborate wedding ceremony in Persepolis, where she still had family. Artaynte seemed quiet and shy; she giggled each time Darius offered her a sip of mead from his wineskin.

Artabanus stood beside the hunting party, an inscrutable look on his face. Esther shook off puzzling thoughts and they waited for his signal to move out.

She shot a deer and several pheasants. She applauded along with the king when Darius and Artaxerxes were also successful with their shots. Artaynte did not hunt, not being proficient yet with bow and arrow. Esther made a point to talk with her, but the princess did not say much.

Later, at their campsite, the royal party watched a hand-to-hand combat exhibition between some of the soldiers. Xerxes and his sons cheered the soldiers on. When one emerged victorious, he bowed to the king, scarcely able to hide his pleasure.

Esther marveled at the skill of the king's immortals. She had often wondered why they were called that. *Many of them had not proved to be immortal during the battle with Greece.*

Xerxes had been most attentive since Haman's death and Mordecai's elevation as his prime minister. Esther rejoiced in his love and favor. He seemed to derive particular joy from hunting. Although the meat was always a welcome addition for their table that the king often shared with the palace servants, he seemed to most enjoy being out in the countryside. He laughed more when they were away from the palace, seeming relaxed and at ease.

The king's son-in-law Megabyzus, husband of Xerxes' daughter Anytis, had paid the king a rare surprise visit. While he enthusiastically took part in the hunt, Esther noticed that Megabyzus seemed agitated. She found him watching her from time to time. Sometimes, she felt a shadow of apprehension move over her heart. But she brushed it off as foolish fears. She had been married to Xerxes for almost six years and now, in the thirteenth year of his reign, all was fairly peaceful in the empire and their marriage was never better. She had learned how to be a queen, oversaw an estate and rich farm lands, was on good terms with Darius and Artaxerxes, and was beloved by her husband.

Darius now stood behind Xerxes during matters of state, signaling the crown prince's eventual authority. At the king's insistence, Esther sat on the throne beside him while he attended to some of the business of the kingdom. Knowing that Mordecai was near, praying for her, and in the king's good graces gave her much comfort.

Mordecai had proved to be an excellent prime minister. He did not wish to be known by the Persian term *grand vizer* and Xerxes had acceded to his request. The king had come to depend on Mordecai and trusted his advice. Mordecai's reputation spread throughout the kingdom and the Jewish people revered him.

Esther rejoiced that she was able to speak with her Abba every day after years of only sending messages back and forth through Hathach. It was a blessing to hear his wisdom. She marveled that Mordecai had also won over the other advisors. Observing the matter with Haman, they had come to the conclusion that he was blessed by the gods and listened to his counsel.

⁓

One day, while Esther and Mordecai were talking, she brought up an issue she had with Haman's property. Her cousin oversaw the estate for her and she had to confide her innermost thoughts to him concerning it.

"I do not wish to keep the property, Abba. I could not walk the halls that once belonged to a man as evil as Haman. There has been too much bloodshed there. His ten sons killed, Haman impaled on that pole, his wife poisoning herself. What should I do? The king says it is up to me to do with it as I choose."

Mordecai stroked his beard and considered her words. "I understand fully what you are saying. If it is pleasing to the king, let the property be sold and the proceeds put in your account in the treasury."

It was so ordered and to Esther's relief, a wealthy merchant from one of the provinces purchased the estate. He had no connection to its history and seemed pleased to be able to expand his business in Susa.

Now, as she walked in the king's garden with Xerxes in the evening, she carefully brought up another subject that had been in her thoughts.

"My lord, it is so peaceful here. I pray it refreshes you, as it does me. The palace seems quiet but...I must be forthright with you, beloved husband. I have been wondering about Aspamitras."

He turned to her with a puzzled look. "Aspamitras? What about him troubles you?"

"Does he come to Susa often? I've hardly seen him while I've been here and yet…"

A change came over his face. "When did you see him?"

"Just recently, on the day of our hunt."

Xerxes frowned. "He is usually in Persepolis this time of year." He was quiet, then murmured, almost to himself, "Megabyzus and now Aspamitras." Then he turned to her with a familiar gesture. Tipping her chin up with his finger, he kissed her lightly. "I had other plans for us this evening, beloved, but there is something I must take care of. I will see you tomorrow."

She was disappointed, but he was a man of many moods. She touched his cheek. "Tomorrow then, my lord."

As she walked back to her quarters, Hathach at her heels, she glanced back and saw Xerxes striding quickly toward his court. His bodyguards, ever nearby in the shadows, fell into step behind him as he disappeared into the palace.

49

*E*sther felt restless and could not sleep. She didn't know the source of her disquiet. Her maids slept soundly, so she got up quietly, went to the window overlooking the garden, and sought her God.

Adonai is my light and salvation; whom do I need to fear? Adonai is the stronghold of my life; of whom should I be afraid? If an army encamps against me, my heart will not fear; if war breaks out against me, even then I will keep trusting....

She had been praying for only a short time, when she heard shouting from somewhere within the palace. Then someone pounded on her door. Nadia rose quickly and opened the door to admit several of the king's immortal soldiers.

Fear coursed through Esther's body. She faced them and waited for one to speak.

"Majesty, forgive us for this disturbance. The king charged us that if anything ever happened to him, we were to protect you at all costs."

Her fear became almost a tangible thing. Her hand went to her chest, her heart beating rapidly. "Has something happened to the king?" If he was ill, she wanted to go to him.

A solder put a hand up. "Majesty, I am the bearer of terrible news. I regret to tell you that our king was murdered in his bed this night."

Shock and horror caused her to take a step backwards. Her cry was almost a wail. "Who has done this terrible act?"

"Artabanus is searching the palace and questioning everyone who might have been near the king."

Just then, Mordecai strode into the room. "I just heard and came right away. The captain of the king's bodyguard is questioning everyone."

Her husband, the king, was dead! Her heart racing, her mind awhirl, Esther felt herself blacking out. Mordecai reached her just in time and lifted her, placing her on her bed. Her maids covered her and gathering around the bed, they began to weep.

Mordecai turned to the guards. "Let no one near her. I must speak with Darius. It seems he is now king."

⌒

Mordecai found the crown prince in the throne room with the king's advisors. He bowed low. "Majesty, I grieve with you at the loss of your father."

Darius seemed to be in shock. He acknowledged Mordecai and then asked, "How is the queen?"

"Her maids are looking after her and some of your father's immortals are guarding her. She has had a severe shock, as have you."

"I spoke to him only yesterday. It is hard to believe he is dead. Artabanus vows he will find the assassin soon."

⌒

Artabanus came to the council chambers a few days later and accused Darius of killing his father. Darius looked at him with amazement.

"You think I killed my father? You are wrong, Artabanus. I would do no such thing!"

But Aspamitras, the king's eunuch chamberlain, stepped forward. "I saw him go into his father's chamber the night he was murdered."

"You are lying, Aspamitras! Both of you are lying! This stinks of a plot—perhaps your doing!" Darius's face was red with anger.

But despite his cries of innocence, the king's guards stepped forward. At a nod from Artabanus, they drew their swords and killed Darius.

When Esther heard the news from Hegai, she began to weep uncontrollably. *How could Darius do such a thing? When Darius was with her and Xerxes, he never gave any sign that he was unhappy with his father—quite the opposite. And to murder Xerxes? That didn't sound like Darius at all.* She pictured the tall, young prince and thought of his new wife, Artaynte. It was as if one of her worst dreams was coming true.

Esther gathered her courage and drew herself up. "Where is Artaxerxes?"

"He has been named king with Artabanus as regent, majesty."

It was almost too much to comprehend: her husband dead, the crown prince killed, and the younger brother suddenly king. Suddenly the door opened and Mordecai rushed to her side, along with more of the king's immortals.

"Abba!" She clung to him. "What shall I do?"

"Hegai came for me only a short time ago. I'm here, my Hadassah."

Soldiers were stationed both within her chambers and outside her door. It gave her some relief that they had pledged to the king that they would protect her even to the death. They were keeping their word. Her maids wept along with her and tried to alleviate her anguish. As the rays of the dawn began to pour light in the window, there was a small commotion outside her door and it opened again to admit Artaxerxes, now a very young king of the Persian Empire. He stood a moment, as if to gather his emotions, and then spoke to the guard.

"Leave us, but remain outside."

The guards obeyed and when he nodded to Mordecai and her maids to leave also, Esther was apprehensive. *What did he have in mind?*

Mordecai had to obey and left reluctantly. "I will be nearby."

Her maids, with a fearful look back at their mistress, left also. When they had all gone, Esther waited, seeing the turmoil in Artaxerxes' face. He came closer and she could see he was having difficulty holding in his emotions. And then she knew. He had come to her for comfort.

"I know you loved my father, too," he managed to say, his voice cracking.

She reached out her arms and embraced the young man, now with the weight of a huge empire on his shoulders. He sobbed in her arms, quietly, so the guards could not hear. They would consider such a display of emotion a sign of weakness.

When Artaxerxes had regained his composure, he stood back. "I did not want to be king."

"Do you believe Darius killed your father?" She had to ask.

He frowned. "It is not like Darius. He gave no indication he was thinking of such a thing. He talked about the hunting trip we had and how much he looked forward to another one. He even mentioned that perhaps our father might be willing to teach Artaynte how to use the bow, since he was so successful teaching you."

She looked into his face, pinched with sorrow. Artaxerxes had come to her privately. He must believe that he could trust her—and she knew she had to do all she could to protect him.

"Did Artabanus tell you that Darius killed your father?"

Artaxerxes nodded. "He said the king's chamberlain saw Darius enter my father's chambers the night he was killed. My brother denied it, but Artabanus ordered the king's guards to kill him." A mix of anger and agony seemed to fill him and his eyes watered again even as he pounded a fist into one palm. "I did not have a chance to talk with Darius or decide for myself if he was guilty! I am not of age and Artabanus has the authority. He has been head of my father's bodyguard for many years and my father trusted him implicitly. I had to believe him. It was too late to confront Darius." He paused, his eyes were filled with pain.

Esther drew in a deep breath and could feel the color draining from her face. *With Xerxes assassinated and the crown prince accused and slain for the murder, how safe was Artaxerxes?* She knew she was on tremulous ground, but had to proceed. "Majesty, I saw Artabanus speaking with the eunuch, Aspamitres, in the corridor, several days ago. I assumed they were discussing matters in the palace."

"The two of them were talking? When?"

She hesitated. "It was early morning on the day of our last hunt, when I left your father and was on my way back to my quarters." She put out a hand. "Majesty, speak with Mordecai. He is my adopted father and a man who can be trusted. Your father made him prime minister because of that. He is wise and can help you."

The young king nodded. Pulling himself together, he opened the door to admit Mordecai—and standing there, in the midst of the immortals, was Artabanus.

"Majesty, is the queen all right?" Artabanus seemed almost too solicitous.

"I wished to speak to the queen privately about Darius, since she has already been through so much." He leveled his gaze on the older man. "And I now wish to speak with my prime minister... alone."

Artabanus bowed. "As you wish, majesty, but as your regent, I should remain." His eyes glittered with animosity.

Drawing himself to full height, Artaxerxes waved his hand dismissively. "That won't be necessary."

50

*S*urrounded by ten of the king's immortals, Mordecai and Artaxerxes went to the young king's private chambers. Artaxerxes had the soldiers wait outside. He looked around, making sure no one was hiding in his quarters or anywhere nearby who might overhear their conversation. Then he closed the door.

Mordecai spoke up. "How can I be of service to you, majesty?"

"Queen Esther said you would have wise words for me and I have no one else to turn to. I must know what to do—and who to trust."

"May I have your permission to speak freely, majesty?"

"Please do."

Mordecai gathered his thoughts about what he had seen and the little bits of conversation he had overheard during the last several weeks. He had seen Artabanus and Aspamitras talking together many times, but had not considered it of any importance. The commander of the royal bodyguard—now regent!—and the king's chamberlain must surely need to speak of matters pertaining to the kingdom from time to time. However, something did not add up in his mind. Then it suddenly occurred to him: Artabanus had quietly installed his seven sons in key positions in the kingdom. *What did it mean?*

"Majesty…" Mordecai hesitated. "Forgive me, majesty, but I'm not sure how much your father schooled you on the affairs of the kingdom, nor whether he himself knew every detail or every promotion. I am just wondering whether your father was aware that Artabanus had placed his seven sons in important positions."

Artaxerxes studied him intently. "What are you saying?"

Mordecai took a breath and finally plunged on. "I do not believe Prince Darius killed your father."

"Are you saying…Artabanus? Why would he tell me…?"

"Your father is dead and the crown prince is dead. That makes you king. Due to your age, Artabanus rules as regent. He is an ambitious man and I have watched him a great deal. I believe he wishes to take the throne, one way or another. Your own life may be in danger."

Mordecai waited, hoping he had not sealed his own death warrant by accusing the commander of the king's bodyguards. If what he suspected was true, Artabanus had killed Xerxes and then killed Darius to cover his horrific deed.

Artaxerxes' eyes were wide with shock. "You are accusing the commander of assassinating both my father and my brother? How can that be? My father trusted him!"

Mordecai nodded. "I have spent my life observing people. The information I have gathered has been most disturbing. I would suggest that you not be alone with Artabanus, majesty."

The young king shook his head. "Who can I trust?! I must trust you, as my father trusted you."

Mordecai bowed his head. "I saved his life once and I will do everything in my power to protect yours."

Artaxerxes pounded a fist into his palm. "I must confront Artabanus!"

"Forgive me, majesty, but that might be unwise. Gather your own forces and when you are ready, confront him openly. Many of the king's guards may be loyal to him and wish to see him crowned, especially if he has promised them positions of power. If you confront Artabanus now, you may find their blades trained on you. Rest assured, we will out the traitors in our midst. Nothing remains a secret for long in this palace. Sooner or later, the servants know—and I will find out who is on his side. In the meantime, we must perform our expected roles. There needs to be a coronation ceremony, where you are officially crowned king, with Artabanus as your regent and myself as your prime minister."

Artaxerxes let his breath out slowly. "I believe I know why my father trusted you, Mordecai." He searched the older man's face. "I must know the truth, one way or another. I will take your advice. You will remain prime minister and when you have all of the information we need, I will confront Artabanus."

"Have confidence in yourself, majesty. I have also watched you. I believe you will make a good king. You are compassionate, but have strength."

Mordecai opened the doors and with a nod to Artabanus, who seemed to be impatient to be left standing outside and not privy to their conversation, went to consult with the king's other advisors. He looked back at the immortals surrounding the king. By now, he knew most of the soldiers in the palace and seeing their grim faces, he was assured that none of them would touch the young king while they had breath.

⌒

Too soon, the ceremony Esther dreaded took place as the bodies of Xerxes and Darius were taken to the Tower of Silence in Susa. Unmoved by the protests of Artabanus that Darius was a murderer, Artaxerxes insisted that his brother's body be treated as befit his royal birthright.

Wearing the Persian veil of mourning, Esther stood next to Artaxerxes and Mordecai as the Zoroastrian priests prayed over the bodies. While they prayed to their god, she silently prayed to the one true God for strength to get through these next few days. She knew Mordecai did the same.

Oh, Adonai, full of mercy and compassion, who dwells in the heights, provide a sure rest upon Your wings, within the range of the holy, pure and glorious, to Xerxes and Darius....

When the bodies had been carried into the tower and placed in two crevasses at the top, she continued to stand resolutely, knowing what would happen when they were unwrapped and left there to the birds and the elements. Just as in Persepolis for Atossa, the birds were already circling. She resisted the urge to spill the contents of her stomach. She thought of the times she had lain in Xerxes' arms...when he had made love to her...when they had stood together watching the sunset, or talked over a meal. She thought of the hunting trips and almost anything she could think of besides the fate of her husband and his son.

Susa was in mourning and the sorrow hung like a heavy curtain over the city.

Thousands gathered to pay their respects and silently watch as the bier was carried into the tower. Many then burst out weeping and wailing. They threw dust into the air so that it fell on their heads in much the same manner that her people covered themselves with ashes when mourning. Esther, too, wanted to cry out and moan aloud, but as a queen, she had to maintain her dignity, not only for her own sake, but also for the sake of the young king who stood beside her. Mordecai stood stoically on her other side, lending his strength. He also was appalled at the ceremony, but having lived in Susa all of his life, he was familiar with the Persian burial customs.

When at last it was over, the royal party slowly made their way back to the palace. Mordecai had told her Artaxerxes would not take any action against Artabanus after the coronation ceremony and the ossuaries were placed in the tomb.

Esther finally reached her room and collapsed on her bed, her maids surrounding her as she wept. After removing her veil and slippers, they pulled soft coverings over her. Then they left her alone to cry and mourn until she fell into an exhausted sleep.

The evening shadows were gathering when Esther finally awoke. Ever cautious, Hathach had personally watched as servants prepared a meal for the queen and her maids and carried it himself to her chambers. Her maids bathed her and dressed her in fresh clothes. Their eyes were red from weeping for her, but they tended to her gently and lovingly. They had become close, almost like sisters, and although they kept their place, she felt surrounded by loving friends.

A few days later, the bones of Xerxes and Darius were finally recovered and placed in ossuaries. Esther had become ill and so Artaxerxes, with a contingent of his most trusted immortals, Artabanus, and other court officials, made the long trip to Persepolis to place the ossuaries in a tomb to the east of that of Xerxes' grandfather, Cyrus.

For days, Esther lay in her bed, a fever raging through her body. The physician came to see her several times and prescribed herbs to bring down the fever. Mordecai had been given charge of the palace while the king and Artabanus were away. Many times, he came and prayed over Esther. She heard his words vaguely, but could not respond. He told her that their people all over Susa were praying and beseeching Adonai for her recovery. She had saved them and they revered her.

On the sixth day, Esther opened her eyes and looked around. "How long have I lain here?"

At the sound of her voice, Mordecai jumped up from his chair and went to her bedside. Her maidens had also been praying to the Jewish God and rejoiced to see their mistress come out of the fevered dreams that had made her thrash about and cry out in fear.

"Hadassah, you have been grieving, but you will be well." He felt her forehead, then motioned to the maidens. "She needs a little something to eat—some bread and cool water would be good." Parisa hurried to the door to tell Hathach.

Mordecai leaned down and kissed Esther's cheek. "Now I can tend to my duties in peace." He left the room.

Esther gradually regained her strength. She sat in the garden in the warm sun, tended to by her maidens, who brought her food and drink. She missed Xerxes so much, it was like a part of her had been cut away. For long hours, she thought about her situation and wondered what her next step would be. *Without Xerxes to cherish and protect her, what would become of her? Would Vashti now return to the palace—and if so, what might she do? Atossa had called Vashti vain and foolish yet also courageous. Would she resent Esther still, after all these years?* Esther knew her future was precarious. She must wait for the return of Artaxerxes, for he had the power to grant her the petition she sought...

51

Artaxerxes returned three weeks later and, learning that Esther was no longer ill, he graciously called on her instead of summoning her to him. She did not fear his coming, for she had supported him when he took the throne under such difficult circumstances. She suspected Artaxerxes wanted to take control of the kingdom and wrest power from Artabanus. As she faced the young king, she saw determination in his face and a burden lifted from her heart.

He sat down next to her in the garden and smiled. "I am glad to see you are feeling better." He paused, contemplating his words. "I wished to tell you, before you heard it from someone else, that I wish to bring my mother, Vashti, back to the palace from the *haremsara*. Artabanus opposes the idea, even though she is now queen mother. I was not her favorite, but cannot in good conscience leave her there." Artaxerxes glanced at Esther to gauge her reaction.

"That is compassionate and the right decision, majesty. I agree with you." She turned to look him in the face. "When your mother comes, it is best that I do not remain in the palace. I have no sons to seek the throne and my time here has come to an end."

"Where would you go? I know my father gave you the estate and property of Haman."

"I have sold all that belonged to that man. A wealthy merchant purchased it. He knew nothing of Haman, he merely wanted to establish business in Susa. The bloody history of Haman's estate made it impossible for me to live there." She paused. "Your father gave me one of your grandmother's estates in Ecbatana. With your permission, I wish to go there. It oversees a small town and the people there have many needs."

He raised his eyebrows. "I'm glad to hear that you have another place to go. I understand. If that is your desire, go when you are ready. I will see that your maids accompany you and additional servants will be sent to maintain the estate. Also, you will need a military escort. I will send a company of immortals to protect you on your journey."

Relief flooded her heart. "Thank you, your majesty."

"It is my wish that you stay for a while, however. You have been good to me and I know you were loyal to my father."

She inclined her head. "I will stay as long as you need me. My God will show me when it is time to go. Forgive me for inquiring, majesty, but what of Artaynte? I've only spoken to her briefly. She was very fearful."

"She will be returned to her parents. She is not with child and she is anxious to leave here. I am certain they can find a husband for her." He grinned ruefully. "I think the prospect of being queen was too much for her in any case, or I might have considered marrying her myself."

He appeared to be pondering something, so she waited for him to speak again. "Good Esther, wife of my father, there is always intrigue in the palace and I was forced to take the word of Artabanus and Aspamitras that Darius killed our father. Yet something is not right. I have no proof, only the word of the captain, who's now regent. I wonder, why him? Why would my father assign the regency to the commander of his royal bodyguard? Wouldn't it have made more sense to select one of his advisors?"

Esther spread her hands. "Your father didn't often share the reasons for his actions."

"I do not trust Artabanus but have no choice. I have few I feel I *can* trust." He looked earnestly at Esther. "My father said you were a wise woman and I trust you. My father did. And I have trusted Mordecai."

Esther reached over and placed a hand on his arm. "You and your brother were not enemies. You may never know what happened, but it has fallen to you to rule over this empire. You will be a good king, Artaxerxes. You do not need Artabanus. Your father trusted Mordecai as his prime minister. He is an honest, faithful servant, who served Xerxes well and his father before him. I'm sure he's mentioned that he worked in the king's treasury before his elevation to prime minister. Mordecai speaks many languages and is wise. He will serve you well if you let him." She smiled. "He raised me and I love him, just as much as I loved your father."

His sighed and looked out over the garden. "I know you loved my father, as I did. For that, I would agree to almost anything you suggest. I am king under strange circumstances I could not control and I'm filled with heartache over the events that brought it about."

They heard a commotion from within the queen's chambers and looked up to see Artabanus striding toward them, his face the picture of annoyance.

"There you are! Majesty, I have been looking for you. We have matters to discuss." He looked at Esther expectantly, as if to give her an opening to tell him what they were talking about. She regarded him silently.

Artaxerxes rose. "I have been inquiring after the queen's health. How is it you have access to her private garden without her permission?"

Esther's face was expressionless, but inwardly, she was pleased. *Good!*

The captain raised his eyebrows in surprise, both at the question and the king's tone. "I … needed to find you. As I said, there are matters we must discuss."

"Then send me word and I will meet you in the inner court with my other advisors." Artaxerxes waved a hand. "You may go."

"Yes, majesty. However, as regent, I must be aware of the decisions concerning the kingdom."

Artaxerxes let loose a short guffaw. "You can't be serious, Artabanus. What decisions do you think I would make with Queen Esther that would require your attention?" His face grew stern. "I may have no choice in your being regent, Artabanus, but I am still king."

Artabanus's face turned red. "You are young, majesty. Obviously, you need an experienced advisor."

"I have experienced advisors—a cadre of them—along with my prime minister. I am done here." He nodded to Esther. "Good day, my lady." The king then turned and strode away, leaving the captain standing there. The immortals outside formed a circle of protection around the king and they left the hallway.

Esther was startled at the look of hatred that appeared on the captain's face as he watched Artaxerxes walk away. Then, before she had a chance to request that he depart as well, he stalked out without taking proper leave of her or even a backward glance. The captain was clearly not fond of the king…she did not want to face the thought of what that might portend.

52

The animosity between Artaxerxes and Artabanus only increased over the next months. Esther remained in the palace, for she felt the young king needed both her and Mordecai. Vashti had not yet been brought back from the *haremsara* and the tension in the palace was almost palpable.

Mordecai was in the palace library looking over some documents when General Megabyzus, asked to speak with him. Artabanus was away from the palace on what he'd said was an urgent matter. Apparently, the general knew this. His countenance was grave and he looked like a man at war with himself.

"May we speak in private, prime minister?"

"Of course." Mordecai dismissed the servant who was helping him and motioned to the guard stationed outside to close the door.

"I have learned that you are a just man and a trusted advisor to the king. I realize I forfeit my life for what I must tell you, but my conscience will not let me rest."

Mordecai indicated a chair. "You may speak freely and I will give you my opinion, although you must know, I am not surprised that you have finally come to me. I suspected there was more to your earlier visits than it appeared."

Megabyzus rubbed his forehead with one hand, eyes filled with pain. "I was complicit in the death of King Xerxes and the crown prince. Artabanus planned the death of both of them with the help of Aspamitras. I did not take part, but I knew about it…and remained silent. I was convinced that my wife, the king's daughter, had committed adultery, shaming our family. Xerxes only gave her a brief reprimand instead of what she deserved. I was angry and not thinking rationally. I have since regretted my actions."

Considering the grief Esther was still bearing and the turmoil that Persia had endured, Mordecai's first reaction was anger. He had to fight down the urge to strike the man. But it was obvious Megabyzus was tormented. The look on his face showed that the guilt he carried was eating him up inside.

Still, Mordecai had to get to the bottom of this. "Why are you coming to me now? Your silence cost the lives of our king and his son and hurt the empire."

"Yes." Megabyzus hung his head for a moment, but then looked Mordecai in the eye. "I have come to prevent another tragedy. Artabanus has placed four of his sons in crucial positions and three other sons are stirring up a rebellion among a group of soldiers. Since he is regent, Artabanus intends to kill Artaxerxes and seize the throne for himself."

Mordecai jumped up. "This is terrible news! We must go to the king at once. You may have forfeited your life with your words, but you may have prevented another assassination. Come with me!"

The general rose and followed him. "The rebellion could take place at any time, prime minister. Artabanus went out just this morning to gather his rebels to bring to the palace. I wish to stand with our king if a battle takes place."

Suddenly, shouting outside the palace interrupted their conversation. The two men rushed to the outer court and the general drew his sword. Artabanus had indeed returned and a battle was taking place between his rebels and the king's soldiers. The eunuch chamberlain Aspamitras stood grinning on the sidelines.

To Mordecai's horror, the young king had also been notified of the conflict and entered the court with his sword drawn. He was immediately engaged by one of the rebel soldiers, but Artabanus pushed him out of the way. "The king is mine," he snarled.

In an instant, Megabyzus stepped between them and faced Artabanus. "You are on the losing side, captain. This day, you shall taste my sword."

Rage filled Artabanus. "You would take the side of this child king against me?" He thrust his sword, but the general sidestepped easily.

Mordecai raced to the king's side, together with the immortals he knew were loyal to Artaxerxes. They formed a tight circle of protection around the king and the group moved back against the wall, for Artaxerxes refused to leave the battle scene, despite Mordecai's pleadings.

The soldiers from both sides dropped back as Artabanus, almost swaggering, began to move around Megabyzus. Their swords clashed again and again. Time after time, Artabanus thrust his sword only to have his opponent sidestep, a smile on his lips that seemed to infuriate the regent. He slashed frantically, but Megbyzus ducked, spun, and leapt away with ease. In a moment, the general found his advantage and thrust his sword deep into Artabanus, whose face was a picture of astonishment as he clutched his chest. He staggered toward Artaxerxes, dropping his weapon and trying to speak. The king broke through his soldiers' ranks and springing forward, he snatched up the regent's own sword and, with one blow, lopped off his head. Artabanus's body crumbled at Artaxerxes' feet, blood pooling swiftly around him.

The rebels tried to run, but Artaxerxes cried out. "Cut them down—they have committed treason!"

His soldiers obeyed and slaughtered the now fearful rebels before they stepped foot out of the courtyard. Then Artaxerxes turned and pointed to Aspamitras, whose face had become pale with fear.

"Seize him! I have a special death for one who has betrayed his king."

The frightened man's head was covered with a cloth sack and he was hustled away.

Artaxerxes stood tall and looked around at the bodies of Artabanus and the rebel soldiers. Fortunately, because they vastly outnumbered their opponents, the king's loyal guards and soldiers suffered some injuries, but kept their lives. Artaxerxes motioned to some palace servants who had been watching the battle. "Take the bodies away and bury them. They shall spend eternity in the earth for their crimes." He turned to the immortals' captain who had led the battle against the enemy. "Seek out the remaining sons of Artabanus and any other males of his household and his lineage and put them to death. None of his line shall ever threaten the throne again."

The soldier bowed. "Yes, your Majesty. It shall be done. Three of his sons were here. They are dead, but there are four more."

"Then seek them out immediately and carry out my command."

"Yes, majesty." The soldiers ran for their horses and were gone.

The king turned to Megabyzus. "You have vanquished a hated enemy and perhaps saved my life this day. But why are you here, uncle?"

"I ignored the words of Artabanus when he was talking about assassinating your father and brother." And he related to the king all that he had told Mordecai.

"Then my brother did not kill our father?"

Megabyzus shook his head. "No, majesty, it was Artabanus and Aspamitras."

Artaxerxes put his hand over his eyes as he struggled with his emotions. "He should have been king." He drew himself to full height and looked sternly at Megabyzus. "Did you have a hand in the assassination?"

"Only in my silence, majesty, grieving as I was over my adulterous wife bringing shame to me and my house."

Artaxerxes leveled his gaze at the general. "You have saved my life this day and for that, I will consider sparing yours. However, you will remain in the palace under guard until I determine what shall be done with you."

Megabyzus bowed. "I am your servant. Do with me as you wish."

The king nodded to his guard and the general was taken away.

Mordecai looked after him and then back to Artaxerxes. "You are merciful, my king. It is a wise ruler who can forgive a truly repentant man."

Servants were ordered to wash the blood off the stones of the courtyard as Artaxerxes departed. The faces of his men showed obvious admiration for their young king, who stood bravely steadfast in the face of a betrayal and revolt. They bowed deeply as he passed. Mordecai knew they would now follow him without question.

A short time later, Artaxerxes and Mordecai entered the queen's quarters, where Esther had been watching the battle from a balcony overlooking the courtyard. She turned and greeted them, her hand on her heart.

"I was so afraid for you, majesty."

Mordecai regarded the young king. "You acquitted yourself magnificently, majesty."

Artaxerxes smiled ruefully. "It seems the hours of sword practice and tutoring were well worth the time I spent." His shoulders drooped. "I am grieved that it was Artabanus's plan all along to kill my father..."

"And your brother," Esther murmured softly.

"Yes. He was groomed for the crown, not me. At least he was treated like a king in the Tower of Silence, before we were certain of his innocence. And now his bones lie beside my father's...."

He looked away, getting control of his emotions and then turned back to Esther. "Do you still wish to leave the palace?"

Mordecai frowned. "What's this?"

Esther told him about Vashti's circumstances and how both she and the king thought it best that she return to the palace, while Esther left it.

He stroked his beard, contemplating the idea. "Perhaps your decision to move to your estate is a wise one. But you will be there alone."

"My maids will come with me and I'm sure you will find time to get free from your duties to visit me. There is much to do in the town, Abba, and they are my people now." As she said this, she turned to the king. "Forgive me, majesty. I was presumptive. You have not said what you wish Mordecai to do."

The king put a hand on Mordecai's shoulder. "I wish you to remain as my prime minister. I need your wise counsel with all that stands before me as king. It is my desire that you stay."

Mordecai nodded. "I thank you for your confidence, majesty. I will stay as long as you need me."

Artaxerxes seemed greatly relieved. "Tonight, we shall have a banquet for all the court officials and celebrate my victory." He turned to Esther. "Join us, Queen Esther, and let us remember your service and love for my father before you leave."

"I will come. Mordecai can escort me."

∽

Still feeling a little weak, Esther leaned on Mordecai's arm and took her seat on the dais next to the king. A table was brought before her so she did not have to eat beside the men.

Halfway through the banquet, the king stood and raised his cup of wine. "I wish to recognize Queen Esther, a woman of wisdom, a helpmate worthy of my father, and someone who will always be a friend of the king."

Cups were silently raised toward her and she could only nod her head briefly in acknowledgement. Word had spread throughout the palace and everyone knew she was leaving. The other advisors and many of the servants went out of their way to wish her well.

As she sat looking around the great hall, she thought of the day almost a year ago when she had gathered her courage and stepped into the inner court to plead for her people. Adonai had made a way for them and she knew now it had been planned long before she was taken captive to the palace. *How His ways were beyond understanding!*

When she returned to her quarters with Mordecai, they discussed her caravan and she agreed to meet him in the morning. Her horse would be waiting for her and wagons were being prepared for her maids. Artaxerxes assigned a small contingent of soldiers to escort her to her new home and remain with her as her personal guard, housed at the estate.

⌐◞

The mood was somber as the sun rose over Esther's caravan. Mordecai embraced her, tears running down his face. "I feel as if I am losing you again. Safe travels, my Hadassah, and may you find peace in your new home."

Esther wiped his tears with a bit of her veil. "Don't fret, Abba, we will see each other again soon, when the king feels he can release you from your duties for a short time. I know you will serve him well. And when your sunset years come upon you, you will have a place with me."

With the soldiers looking on, Artaxerxes remained stoic... but then his face became wistful. "I always did enjoy your stories, Queen Esther. May your God go with you and keep you safe." He gave her a warm smile. "I stayed at the estate in Ecbatana a few times with my grandmother and it is one of my favorite places. I will also come to visit you one day, although not at the same time as Mordecai. One of us must remain here to manage the kingdom."

Esther bowed her head to him. "I will be glad to see you again, majesty.

She then spotted Hathach, wearing his traveling clothes and standing patiently beside Farah, holding her reins.

"Hathach? You are coming with me?"

In reply, to her surprise, he quoted from the story of Ruth:

"Wherever you go, I will go; and wherever you stay, I will stay. Your people will be my people and your God will be my God."

He tilted his head and looked up at her with a beatific smile. "How could I do otherwise, my queen?"

Esther smiled back at him. "And I shall feel safer with your presence, Hathach." He drew himself up, nodded, and took his place in the caravan.

Mordecai watched as the small procession made its way down the long ramp toward the city. He knew the people were waiting to bid her farewell and he could hear their shouts of encouragement.

"Safe journey, your majesty!"

"May God go with you, my queen!"

"We wish you good fortune and long life, Queen Esther!"

Mordecai thought of all his Hadassah had been through: a simple Jewish girl lifted up by Adonai to become queen of Persia to save His people. She had become a woman to be reckoned with, a queen in every way. He watched until the last of the procession had passed through the city gate.

"Hold your head high, my Hadassah, hold your head high," he murmured.

EPILOGUE

*I*n Ecbatana, the people of the town embraced Esther as their ruler. The children in particular loved her, for once a month, she invited them to her estate to hear stories and enjoy some refreshments. If her kitchen staff made too many little cakes—and she made sure they always did—she sent the children home with the extra sweets to share with their parents. She was also generous to the people who tended her fields.

Esther was exceedingly glad to be able to observe the Jewish holy days again. Mordecai traveled there on each occasion to maintain them with her.

Artaxerxes turned out to be the benevolent king Esther had felt he would be. He had mercy on Megabyzus and sent him to Syria to serve as governor.

Artaxerxes married Stateira, the daughter of the Persian nobleman Hydarnes, and made her queen. He reigned in Persia for forty-one years.

In the first year of his reign, he brought his mother Vashti back from the *haremsara*, but was informed of a plot involving her to put his brother Hystaspes on the throne. Vashti had sensed that she would have little power under Artaxerxes. After she instigated a coup attempt on his life, he was forced to put Hystaspes to death. Although stunned and heartsick at his mother's betrayal, the king was reluctant to kill Vashti, so once again, she was relegated to the *haremsara*, where she spent the rest of her life.

Mordecai served King Artaxerxes for seven years, at which time the priest Ezra received permission to return to Jerusalem and teach the law again to the exiles living there. Mordecai considered going also, but his health was waning and he chose instead to join Esther at the estate in Ecbatana.

AUTHOR'S NOTE

*H*istorical accounts, no matter what the subject, always seem to vary. In this case, there were many versions of the story of Esther. Some said she didn't exist at all, that Esther's story was a Jewish fable. Others said she had lived and had children. Still others said she had no children. There were so many conflicting accounts that I chose to follow the biblical account for most of the story. In the book of Esther, the entire Greek/Persian War is covered in the three words, *"After these things…"* I wove in what I felt was necessary to the story. The Scriptures state that the king *"loved her above all the other women."* Whether Esther loved the king or just made the best of her amazing circumstances is anyone's speculation. I chose to make it a love story: a beautiful young Jewish girl, unexpectedly beloved by a pagan king. Esther was only about seventeen when the Persian king took her for his wife and had much to learn about being a queen. I pray I've portrayed her journey successfully.

The name of God is not present in the biblical account, but when the Jewish people fast, they pray. Also, I wanted to show how

Esther adjusted to her Persian surroundings, where she was unable to celebrate her Jewish holy days. She was raised by Mordecai as a Jewish maiden and I didn't feel she would stop believing in Adonai nor stop saying the prayers she had grown up with once she started to live in the palace. Those were woven into the story.

According to one historical account, Mordecai served the king of Persia for seven years. The date of Mordecai's death is not known, but there is a tomb in Ecbatana, now in present-day Iran, that carries the names of Esther and Mordecai. It is believed their bones were interred there.

The biblical story ends with Mordecai serving the king as prime minister; it does not say what happened to Esther. I wanted to wrap the story up and with the tomb of Esther and Mordecai mentioned in Ecbatana, it seemed logical that they lived there until their deaths.

As always, I learn many new things when writing a biblical novel and this time, I enjoyed delving into the Persian Empire as well. I hope you enjoyed the story as much as I enjoyed writing it.

—*Diana Wallis Taylor*

ABOUT THE AUTHOR

*D*iana Wallis Taylor is an award-winning author of more than a dozen books, including *Lydia, Woman of Philippi; Mary, Chosen of God; Ruth, Mother of Kings; Shadows on the Mountain; Claudia, Wife of Pontius Pilate; House of the Forest;* the novels *Mary Magdalene* and *Martha; Smoke Before the Wind; Journey to the Well;* and *Halloween: Harmless Fun or Risky Business?*

Her additional published works include a collection of poetry, *Wings of the Wind;* an Easter cantata, "Glorious," written with a musical collaborator and available on Sheet Music Plus; and contributions to various magazines and compilations. She is currently completing a book on Abigail, King David's third wife.

Diana received her B.A. in Elementary Education at San Diego State University and was an elementary school teacher for twenty-two years. She operated two coffeehouse/used bookstores and later retired from a private Christian college as Director of Conference Services.

She makes her home in San Diego, California. Readers are welcome to reach out to her and read her blog at www.dianawallistaylor.com.

Welcome to Our House!

We Have a Special Gift for You ...

It is our privilege and pleasure to share in your love of Christian fiction by publishing books that enrich your life and encourage your faith.

To show our appreciation, we invite you to sign up to receive a specially selected **Reader Appreciation Gift**, with our compliments. Just go to the Web address at the bottom of this page.

God bless you as you seek a deeper walk with Him!

WE HAVE A GIFT FOR YOU. VISIT:

whpub.me/fictionthx

WHITAKER
HOUSE